When the servant left the room, closing the door behind him, Colin filled a glass with champagne and handed it to Chantele. She sipped it slowly, and looked around the room with curiosity.

"Like it?" Colin asked.

"Very much, but I thought you stayed with your cousin Lucien."

"I prefer my own quarters," Colin said cooly. Then he detected the slight tremor of Chantele's hand holding the glass. "Relax," he said gently. "We have plenty of time."

Colin rose from the sofa and crossed the room to join Chantele as she examined the books that filled the shelves. "I didn't know you like poetry," she said, pulling out a book.

"There's much you don't know about me, fair princess," he said, taking the book from her hand, "but there's one thing you do know," he whispered in her ear before touching his lips to the pulse of her throat. His mouth traveled the long column of her neck and pressed soft kisses to her eyelids, before brushing her cheek and finally covering her parted lips. And with this kiss, Chantele decided that Colin was right. She knew one thing—that she loved him—and what she didn't know, he could teach her. . . .

HISTORICAL ROMANCE IN THE MAKING!

PASSION'S PLEASURE

BY VALERIE GISCARD

ZEBRA BOOKS
KENSINGTON PUBLISHING CORP.

ZEBRA BOOKS

are published by

KENSINGTON PUBLISHING CORP.
475 Park Avenue South
New York, N.Y. 10016

Prologue

"I could kill you!" he said, advancing menacingly toward her. His hands went around her throat and began squeezing, squeezing, until her temples were pounding and everything was growing dim. And she was cold, so cold . . . Just before she closed her eyes, through the fog that was beginning to envelop her brain, the notes of a waltz drifted in, evoking images of the past. . . .

One

The sudden rush of panic she felt when he reached for her mask and unveiled her face abated at the pleasure she saw reflected in his deep gray eyes.

"You are indeed fair, my princess," he said wonderingly. His eyes delved into limpid ambers that slanted slightly under delicate arched brows, giving her face a rather exotic look, and fastened on the ripe, pouting lips that seemed made for kisses. The ample decolletage of her gown displayed softly rounded shoulders and a firm bosom, surprisingly full for so slender a girl, and its whiteness enhanced the golden tone of her skin that set her apart from the other pale, painted beauties. Her waist was so small that he could span it in the circle of his hands. "Lovelier than I had imagined, my Chantele."

He knew her name and yet she had no idea who he was. But it did not matter; for her, everything else had ceased to exist since that first moment when he had claimed her on the dance floor and she had looked into those strange gray eyes that seemed to reach into her soul. She had forgotten that she had not wanted to attend this masked ball at the Tuileries after she had overheard her parents urging Noelle to encourage Jean-Philippe's suit; she had forgotten her disappointment when Jean-Philippe had not even asked her for a dance; nothing mattered but to bask in the warm glow of the stranger's gaze.

He removed his mask and she saw that his long, aristocratic nose had been broken at one time, adding a rugged, angular quality to a face of virile beauty. Under thick and well-defined brows as dark as his hair, his eyes were thickly lashed and enigmatic; his mouth was wide and full-lipped.

The arms that held her were strong, and his lips descended upon hers in a kiss that was long and deep, almost bruising. Like a caged bird her heart beat wildly as his probing tongue explored and savored her mouth. She felt the rush of blood through her veins and her breasts become taut, as if they had a life of their own; her knees were so weak that she suddenly had to lean on him for support.

He drew his mouth from hers and gazed deeply into her eyes. "You've never been kissed before, have you, princess?" he said huskily.

"Not like this," she answered breathlessly.

He kissed her again and again, robbing her of her will, and all she could think was that she didn't want him to stop. She wrapped her arms around his neck, and when his hand slipped inside her bodice to cup her breast, she sobbed and pulled away, frightened by the intense desire his touch had awakened.

"Don't be frightened, little one," he said, gently caressing her cheek. "I'd never hurt you."

Had she not been so bewildered, Chantele would have found it amusing. No man had ever called her "little one". How could they, when she stood almost as tall as they? But this man was so tall that he made her feel small and fragile, and she was too conscious of the effect of his nearness on her emotions and of the strong attraction she felt for him. She pulled

9

away from the arms that encircled her waist and struggled to regain her senses.

"I want to see you again, Chantele," he said. "May I call on you?"

She sensed danger, but somehow she could not bear the thought of never seeing him again. "My parents . . ."

"Everything will be proper, princess, I assure you."

He gave her a boyish grin and a flash of gleaming white teeth before he adjusted his mask. He waited for her to replace her own before he danced them back into the salon, where they were lost in the sea of silk and satin and jewels illuminated by huge chandeliers resembling cascades of crystal, and where the ripples of laughter, wafts of perfume, and sounds of music filled every corner.

His name was Colin Marquandt, she learned later, when his cousin Lucien Pellisant introduced him to her family, and he was from America. Colin was polite and charming, and with a sinking heart Chantele saw how her sister bestowed on him her most seductive smile. Noelle was never satisfied, always wanted more; especially if it was something her sister had, and she could not miss the way Chantele's eyes lit up at the sight of the Creole. It had always been the same, ever since they were children.

But it was Chantele whom he asked for the

next dance, much to Noelle's chagrin, and the rest of the evening was like a dream. She wanted the ball to go on for ever. When the family was ready to leave the party, Chantele was oblivious to Noelle's peevish glares.

It was cold outside in the snow-covered courtyard, waiting for their carriage to be brought around, but Chantele was still warmed by the memory of Colin's kisses. Inside the carriage, the conversation was of the events of the evening, the gowns they had seen, the jewels, and gossip about the emperor's flirtations with his current mistress right under Eugenie's nose.

"She doesn't care," her mother Veronique said, unable to disguise the envy in her voice, "all she cares about is buying more clothes."

At this time of the morning, only a few figures moved in the deserted streets of Paris, the rag-pickers carrying their bundles on their backs and hooks and lanterns in hand as they moved from one pile of garbage to another. Chantele saw a few bundles of rags moving in the shadows, probably beggars seeking the warmth of a portal against the chill of the night, and felt a rush of pity for the poor, unfortunate souls. She would never complain again of having to wear Noelle's hand-me-downs or of there being no fire in her room to ward off the cold. How could she be so petty, she thought guiltily, when there were people who didn't even have a roof over their heads on a cold winter night such as this; and here she was, on her way to a warm bed. No, she had too much to be thankful for: a comfortable home, her painting, her music, and most of all, the love of her Rosalyn. And now, Colin. Who was this man who in the span of a few hours had been able to move her so? Was he as passionate and as gentle as she believed him to be, or was it all a figment of her imagination? What was he really like?

Wrapped in her own musings, she had been oblivious to the conversation going on around her until the word "creole" sparked her interest. It was her mother talking.

". . . he asked to be received."

"And?" Noelle inquired with interest.

"I asked him to tea next Friday," replied Veronique.

"Lucien told me his family owns a large plantation in Louisiana," interposed Antoine, her father.

"I think he was horrible!" exclaimed Noelle. "The man has no manners!"

"He seemed personable enough," Antoine offered placatingly.

"But did you not see the way he cut in on Chantele before they had been introduced?" Noelle said angrily. "Of course, it was all her fault, flirting with him the way she did."

"But I . . ." Chantele tried to protest.

"Oh, pooh!" Noelle cut her off. "It was embarrassing the way you kept throwing yourself at him. You danced with him practically all night.''

Chantele suppressed an angry retort. She had never won an argument with Noelle, and now her parents were regarding her with open disapproval. Besides, she was feeling guilty about the liberties she had allowed Colin. Had she really made such a fool of herself?

Noelle said something, but there was a humming in Chantele's ears, and she needed all her concentration to hold back the tears that were threatening to flow, and she didn't want to give Noelle the satisfaction of seeing her cry.

''Enough!'' Antoine said angrily.

Noelle sank into a sullen silence, but Chantele knew she had not said her last word. Finally, they reached home and trying to avoid her sister, Chantele ran to her room. She found that Rosalyn had waited up for her, nodding half-asleep in a chair, and Chantele rushed into her arms, letting tears flow.

''Now, now, *ma petite,* it can't be all that bad,'' Rosalyn said stroking the girl's hair. ''What happened?''

Rosalyn Hastings waited for her sobs to subside. In her ten years as a governess in the Daladier household, she had seen Chantele shed many tears over her parents' indifference, over Noelle's cruelty. Because of her beauty, Noelle had always been the recipient of the

13

parents' praise and favor; Noelle, with her pale blond hair, china-blue eyes, marble complexion and sophistication who turned the heads of a society that took superficial beauty as the ultimate value of a woman. But Chantele was no longer the ugly duckling, and this, Noelle resented.

Rosalyn vividly remembered the first time she had met the girls. The sisters had been opposite poles, even then. Noelle, secure in her beauty, poised beyond her nine years. But it had been Chantele, with her honey-blond hair curling and tangling in disorder, a smudge on her cheek, a rebellious expression in the small, gamin face, and a look of challenge in her amber eyes, who had immediately captured the governess' heart; probably because behind that defiance, in the thrust of the little chin, Rosalyn had seen her terrible vulnerability.

Her initial appraisal of the situation had proven correct; Antoine Daladier was an elegant, ineffectual man married to a regal beauty whose interests went little beyond herself, gowns, jewels, and a life of luxury and gaiety. A beautiful child like Noelle was pampered and paraded with pride; the second daughter, Chantele, had been a terrible disappointment. The ungainly child was their despair and, consequently, was ignored. In rebellion, the girl had become a tomboy whose antics were the terror of a parade of governesses who, unable to control her, resigned one after the other. It had not been easy for Rosalyn to win Chantele's confidence, but the girl, starved for affection, had eventually responded to her efforts and delighted the childless widow with her quick mind and natural charm. And what a sweet, sensitive child she was!

A voracious reader, Chantele had a tremendous eagerness to learn and explore new things. She had a good ear for music and languages, and could play the pianoforte beautifully by the time she was ten. Learning English was easy, and Rosalyn was able to speak her native language with the child, who spoke it without a trace of French accent.

Through the years, Rosalyn had hoped Veronique and Antoine would learn to appreciate the efforts of their youngest daughter to win their approval, but it had been to no avail; Noelle had continued to be the center of their attention, a place she had been forced to share after the birth of Claude, their only brother. In time, Chantele had become resigned to the situation, but now she had Rosalyn, and the affection between them had deepened with the years.

And now the Daladiers were facing ruin. Their lavish living, combined with disastrous investments, had exhausted what Veronique and Antoine had considered unending riches, and they had placed all their hopes on Noelle's beauty to save them from ruin by catching a rich husband. They had cast their greedy eyes upon the Bisant fortune, and Rosalyn was aware that Chantele was entertaining romantic ideas about the handsome Jean-Phillippe Bisant.

Rosalyn Hastings was a small, plain woman of indefinite age. Although her dark hair was sprinkled with gray, her gentle face remained unlined; but her brow creased now in a frown, witnessing Chantele's tears. When the girl did not answer, Rosalyn knew that Chantele's state had to do with her sister.

"Don't cry, my pet," she said soothingly in English, the language they spoke when they were alone. It had started many years ago as practice for the girl and had soon become their custom. By now, Chantele was just as at home in English as she was in her native French. "What did Noelle do to upset you? Is it about Jean-Philippe?"

"Jean-Philippe?" Chantele repeated, somewhat puzzled. And then she smiled, and said, to Rosalyn's surprise, "No, it's not about him at all! Oh, Rose, I met the most handsome, most wonderful man in the whole world! His name is Colin Marquandt, and he's from New Orleans, in America. And, Rose," she added dreamily, "he didn't even look at Noelle, no matter how hard she tried to get his attention. She's furious!"

16

Rosalyn smiled. "Tell me all about it," she prompted, and while Chantele changed into her nightgown, Rosalyn listened to her recount of the ball, and of meeting Colin. When she finished, Rosalyn's frown of disapproval told Chantele that she had made a mistake confessing that Colin had kissed her.

Later, in her bed, thinking of Colin's warm lips on hers, it was almost as if he was kissing her again; her body tingled at the memory of his caresses, and she felt again that curious mixture of joy and pain she had experienced. Nothing she had ever known before had prepared her for this, and it frightened her. What was happening to her? In her heart she knew that from the moment she had gazed into those strange gray eyes her fate to love him had been sealed; yet the feelings she was now experiencing were not what her ideas of love had been.

And what of Colin? Had she acted the fool, as Noelle had pointed out? Had he simply taken advantage of her recklessness, or had he felt as she did?

It was going to be a terribly long wait until Friday.

Noelle did not disappoint her sister when the following morning, still smarting from her failure with Colin, she swept into Chantele's room, catching her sister by surprise. It was too late to try to hide the picture she was sketching, and Chantele braced herself for Noelle's mordant remarks.

"Not bad," Noelle conceded, examining the sketch of Colin's face, and Chantele determined not to rise to her sister's banters. In this mood, Noelle was at her worst.

Noelle studied the drawing critically. "I think his eyes are closer together," she said maliciously, "and his nose is much larger."

When Chantele made no comments, Noelle regarded her with sarcasm. "He made quite an impression on you, didn't he?"

"He was very nice."

"Nice?" Noelle exclaimed rolling her eyes to the ceiling, "My dear sister, last night you made a spectacle of yourself with that . . . that *Creole,*" she spat, "and all you have to say now is that he was nice?"

"I did not do any such thing."

"Ha! It's obvious you know nothing about men," Noelle said caustically. "The only reason he was so nice, as you put it, was because you kept throwing yourself at him. Really, Chantele," she added with a pout, "it was disgusting."

Chantele bit her lip, refusing to enter into an argument. But Noelle was not finished. No matter how many attentions she had received, she bitterly resented any Chantele attained. Now that she had Jean-Philippe at her beck and call, her vanity demanded some tribute from Colin Marquandt simply because he had indicated a preference for Chantele; and, obviously, her sister was interested in the man.

"I can't understand what you see in him," she said caustically. "Jean-Philippe is much more handsome than the Creole."

"Perhaps you're right." Chantele didn't want Noelle to know how much she wanted Colin. If she did, Noelle would not rest until she had taken him away from her, and Chantele was not sure enough of herself to withstand the test.

"Still," Noelle said thoughtfully, "he's not too bad." Obliquely, she observed Chantele's reactions, and the tightening of her sister's jaw told Noelle of her anxiety. "You don't really believe he's interested in you, do you?" she said mockingly.

"I have no idea."

Noelle shrugged, and sauntering across the room she came to stand before the oval cheval mirror. "I think a man like that would prefer a more . . . sophisticated woman," she said striking a pose. She pushed aside the robe de chambre she wore to expose a creamy shoulder and smiled at her own reflection. "What do you think?"

"Perhaps," Chantele shrugged.

Angrily, Noelle whirled about "Perhaps," she mimicked. "Is that all you can say this morning?"

19

"I think you're saying enough for both of us!" Chantele snapped.

Noelle gave her a cattish smile. "You know he's going to look at you only until I decide whether I want him or not," she said and was gratified by the fear that involuntarily flashed in Chantele's eyes.

"If you want him, you can have him," Chantele said noncommittally.

"My, what a condescending little sister you are, my dear," Noelle said derisively. "Well, then, since you have no interest in him, I suppose I'll have to be polite to the poor man." She waited for an outburst from her sister and was disappointed when none came.

Chantele was too busy pretending to ignore Noelle's malicious grin when the door opened and Rosalyn walked in. The tension between the sisters was almost tangible.

"Hello, Noelle dear," Rosalyn chimed in, "I heard you had a wonderful time at the ball last night. Has Jean-Philippe proposed yet?"

If looks could kill, Rosalyn would have died on the spot. Noelle hated her; she was the only person whose affection for Chantele she had been unable to sway. Angrily, Noelle stalked out of the room, slamming the door behind her.

"I see Noelle *la Belle* is in one of her charming moods this morning," Rosalyn observed. "What did she say to upset you, my pet?"

"Oh, Rosalyn," Chantele turned haunted eyes on her governess, "she wants to take Colin away from me!"

Rosalyn expelled a sigh of exasperation. "Darling," she said persuasively, "when are you going to learn that when the right man comes along no one, not even Noelle, will be able to take his love away from you?"

"But she has always taken my friends away from me!" Chantele cried in despair.

"Only those who were not truly your friends, my darling, and tell me, did you really care for any of them?"

"Only Jean-Philippe."

"And now?"

Chantele shrugged, "I don't care about him, either."

"You see, darling? It's not the end of the world. Any one who can be blinded by Noelle does not deserve your friendship, much less your love."

"But she's so beautiful," Chantele said wistfully.

"And so are you!" Rosalyn cried angrily. "Look at yourself, Chantele," she said propelling the girl before the mirror. "You have a rare beauty, my dear. Noelle's beauty is too perfect, too cold. Those little imperfections you find so discouraging are what give you that special charm, my darling."

"I know you're not a vain creature," she

continued, "and why you long to be as beautiful as your sister. But let me tell you something. You are far more beautiful than she is, and you know why? Because you are beautiful inside, my pet, and that's even more important than superficial beauty. You are sensitive, and warm, and loving, and honest, and those qualities shine in your eyes, in the way you talk, in your every gesture."

Chantele's confidence was beginning to return. "And do you think Colin will see that?"

"If he doesn't, then he's not as wonderful as you think he is."

Chantele remained silent, trying to accept that theory. After a pause, Rosalyn moved into action. "We have work to do," she said, beginning to make the bed. The drawing of Colin's face, left on the bed by Noelle, drew her attention, and she carefully studied the virile, ruggedly handsome face of sharply chiseled features so aptly caught by Chantele. There was something in that face that made Rosalyn shiver with apprehension; perhaps the intensity in the eyes, or the curl of the sensual mouth. She regarded Chantele with alarm. "Is this Colin Marquandt?"

Chantele bobbed her head and smiled. "Isn't he beautiful?" she said dreamily. "And his eyes, Rose, are of such a strange color like I've never seen before. A dark gray, almost black, but not quite."

Her words only increased Rosalyn's apprehension. This was not a young man like others Chantele had known. There was a certain . . . she searched for the right word . . . a certain danger in those eyes that made her tremble for Chantele. Rosalyn detected a certain ruthlessness about him that frightened her. Chantele was completely out of her depth with a man like him. "He's handsome indeed," she had to agree, hiding her uneasiness in her chores. How could she warn Chantele against this man? She knew that saying anything against him would only alienate Chantele, but for the first time in her life, Rosalyn wished with all her heart that Noelle would take something away from her sister.

There were no traces of declining wealth to be seen in the opulent home of the Daladiers as Colin Marquandt followed the saucy maid into the salon where the family received their guests. In a society where appearances were already paramount, and in a gallant effort to present an affluent facade, the Daladiers had assembled in this room the few paintings and *objets d'art* that still remained in their possession and added that extra touch of luxury. The furniture was in the again-fashionable rococo, reminiscent of the style of Louis XIV, upholstered in delicate pastel brocade, gilded, and embellished with elaborate scrolls. There were gilt chairs set around a table so spindly that it seemed incapable of supporting the heavy silver tea service on top. A console topped by white marble offered a striking contrast with the *pouffe,* an upholstered stool with legs whose carved and gilded wood simulated knotted rope. And ormolu clock tic-tocked softly on the mantle of the fireplace where a cheery fire crackled, adding its golden glow to that cast by the gaslight, and giving the room an almost dreamlike quality. Colin had the curious feeling that he had walked into the carefully staged scene of a play.

Antoine, wearing an elaborately embroidered vest under his frock coat, stood behind the *canape de l'amitie,* the settee occupied by the ladies. Veronique, looking almost as young as her daughters and stunning in purple velvet embellished with feathers, was gratified by the admiration she read in Colin's eyes as he gallantly kissed her delicate hand. Noelle, who had taken great pains with her toilette, was a portrait of beauty in solferino taffeta embroided with crystal beads and offered her most welcoming smile. Chantele was lovely in a simple gown of pale green silk embossed with roses and trimmed with lace. Her hair was parted in the middle and swept in two soft waves that framed her face and then coiled at the sides of her face. Her greeting was demure, but the look in her eyes was more eloquent than words.

24

After the initial pleasantries, Colin took his seat and accepted a cup of tea from Veronique and a plate of delicate tea cakes from Noelle.

"I understand that you are from America, *Monsieur* Marquandt," Veronique opened the conversation.

"Yes, *madame*. From Louisiana."

"We have never traveled to America," Veronique said pleasantly, "but we have heard many nice things about New Orleans."

"Indeed, *madame,* it is a beautiful city with a character all its own. Since it has been under the domain of several countries, New Orleans is a charming mixture of cultures."

"And is this your first trip to France?" inquired Noelle.

"No, *mademoiselle*. Like most Creole young men, I made my studies in France. My mother was a *Parisienne,* you know. Madame Pellisant, Lucien's mother, is my aunt."

"A very distinguished family," commented Veronique with approval. "I understand some of them remained in England after the Revolution."

"And by now they are second-generation British," Colin said. "I used to spend my holidays with them while attending Cambridge."

"You seem to be a very accomplished young man, M. Marquandt," Veronique said with a charming smile.

"You're most kind, *madame.*"

"And are you planning to make Paris your home?" inquired Noelle.

"No, *mademoiselle*. The trip has been a . . . a holiday for me before I return to New Orleans and relieve my father of some of the burdens of running the plantation."

"Ah, yes," Veronique interposed. "Lucien mentioned something about a plantation. But, surely, you don't run the plantation yourself," she said somewhat surprised. "Isn't there an employee to do it for you?"

"There is an overseer, of course," explained Colin, "but it's been the tradition that the head of the family runs L'Esperance. Even the women. When my great-grandfather died at the age of 35, his widow ran the plantation herself until her son, my grandfather, became of age."

"How marvelous!" exclaimed Chantele, who had been unable to get a word in all afternoon. She seemed to have something to add, but her mother interfered.

"Do tell us about L'Esperance, Monsieur Marquandt. What a lovely name."

"It's located north of New Orleans, on the Mississippi River. We plant sugar cane and some cotton."

"It must be a very extensive property," interposed Antoine, visibly impressed, "and require a tremendous number of field hands."

Before Colin could reply, Noelle interposed

avidly, "Are there many slaves in L'Esperance?"

"Yes," Colin replied, and detecting a note of disapproval in his voice, Chantele risked another question. "Don't you approve of slavery, *Monsieur?*

Colin stirred his tea thoughtfully before he replied. "It's been pointed out to me that I'm in no position to criticize the system which has provided several generations of Marquandts, myself included, with certain privileges, *mademoiselle*. The entire system depends on slavery. Plantations like L'Esperance and others are so extensive that a great number of workers is required. The theory is that paid labor would destroy the economy, and not only Louisiana, but in all the South."

"But you don't agree," Chantele observed.

"No, I don't. I believe that, in the long run, a man who works for wages would be far more productive than a slave. That, of course, aside from the inhumanity of a system that degrades not only the slave, but the master as well."

"But surely the masters take good care of their slaves," objected Noelle. "I remember when Madame LeClair brought that little black boy from the Indies. She was very good to him. She dressed him in very fancy suits and fed him sweetmeats, and took him along wherever she went."

"Just like a little lap dog," Colin said drily.

Realizing Noelle had made a mistake, Veronique rushed to cover her daughter's blunder. "Do tell us about your family, *Monsieur*. Is it large?"

"My mother died when I was 15, and my father's second wife has a son by a previous marriage. That's all there is of the Marquandt family."

The Daladiers seemed very interested in the society life of New Orleans, and Colin continued to answer their inquires until the conversation drifted to gossip. While Noelle offered some juicy tidbits on the current affair of one of her acquaintances, he discreetly observed Chantele. More than ever, he was struck by the difference between her and the other women. It was interesting, he had noticed during the course of his visit, Noelle's patronizing attitude toward her sister and Veronique's indifference toward her youngest daughter. The evening of the ball she had bewitched him, and today he could not wait to be rid of those inquisitive, boring creatures who stood between them. Had it all been an illusion, or was this quiet creature her true self? No, it couldn't be. Her eyes spoke a language much more eloquent than the torrent of words assaulting his ears, and he sought a discreet way to be alone with her. But Noelle, who had monopolized the conversation, had no intentions of allowing him a moment with her sister, and Colin became aware of an anger rising within him.

Before his arrival, the family had been discussing their expected guest. Noelle had been in a huff; despite their efforts to conceal their financial troubles, gossip had reached the Bisants. Jean-Philippe was having difficulties in convincing his parents, and until they agreed, an engagement was out of the question. As a member of a distinguished family and heir to a large plantation in America, Colin offered a splendid weapon to prod the vacillating Jean-Philippe into action. Veronique and Antoine, who found it more difficult every day to maintain their charade, thought the idea of using Colin had merit. Besides, they reasoned, if the plan failed and Jean-Philippe was unable to convince his parents, their beautiful Noelle could always charm the Creole into marriage.

Chantele had listened to all this with a sinking heart and prayed that Colin would not be enticed by the beguiling Noelle. She was delighted that her suitor, although charming and polite toward her parents and sister, did not appear to be succumbing to Noelle's flirtations. From his occasional glances in her direction she could tell his interest still remained with her, and this helped her keep a low profile during his visit.

The weather had been extremely mild, and before he took his leave Colin extended an invitation to the two young ladies to ride to the

Tuileries Gardens the following afternoon. Noelle's delight, when she accepted, would not have been so great had she seen the glance that passed between Colin and her younger sister.

Chantele had harbored no illusions as to the outcome of the afternoon, especially after the conversation she had overheard, but just seeing Colin again was enough for her. She had known Noelle would flirt with him, as indeed she had, but a knowing smile played on her lips as she ascended the stairs to her room after his departure. She could not have mistaken the unspoken message in those strange gray eyes; he wanted to see her, and he would find a way.

Rosalyn, who had seen Colin briefly during his visit, did not feel her apprehension lessen after meeting him in the flesh. All her fears had been confirmed. The man was a threat to Chantele. But try as she might to hide her dislike for him, Chantele became aware of it, and consequently, confided in her no more that day.

Two

The weather was crisp and clear, and Chantele was barely able to contain her excitement when Colin appeared in the company of his cousin Lucien in an elegant open carriage. Immediately assessing the situation, Noelle possessively took Colin's arm and let him help her onto the carriage. Colin accepted her maneuver with good humor, allowing Lucien to escort Chantele, but during the ride their eyes shone with mischief each time they met while Noelle chatted enthusiastically.

"Do you like the theater, M. Marquandt?" she inquired.

"Very much, *mademoiselle.*"

"I understand a new play by Dumas *fils* will be opening soon." She paused, waiting for an invitation that never came. "Have you seen the *Dame aux Camelias?*" she finally asked.

"Yes, I have, mademoiselle. An excellent portrayal of Parisian life as it is today, wouldn't you say?"

"Oh, I don't know," she replied dubiously. "It's so nice to have all this gaiety again, the balls, the beautiful gowns, the elegance of the court. It's a welcome change from what we had before, don't you agree, M. Pellisant?"

"Of course, *mademoiselle,*" Lucien replied wryly.

The little fool, Lucien said inwardly, would not look beyond the ostentation and outward splendor of the court, caring little about its lack of values and immorality. As long as she could find a rich husband there to satisfy her hunger for luxuries, little did she care that while the emperor presented his current mistress an emerald worth hundreds of thousands of francs, the average worker earned between two and four francs for an eleven-hour day, wages that were insufficient even to provide food for his family. But, as a lawyer, Lucien was well aware of that other side of Paris which people like Noelle and her family happily ignored. He had seen a stern judge impose a four-year sentence on a thirteen-year-old serving girl who earned only four francs a month, for the crime of stealing jam from her mistress; he saw the streets full of beggars and cripples and bands of thieving children and twelve-year-old prostitutes. People like the Daladiers did not look beyond the glitter of the court and the elaborate facades of the Second Empire to see the appalling squalor in which the poor of the city lived, sometimes starving to death in the streets.

Lucien was relieved that their arrival at the gardens precluded further comments and was the first out of the carriage to assist Noelle, who alighted with a show of her new tasselled Russian leather boots, threaded with colored silk. Lucien offered his arms to Noelle saying, "Now is my turn for the company of this beauty."

Noelle opened her mouth to protest but immediately shut it seeing Chantele on Colin's arm. Aware that refusing this arrangement would only create a scene, she reluctantly accepted the situation with as much grace as she could muster. The two young couples joined the promenade, Lucien making sure that he and Noelle were several paces ahead.

It seemed as if the entire population of Paris had assembled at the Tuileries for the afternoon, taking advantage of the crisp, but mild weather. The women, beautiful in their billowing crinolines, were escorted by men in top hats, frock coats, and light trousers. Now and then, the flash of a uniform could be seen.

Elegant children in black velvet suits with white lace collars and little white hats topped with pompoms played with their hoops and balloons under the watchful eyes of their nannies. Sitting on chairs under the still leafless trees, little groups of intellectuals carried on animated discussions.

"I see you brought reinforcements today," Chantele said when Lucien and Noelle were out of earshot.

"Do you mind?"

She laughed happily and shook her head, "Not a bit."

"Ah, princess, how difficult it is to steal a few minutes with you!" he said raising her hand to his lips and kissing the inside of her wrist.

Chantele had practiced languid looks, charming smiles, and witty remarks before her mirror, but they all vanished from her mind in his presence. She felt her cheeks grow hot, and trying to recover her poise said casually, "Don't you like Noelle?"

"Surely you're jesting, princess!" he

laughed. "I had to suffer her constant prattle just to be near you." And then, he added, "But I'd slay a dragon just for that."

They paused to watch an artist at work. Unaware of being observed the young man was busy trying to capture on paper the scene before his eyes when suddenly he tore at the paper with annoyance.

"I thought it was going quite well," Chantele said, and for the first time the young man became aware of their presence.

"It could be better," he said with a shrug and began to crumple the drawing.

"Please, don't destroy it!" Chantele cried.

The young man paused, and after a slight hesitation offered the drawing to Chantele saying, "I could never refuse such a lovely young lady. With my compliments, *mademoiselle.*"

Chantele accepted it gladly. "Thank you, *Monsieur* . . ."

"Manet," the young man replied with a flourish, "Edouard Manet, at your service, *mademoiselle.*"

"Will you sign it for me?"

"It's not worthy, *mademoiselle,* but if it will make you happy, of course." He signed the sketch, and Chantele examined the drawing with interest.

"It's wonderful, M. Manet," she said with delight. "I myself like to sketch, but I'm afraid my work will never be half as good as this. And you were going to destroy it!''

"You are most kind, *mademoiselle* . . .''

"Oh, please, forgive me,'' she said charmingly. "Daladier, and this is M. Marquandt.''

"I don't profess to be an art expert, M. Manet,'' Colin said shaking hands with the artist, "but Mlle. Daladier is right. Even I can tell this is excellent. As the matter of fact, I'd like to see more of your work. Where can I find you?''

"Any afternoon after five o'clock at the Cafe Tortoni.''

"Good. I'll look for you there.''

"And thank you so much for your gift, M. Manet,'' Chantele said slipping the drawing into her reticule, "I shall treasure it always.''

Manet gave her a gallant bow and was immediately back to work.

"So you are also an artist,'' Colin said, pleasantly surprised. "I know so very little about you, my fair princess. You know,'' he said turning serious, "Noelle won't fall for the same trick twice, and it's obvious your family won't let me come near you. You saw what happened yesterday.'' He paused before he added, "Kitten, I don't want to make things difficult for you, but I must see you again. Alone. I've thought of nothing but you since we met, my sweet. Have you thought of me?''

How could she tell him that he was in her thoughts every minute of the day?

"Don't be afraid to tell me what you feel, princess," he said when she hestitated. "I want to hear you say it."

"You know I have," she replied flushing with color.

"If we could meet . . . is there someone you can trust?"

Chantele immediately thought of Rosalyn and quickly dismissed the idea. No, instinctively she knew Rosalyn would not help her this time.

"A maid?" he offered.

Chantele brightened. "Juliette!" she exclaimed. "Sometimes she goes shopping with me."

"Good. Will you meet me tomorrow?"

"Where?"

"Tomorrow, at four o'clock, at the Place d'Armes. I'll have a carriage waiting and perhaps we could go for a ride away from the city. Would you like that?"

"That would be lovely," she said, already dreaming of a few stolen hours with him. But then, "What if I can't get away?"

"Then I'll wait for you the next day, and every day until you come."

A rush of excitement ran through the crowd, who parted to let the Imperial couple through. Louis Napoleon's presence was far from imposing; his large nose was the most prominent feature in his somewhat melancholy face. In his hand he carried a walking stick of rhinoceros hide topped by a golden eagle. Eugenie's features were exquisitely chiseled, her complexion flawless, and her deep blue eyes reflected the warmth of her smile as they strolled at leisure, greeting their subjects as they walked by. Except for a small retinue of ladies and gentlemen, they appeared to be unescorted.

When Colin expressed his surprise at the lack of guards, Chantele replied, "They love the Tuileries, and it's not unusual to meet them like this, or at the theater, with only a group of courtiers. I know there's much opposition to the Emperor," she continued, "political meetings are banned, as you probably know, but Louis Napoleon is not overly upset by criticism and allows a great deal of latitude to his dissenters. It is true that agitators receive stiff sentences, but we must also admit that excessive cruelty is not used. To give the Emperor his due, I think he's really interested in improving the lot of the people. A new aqueduct to supply the city has been planned, and the new sewer should go a long way in improving sanitation. Much more than that will be necessary to help the poor; I'm well aware of the appalling conditions in which they live, but at least it's a start. The number of dead during the last cholera epidemic was horrendous, and they were mostly among the poor. But the problem is not a simple one to be resolved overnight; more and more people come into the city each day, looking for work. As you can see all around us, the city is being transformed; unfortunately, too much emphasis is being placed on elaborate buildings that will only increase the Emperor's prestige."

Colin was surprised at the awareness that such a young girl had of the situation, and he listened with interest as she continued.

"As for Eugenie, her fondness for ostentation does not make her popular with the people. They resent her, saying that all she cares about are clothes and jewelry. Already they call her *L'Espagnole* as they called Marie Antoinette *L'Autrichienne.*"

Chantele paused, suddenly aware that Colin was regarding her curiously. The young men of her acquaintance did not appreciate a girl discussing politics, and she flushed slightly and said, "She's very beautiful, isn't she?"

"Not as beautiful as you," he said huskily, caressing her with his eyes, and Chantele knew that, to him, she was more beautiful than Eugenie, than Noelle, or any other woman in Paris. And, for her, that was more than enough.

It was not until two days later that Chantele was able to keep her rendezvous with Colin, and Paris offered its rich variety of movement and color as they rode through streets filled with the clatter of carriage wheels and the shrill cries of vendors. Colin bought a bunch of Parma violets from a flower girl who cried, *"Fleurissez vos amours!"*

May your love flourish, Chantele mused, what a lovely thought. It was only the cry of flower-sellers and she had heard it a million times before without taking notice, but this afternoon, with Colin holding her hand, she took it as a happy omen. Inhaling the fragrance of the flowers, she absently looked out the carriage window to see sunlight reflecting on the plumed helmet of a Cent Gard who was swaggering down the street toward the cafes in his sky-blue tunic and glistening jackboots.

It seemed as if spring were coming early this year; there had been patches of frost on the ground only days before, and yet this day, the air was surprisingly warm and heavy with the scent of pine. Juliette was an ideal chaperone, discreet enough to look the other way when they disappeared among the trees, and young enough to feel a little envious of the *Mademoiselle* and her handsome lover. She approached the coachman, a strapping lad with a florid complexion and dancing brown eyes with whom she would not mind whiling away the time until the *Mademoiselle* returned.

They were barely out of sight behind the trees when Colin pulled Chantele into his arms and devoured her with hungry kisses.

"Oh, my darling," she cried clinging to him,

returning his kisses with a passion unknown to her before, "I was so afraid you would not be waiting for me!"

Colin rubbed his knuckles against her golden cheek. "I told you I'd be there." He took her hand, and continuing their exploration of the forest they came upon a small pond which had been concealed by the trees. "What happened yesterday?"

"I was not allowed to go out," she replied. "I think Rosalyn suspected."

"Rosalyn?"

"She was my governess. I can't understand it," Chantele said with a frown, "she's always been on my side. Suddenly, I feel I can't confide in her anymore."

"She disapproves of me, doesn't she?"

He knew her answer when she hesitated. "But she doesn't even know you!" Chantele objected.

"She's very important to you, isn't she, princess?"

"Yes," Chantele replied thoughtfully. "She's been like a mother to me, Colin. She's the only one who truly loves me."

"The only one?" he said teasingly and pulled her down on the grass. His lips found the pulse of her throat and Chantele lost track of everything but the feel of his lips and his hands. Colin loosened her bodice and caressed her breasts. Her emotions in turmoil, Chantele

41

tried to remind herself that she should not let him take such liberties, but she was unable and unwilling to make him stop teasing and nibbling her flesh.

"You like that, don't you, kitten?" His tongue teased the tips of her erect nipples, and she thought she would die of pleasure. Striving to get closer to him, her fingers entwined in his hair and her mouth searched hungrily for his.

"I was right about you," he said gazing into her eyes that were clouded by her desire. "You are all fire and passion, my love."

Her cheeks blushed crimson and she tried to cover herself, but he stopped her. "Don't," he said, gently pressing her wrists to her sides, "let me fill my eyes with your beauty."

She lay on the grass, abandoning herself to his caresses, and her eyes fluttered open when he stopped.

"You are too much of a temptation," he said in a tight voice. "Let's get back."

Chantele sat up, confused by his sudden anger. What had she done? She began to adjust her clothing, trying not to cry, and at the sight of her quivering lips his expression softened.

"Chantele," he said gently, "It's better to stop now, or I'll take you right here and now."

"You're not angry?"

"No, kitten, I'm not," he replied, and framing her face with his hands, he added, "You're too precious to me, princess. When I make love to you for the first time, it will be where we can take our time. I want make you happy, my love, but if we don't stop now, I won't be able to hold back. Do you understand?''

She didn't, but obediently bobbed her head. A honey-colored curl escaped her bonnet, falling softly on her brow, and Colin coiled it around his finger.

"I want you so much," he said, kissing her softly on the lips. He rose to his feet and hoisted her by the hand. "It's getting late and I don't want to get you in trouble at home. Will you meet me tomorrow?"

"I'll try to get away."

"Don't take chances, kitten."

Take chances, she thought. To see him again, to be in his arms again she would walk on fire! "I love you, Colin."

He was startled by her confession. He had always found experienced partners more satisfying than the blushing virgins other men sought in their conquests; but if ever there was a woman made for love, it was Chantele. Her innocence, rather than a deterrant, was only increasing his desire for her. He wanted to possess her, to discover the delights hidden in that beautiful body, to teach her all the secrets of love and passion, because he knew that they were one and the same. He had been in love often enough to know that once passion was expended, there was nothing left of that emotion so much heralded by the romantic—love. And a romantic he was not. But he wanted her more than any other woman he had ever known.

"And I love you, kitten."

How she had longed to hear those words! Her heart grew wings, and she had never known such happiness. She glided rather than walked back to the carriage, where Juliette waited, and she held on to Colin's hand all the way back to Paris.

Everything, everything around her had changed. The colors seemed brighter, the sky bluer, and the world had become a better place. With supreme effort Chantele tried to behave as usual, but Veronique's criticism and Noelle's banters didn't bother her any longer. What did it all matter? Colin loved her! How she longed to see Noelle's face when she told her that Colin thought her more beautiful, more desirable than any other woman on earth. She counted the hours until she could be in his arms again, to see her own reflection in his eyes, to listen to his husky voice whispering sweet words of love. She counted the minutes until she would see him again, and their meetings were full of kisses that made her blood run hot and left her wishing for more. Her need for him was becoming an obsession; no longer an hour or two of stolen caresses satisfied her. She wanted to belong to him as her heart already did, and when the false spring retreated behind gray clouds and winter rain made their walks in the forest impossible, Chantele was at her wits' end.

At the appointed hour, Colin was waiting when Chantele appeared with Juliette, and he handed a long-stemmed rose to each of them, a red one for Chantele, a yellow one to Juliette, who blushed prettily.

"Perhaps Juliette would like to visit some friends this afternoon," he suggested looking directly into Chantele's eyes, and she knew it was her decision to make.

"Would you, Juliette?" she asked the girl without hesitation, holding Colin's gaze.

Juliette looked from one to the other, hesitantly. "If you are sure, *mademoiselle.*"

"I'm sure."

"Will you meet us here at six o'clock?" Colin asked Juliette.

"Certainly, *monsieur.*"

"Thank you, Juliette," Chantele said warmly pressing the girl's hand. Juliette gave her a nervous smile before she boarded the carriage Colin had thoughtfully summoned, which immediately joined the milling traffic.

Colin handed Chantele onto his coach and kept her hand in his.

"Don't be frightened, kitten," he said gently. "You can always change your mind."

"I love you, Colin," she replied, leaning against him with a sigh.

After a short ride, his coach stopped in front of an elegant three-story building. The ample vestibule was deserted as they ascended the stairs to the top floor, and Colin extracted a key from his pocket.

"This is my flat," he said, unlocking the door.

Chantele stepped through the foyer and into a parlor elegant in its simplicity, with no trace of gilt or frills. The furniture, of veneer wood and leather, had a solid, comfortable look. Colin took her cloak and rang for a servant. A black man appeared immediately.

"Will you bring us some champagne, Gideon?"

"Yes, sir, Mister Colin."

"Is he . . ."

Colin shook his head. "Gideon is a free man, and so is his wife, Bess," he replied taking a seat by her side on the leather sofa. He reached out and removed her bonnet.

Gideon returned with a bottle of champagne and two long-stemmed glasses on a silver tray. Chantele watched the black man open the bottle and gave a start when the cork popped, betraying her uneasiness.

"Chantele, I want you to meet Gideon," Colin said, "Gideon, this is Mle. Daladier."

"At your service, *mademoiselle,*" Gideon bowed slightly.

She was surprised. Never in her life had she

been introduced to a servant, but she liked the white smile that flashed in the dark face.

"I'll serve, Gideon, thank you."

"Yes, sir."

Gideon left, closing the door behind him. Colin filled the glasses, handed her one, and clinked hers with his own. "To us, kitten."

Chantele sipped her champagne, looking about the room with curiosity.

"Like it?"

"Very much, but I thought you were staying with your cousin Lucien."

"I prefer my own quarters."

He detected the slight tremor of her hand holding the glass. "Relax, fair princess," he said gently. "We have plenty of time." He rose from the sofa and crossed the room. "I have a little surprise for you," he said returning with a package in his hands. "I think you'll like it."

Chantele accepted the parcel and unwrapped it eagerly. It was a charcoal sketch, already in its frame. Edouard Manet had captured all the lively confusion of an afternoon at the Tuileries Gardens. The scene was urban and elegant, charged with movement and anticipation.

"They seem to be waiting for something to happen," she said studying the scene. "And look at the individual figures. You can almost feel the softness of the fur this lady is wearing." Her eyes were bright with excitement. "Oh, Colin, this is wonderful!"

"Come, and I'll show you the others I got from our friend," he said, taking her by the hand and guiding her to the east wall, where Manet's sketches were displayed.

Chantele examined the drawings with interest, commenting on their merits, and then proceeded to read the titles of the books that filled the shelves. "I didn't know you liked poetry," she said pulling out a book.

"There's much you don't know about me, fair princess," he said taking the book from her hand, "but there's one thing you do know," he whispered in her ear before touching his lips to the pulse of her throat. His lips traveled the long column of her neck and pressed soft kisses on her closed lids before they brushed the silken cheek and finally covered her parted lips. His kiss, deep and long, erased all her fears. He released her lips and gazing deeply into her eyes saw that her doubts had disappeared. Effortlessly, he lifted her in his arms, and she leaned her head on his shoulder, letting him carry her into the bedchamber.

He put her down before a crackling fire, and Chantele could hear the patter of rain against the window. Colin removed her garments one by one, kissing her gently as he uncovered her flesh, and when he finished she stood still, letting his eyes travel slowly over her body on which the flames traced dancing patterns of light and shadow.

"My God," he said in wonder, "you are even more beautiful than I ever dreamed." She was long limbed and willowy, and her softly rounded curves invited his touch. He reached out and pulled the pins from her hair, and the long tresses trumbled around her shoulders like a mantle. Burying his fingers in her hair, he held her head back, and his kiss was gentle, yet passionate. "Come, my love," he said taking her hand.

Meekly, she followed him to the bed, where they sat on its edge. Colin had removed his coat and the front of his shirt was open, but he had refrained from completely undressing not wishing to frighten her with the sight of his desire. She could feel the tumult of his heart when he took her hand and placed it on his bare chest as he covered her face with kisses. He pushed her down gently, and his lips left hers to explore the softness of her throat. He stroked her breasts in circling caresses, her belly, her inner thighs until she was moaning with pleasure, and he smiled at her protest when he had to leave her for a moment to discard his clothes. Then, he came to her, and she tensed suddenly when his fingers touched and fondled her most secret places, but the wave of pleasure was too strong to resist. Rivers of honey flowed through her, and he knew that she was ready. He was poised above her for an instant, and his entry was swift and sure. A cry escaped her lips and she became still in his arms, sobbing quietly. He brushed her hair away from her face and gently kissed her salty tears. "I'm sorry I had to hurt you, my love, but there was no other way."

She gave him a tremulous smile.

"Ah, kitten, I love you!"

He began moving slowly within her, and when pain gave way to pleasure, together they roamed the wild fields of passion. As wild beasts of a primeval forest they thrust and tore into each other; as fallen angels they soared through the communion of their heightened yearnings that for a brief, magical moment bonded their flesh and blended their souls.

When it was over, he stroked her gently, soothing her quiet sobs. "Are you all right?" he asked brushing her brow with a gentle kiss.

"Yes," she said dreamily.

"Was it as you had expected, my love?"

She took a moment before she answered, "Somewhere I read that to love is to be two and yet one; that a man and a woman blended as an angel, heaven itself." She propped herself on an elbow and gazed deeply into his eyes. "Until this moment, I never understood what it meant, my love, but it was that, *le ciel.*"

Three

In how many ways he could give her pleasure, she thought in wonder as she dressed, loathing to leave his warm embrace. Colin pushed aside the curtain of her hair and finished fastening the back of her dress.

"Bess will help you with your hair," he said, planting a kiss on the nape of her neck before he went out of the room.

Chantele was sitting at the dressing table when Bess came in, moments later. The Negress was almost as wide as she was tall, and exclaimed in surprise when she saw Chantele. Muttering under her breath, Bess picked up the brush and began dressing Chantele's hair, who sat stiff and erect under the black woman's open disapproval. Bess looked into the mirror, and seeing the girl's discomfiture, smiled widely.

"You sho' has beautiful hair, chile," she said to Chantele's surprise. "Don' pay me no min' chile," Bess said shaking her head, "Ah's an ornery nigger, not like dat fine husband o' mine. It's jist dat . . ." she bit her lip, as if considering to continue and then she did. "Ah don't think Mastah Colin should have brought you here, missy."

"I love him, Bess," Chantele said quietly.

Bess regarded her for a moment, shook her head, and then finished pinning Chantele's hair. "My, you sho' is a pretty chile," she said.

Chantele was smiling happily at Bess's reflection when Colin returned. "Ready?" he inquired.

"Just."

Bess gave him an angry glare and shuffled out of the room, shaking her head and muttering under her breath.

"I'm afraid I have incurred Bess's anger by bringing you here and seducing you," he said with amusement. Then, he turned serious, "She's right, you know."

Chantele regarded him with apprehension.

"I told you there's a lot about me you don't know," he said soberly. "At least now you know I'm not a gentleman."

"I know something else, too."

"And that is?"

"That you make me very happy, and that I love you very much."

Days passed in a whirl of excitement, with Chantele counting the hours until her next meeting with Colin. His flat on the rue de la Paix became their haven, and the happy hours she spent became her reason for being. Her only sorrow was that she could not confide her joy to the woman who had been a mother to her through her childhood years, but Rosalyn's dislike for Colin seemed to grow as her watchful eyes observed the changes in Chantele. Rosalyn could not miss the faraway look the girl had on those days when she was unable to leave her home. Her beauty seemed to grow with each passing day, and as Rosalyn was helping Chantele with the alteration of a dress, her suspicions were confirmed.

After three days of absence, when Chantele had arrived at the flat on the rue de la Paix, Colin had swept her in his arms and carried her to their room without even giving her the chance to remove her bonnet. Their desire for each other seemed to grow each day rather than diminish, and their lovemaking was violent and passionate.

Colin was delighted with the remarkable lover Chantele had become, demanding and generous at the same time. No professional virgin was she, but giving herself fully and demanding as much from him. Eager to please him, she had learned his body so well that she was able to arouse his desire to heights never before experienced. How they enjoyed exploring each other, giving pleasure to each other, becoming one.

"Noelle has been more impossible than ever these last few days," she commented when they were lying side by side on the wide bed. "She's driving the servants crazy."

"And you?"

"No, not me. Not for lack of trying," she added, "but it doesn't bother me any more. Not as long as I have your love."

She sat up and poured herself another glass of champagne, and after she had emptied it, she refilled it and offered it to Colin. "Champagne?"

"Of course."

She laughed throatily when he refused the glass. It was a love game they both enjoyed, a prelude to passion, and he drank the wine from her breast until they became one again.

As usual, Juliette was already there when Colin alighted from the carraige and handed her in. "Until tomorrow, my love," he said kissing Chantele's hand.

"I don't think I can, darling. We're going to a ball tomorrow night."

"At the Carreres?"

"Yes."

"Then, I'll see you there."

"Until tomorrow, then," she said with a happy smile. They had not danced together since the night they had met.

Chantele leaned against the seat and heard Colin's instructions to the driver. Suddenly, she was feeling very queasy. Everything around her was spinning. Juliette was talking and she couldn't understand a word. Her ears were buzzing.

"*Mademoiselle,* are you all right?"

The dizziness passed and she took a deep breath. "Yes, Juliette, I'm fine," she said dismissing the subject. "I guess I drank too much champagne."

As usual, Rosalyn helped Chantele to dress for the ball. The gown, altered only the week before, was too tight at the bosom. Chantele's breasts strained against the fabric and overflowed generously over the low decolletage.

The ballroom was crowded when the Daladiers arrived, and Noelle and Chantele were immediately surrounded by gallant admirers. Noelle and her parents were deliriously happy. The Bisants had finally consented to the engagement, and at long last the match they had been hoping for would take place.

Noelle's engagement to Jean-Philippe removed any possible objections her parents might have had to a marriage between herself and Colin, Chantele mused, but she refrained from bringing up his name because, as she reminded herself with sorrow, not once had he mentioned marriage. But, as usual, her worries vanished at the sight of him, and even though he was attentive and charming when he came to claim her, by now she knew him well enough to notice a certain restlessness about him.

The music ended, and Colin took two champagne glasses from a passing servant and handed her one. "To us, kitten."

They sipped their wine and she found his eyes resting on her bosom. He looked into her eyes giving her one of his lazy smiles, and she colored slightly, reading his thoughts.

"You look absolutely delicious," he said caressing her with his eyes.

"I'm in love."

"I hear it's the most wonderful beauty secret," he said taking her glass and pulling her into the dance floor. A feeling of nausea washed over her as they came out of a spin.

"Are you all right?" he inquired, noticing her pallor.

"It's too warm in here," she replied.

"Shall we go out on the terrace?"

"Please."

She felt better in the cool breeze, and the nausea passed. Chantele leaned on the balcony rail, and Colin stood behind her, encircling her waist.

"Better?"

"Much better."

"Let's walk in the gardens," he said pulling her by the hand.

"Do you think we should?"

"Unless you want me to kiss you right here."

Without further protest, she followed him. Shielded by a tall hedge, he pulled her into his arms and kissed her savagely. His lips were bruising and seemed to devour her.

"I want you."

"Colin, please!"

"I want you now."

"Darling, someone might see us!"

He took her deeper into the gardens, ignoring her objections. There was a gazebo at the end of the gardens, and he directed their steps in that direction. A climbing vine entwined in the lattice work afforded privacy, and he sat on a bench and pulled her on his lap. His lips pressed to the base of her throat and his hand slipped inside her bodice and freed her breasts.

"Don't, Colin, please!"

His mouth covered her protests, and she

57

felt his hands probing the inside of her thighs. Before she knew it, he had stripped her pantalettes and had her pressed against the wall of the gazebo. His hardness within her, he pounded savagely into her. His body tensed with a final thrust, and she knew he had found release. He kept her pinned to the wall and she could feel the wild beating of his heart against hers.

Finally, he released her and ran a hand over his grim face.

"Why, Colin?"

"I needed you," he answered gruffly and turned away.

Chantele adjusted her clothing and followed him back to the terrace. Before they reentered the salon, Colin examined her critically and nodded.

"You look fine."

He took her back into the dance floor, where minutes later he relinquished her to another dancing partner who claimed her.

He didn't ask her for another dance, and she didn't see him again. Had he left the party? What was wrong, she asked herself over and over. Only yesterday he had been the same Colin she adored. Tonight, a stranger had ravished her. It had not been her Colin who had taken her so savagely in the garden. It was a blessing when it came time to go home.

Noelle was not to be ignored, speaking of her

wedding plans, and mistaking Chantele's silence, she asked petulantly, "Aren't you going to congratulate me?"

"Of course," Chantele replied absently, "I'm very happy for you."

"Are you really, my dear sister?" she said derisively, but refrained from needling her sister in front of their parents. Chantele returned to her own musings, ignoring the conversation.

She wanted to be left alone, but found Rosalyn waiting up for her.

"I don't need any help, Rose."

"I think you do, my pet," Rosalyn rebuffed and began unfastening her gown. With alarm, Chantele noticed the marks Colin had left on her and tried to cover them, but it was too late; Rosalyn had already seen them.

"It's Colin Marquandt, isn't it?"

There was no use denying it any longer. She had to confide in Rosalyn. "Yes," she admitted.

"Chantele, are you aware that you are *enceinte*?"

Chantele's eyes widened. "What!" she cried, aghast.

"I know you haven't been feeling well lately," Rosalyn said leaving no room for argument, "and look at yourself in the mirror, my pet. Your breasts are enlarged, your dress barely fits you. It's written all over you."

Chantele covered her face with her hands. It was too much to take at one time. First, she had been raped by the man she loved; and now, this.

"Will he marry you?"

"I don't know," she admitted with defeat.

Rosalyn gave a sigh of dismay. "I suppose he doesn't know, either."

Did he, Chantele asked herself. Was that the reason for his strange behavior? Had he known she was with child and didn't want her any more?

"I don't think he does."

"Then you must tell him."

"I . . . can't."

"But you must," Rosalyn said firmly. "If you don't, then I will."

"No!"

Rosalyn gave another sigh of exasperation. "Very soon you won't be able to hide your condition, my pet," she said persuasively. "Your parents will know and so will Noelle. What are you going to do then?"

Chantele remained silent. Rosalyn waited.

"I'll tell him," Chantele said finally.

"When?"

"Tomorrow."

"You mean, today." Rosalyn hugged her. "Good night, my pet, sleep well."

"Good night, Rose."

Mechanically, Chantele got into bed and

pulled the covers up to her chin. She felt cold and lonelier than ever. What would be Colin's reaction? Did he love her? Yesterday, she would have answered yes without hesitation. Tonight, she wasn't sure of anything anymore.

Colin had told her that there were many things she didn't know about him, and he had been right. There were so many facets to him, she mused. He could be the most charming man in the world, playful and boyish one moment, passionate and wild the next; and that other part of him she had just discovered, ruthless and frightening. But she realized that she loved him, no matter what. Her life had been a constant struggle with her own family, but where Colin was concerned she had no will of her own. Her lips were swollen from his savage kisses; her body was bruised from his brutal passion, and still she longed for him.

The night was long, and morning brought closer the moment of recognition.

She took special care with her appearance, arranging her hair the way he liked, a dress he had particularly admired, and perfume he had given her, and keeping a tight rein on her fears left the house in Rosalyn's company. The cab crossed the streets of Paris—now filled with music and the perfume of lilacs and roses—and when they reached the flat on the rue de la Paix, Chantele alighted alone.

"Should I come with you?" inquired Rosalyn.

Chantele shook her head.

"Then I'll wait here."

Slowly, as if each step led to the scaffold, Chantele ascended the stairs to the top floor. Her hand was trembling when she knocked on the door. Colin had given her a key, but somehow she was reluctant to use it. Gideon opened the door and admitted her in. She could tell he was trying to mask his surprise. Colin, in his shirtsleeves, was working at his desk, but he rose and came to meet her when she came in.

"Chantele," he said taking her hand and kissing her icy fingers.

She searched his face and was not encouraged by his slight frown.

"You were not expecting me."

"I'm glad you came."

"Are you?"

"Of course," he replied, but he had hesitated for an instant.

Several wordless seconds went by, and then they both started to talk at the same time. She fell silent.

"I'm sorry about last night," he said. "Are you all right?"

Chantele nodded. "What happened, Colin?"

He took a deep breath and shook his head. "I don't know," he confessed. Then he turned away and sauntered to the desk. "I had a letter from home yesterday," he said with his back to her. "My father is ill. I'm returning to New Orleans."

Chantele felt faint. "When?"

He turned to face her. "My ship leaves Saturday."

Her legs refused to support her, and she sank on the sofa.

"I didn't want to tell you last night," he tried to explain. "I thought it would be better to wait until we were alone."

"Of course," she managed.

Seeing her dismay, he came to stand by her. "I'm sorry, kitten," he said gently. "I'm going to miss you very much."

She couldn't say anything.

"It's better this way, my love," he was saying. "After what happened last night, you must realize I'm not what you thought."

She couldn't reply. All her efforts were directed at holding back the tears that were threatening to flow.

"You'll find someone else, princess," he continued gently. "Someone who will make you happy, as you deserve."

She stood up and bravely tried to smile. "Good bye, Colin."

"Let me take you home."

"No," she refused, "I have a cab waiting downstairs."

She almost cried out when he kissed her hand. "Goodbye, kitten."

Chantele didn't know how she had made her way back to the carriage when she realized

Rosalyn was patting her hand.

"He's going home," she said in an empty voice.

Rosalyn bit her lip, anger and sorrow struggling in her heart. "Did you tell him about the child?"

Chantele shook her head. "I couldn't."

"But wouldn't he . . ."

Chantele didn't let her finish. "No!" she all but screamed, "I don't want that!"

She was too proud, she had been hurt too deeply, Rosalyn realized. Her pain was too fresh to let her see reason. "As you wish," she conceded, and they continued their ride in silence.

"You're finally home!" Noelle cried as soon as Chantele and Rosalyn walked into the house. "Father wants to see you in his study right away."

What now, thought Chantele. Such summons were always ominous, and with a sigh of resignation she made her way to her father's study. Before she reached it, the door opened and tearful Juliette came out.

"I'm sorry, *mademoiselle*," Juliette said between sobs, "I had to tell."

"Oh, no!"

"Oh, yes!" Noelle said with venom. "You thought you were very clever, didn't you?" Her malice made Chantele quail. "You little harlot!

You have disgraced us all!''

Chantele opened her mouth to speak, but no sound came out. Suddenly, the floor rose up to meet her.

She was lying on a sofa and someone was pressing a cold compress to her forehead. Voices were raised in anger in the background. Chantele closed her eyes again, wishing that she were dead.

''She's awake now.'' It was Noelle's voice.

Antoine loomed before her, the stamp of accusation. ''You have always been a disappointment to your mother and to me, Chantele,'' he said, barely able to contain his temper, ''but this . . . this is unforgivable.''

''Father . . .''

''You have brought shame and dishonor to our house.''

Chantele hung her head. He was right, of course.

''Who's the man?'' Antoine demanded.

''It doesn't matter, father.''

Noelle snickered and Antoine cursed. Chantele realized she had never heard her father curse before, but she felt curiously detached from the whole scene. It was as if she was at the theater, watching a play. The actors were on the stage, she was sitting in the audience. Now the actor playing the role of her father was saying something in a very loud and angry voice. She wanted to get away.

"Who's the man?" Antoine was screaming, his composure all gone.

"I saw her with the Creole last night," Noelle volunteered.

"Marquandt?"

"Yes," Noelle said with venom. "They went out on the terrace, but when Jean-Philippe and I got there, they had disappeared."

"Where did you go?" demanded Antoine.

"To the gazebo," someone said, and Chantele realized she had spoken.

"So far we know only of the Creole," Antoine said with a frown. "Were there others?"

Chantele didn't reply, staring defiantly at her father.

"If he's a gentleman . . ."

"A gentleman!" snorted Noelle derisively, and then, she cried, "Oh, Papa, what are we going to do? How can we ever face people again? What can I say to Jean-Philippe, to his parents? What if he breaks our engagement?"

"Don't worry, darling," Antoine consoled her. "Everything will be all right. Perhaps the man could be persuaded to marry her."

"I won't marry him!" Chantele cried.

"Enough of you!" Antoine ordered curtly. "Get out of my sight! Go to your room and stay there!"

Gideon read the calling card and, recognizing the name, admitted the visitor. "Please come in, M. Daladier."

Antoine was shown to the parlor where he waited studying his surroundings with interest. Everything in the room indicated good taste and luxury. Colin came in, and his greeting was polite if somewhat cold.

"You know why I'm here," Antoine said soberly.

Colin nodded. Chantele had wasted no time in running to her father, he thought wryly.

"Then you know what I must ask of you."

"I suppose you want me to marry your daughter."

"If you are a gentleman, *monsieur*, you will do so."

"And if I refuse?" Colin said raising a mocking brow.

Antoine stretched to his full height. "Then you'll leave me no choice but to ask for a redress, *monsieur*."

Colin laughed, without humor. "You mean a duel? If that is meant as a threat, *monsieur,* I must warn you." He paused before he added, "Swords or pistols, I have no wish to kill you."

At the tone of his voice Antoine felt the grip of the icy fingers of fear and reconsidered his position. His powers of persuasion would be more useful than threats with a man who would not be intimidated.

"Chantele is a very beautiful girl," Colin was saying, "she'll have no trouble finding a rich husband despite the loss of her innocence.''

"What you say might be true," Antoine agreed noticing Colin's grim expression, the tightness in his voice, "under different circumstances. But what man would accept another's child?''

"Child?" Colin's brows went up in puzzlement. "Are you telling me Chantele is with child?''

"Yes.''

Colin turned his back to Antoine, and sauntering slowly across the room came to stand before the open window.

"Surely you won't deny the child is yours," Antoine said, and quailed when Colin turned an angry glare upon him.

"Chantele came to me as a virgin," Colin said in a low, threatening voice. "If she's with child, it is mine.''

Antoine expelled a sigh of relief.

"Why didn't she tell me?" Colin demanded. "Why did she send you instead?''

"She would not even give us your name," Antoine said with a placating gesture. "We had to get that from the maid.''

Colin's anger seemed to abate and he smiled wryly, remembering Chantele's last visit. Perhaps she had meant to tell him before she had discovered he was going home. After learning that he was leaving her, pride had prevented her from telling him about the child. He had to admire her courage. Knowing full well the precariousness of her position, she had walked away without saying a word about her condition. How many women would have done the same?

Marriage was something Colin had avoided for years, despite his father's insistence. He knew he would have to marry some day, but he had been determined to postpone it as long as possible. He was well aware that both his father, Leon, and the Dorleacs, owners of the plantation neighboring L'Esperance, had expected that one day he and Marinette Dorleac would be married. The match would unite the two properties, making L'Esperance the largest plantation in all of Louisiana. Marinette was beautiful and sophisticated, and, Colin thought, as cynical about love in her own way as he was. She expected one day to become Madame Marquandt; he himself had been half-reconciled to the idea. But marriage to Chantele? She was so young, so inexperienced. Like his mother, a Parisienne, how would she adapt to a new life in a different part of the world, as a planter's wife?

Colin's memories of his mother were those of a beautiful woman who, during most of his life, had lived in the seclusion of her rooms. Most of all, he remembered the fragrance of violets pervading her domain. That had been her name, Violette, and like the flower whose name she bore, she had been delicate and frail, never adapting to the new country so different from her native land. He remembered the quiet footsteps and hushed voices when Violette suffered one of her violent headaches or frequent miscarriages; and he vividly remembered his father's despair.

But Chantele was not Violette; she was young, and healthy, fecund as Louisiana soil, and a fighter. Lovely she was, mused Colin, remembering the supple, yielding body he knew so well.

Antoine waited expectantly while Colin ceased his pacing and again stood before the open window, blind to the panorama of the city's rooftops stretching before him. He was thinking of the hours of passion shared with Chantele in this very apartment. Even after all this time, his desire for her had not diminished. Every time he held her was a new, different experience. In his mind's eye he could picture her in her new role as the mistress of L'Esperance. Marriage to Chantele? Why not?

He turned to the expectant Antoine. "Very well, M. Daladier," he said to Antoine's undisguised relief. "I shall delay my departure for two weeks. Will you make the arrangements?"

"Thank you, M. Marquandt," Antoine said offering his hand. "If you wish to discuss the marriage contract, we may do so tonight, at my home."

"I'll be there. Nine o'clock?"

"I'll expect you then." Antoine prepared to take his leave, pleased with the success of his visit.

As Colin had requested, Antoine had arranged for the wedding to take place in two weeks, but when the time came to discuss the dowry, he had trouble broaching the subject.

"I'm afraid that at the moment . . ." Antoine said tentatively, "my eldest daughter is also engaged. And her dowry has already been settled," he lied. "I'm sure you'll understand that two marriages so close together . . . present . . . er. . . ." Desperately he tried to find the right words while Colin, determined not to make things easy for him, let him struggle.

". . . er . . . well, difficulties. However," Antoine rushed to add, "if you will accept my promise, I assure you the dowry will be increased in the future."

Fully aware of the Daladier's reverses, Colin knew the emptiness of Antoine's promises. "The dowry is unimportant," he said finally, and Antoine, who had been prepared for his objections, was pleasantly surprised.

When the details had been completed, Colin stood up. "I'd like to see Chantele, if I may," he requested.

Antoine colored visibly. "She's . . . indisposed," he said.

Valerie Giscard

His embarrassment aroused Colin's suspicions. "Where is she?"

"Upstairs, in her room."

"I'm not leaving until I see her."

Antoine was unable to hide his dismay. "I'm afraid," he admitted, "that she has locked herself in her room and refuses to see any one."

"Did you inform her of our marriage?"

"Yes, or course, but I had to tell her through the closed door, since she refused me admittance."

"Where is her room?"

Antoine was alarmed. "Surely you are not . . ."

Colin's glare silenced him. "We've been lovers, *monsieur*. She's carrying my child. Do you expect me to stop at formalities?"

Antoine shrugged and rang for a servant. Moments later, a maid appeared. "Please show M. Marquandt to Mle. Chantele's room, Marie."

Marie's eyes registered her surprise. "Yes, *monsieur*," she said.

Colin followed her upstairs, and at the end of the hallway Marie indicated the closed door and disappeared. He knocked on the door and waited for a response. There was only silence.

"Chantele," he called and knocked again. "It's me, Colin. Open the door."

There was a small pause before she answered, "Go away!"

"We must talk, princess. Open up."

"I don't want to see you! Go away, leave me alone!"

"If you don't open this door right now, I'm going to kick it down. Open up, I said."

After a pause, he heard the bolt being drawn, and Chantele opened the door a crack. "What do you want?"

He pushed the door open and went into the room.

"What do you think you are doing?" she protested. "This is my room, you can't come in here."

"Why not? You've been to mine often enough."

Chantele colored visibly and bit her lip. Realizing she was about to cry, she turned her back to him. Colin stood close behind her and captured her waist in the circle of his arms. "Why didn't you tell me about the child?"

"What difference does it make?"

"I didn't like learning it from your father. How long have you known?"

"Not long."

"And you came to tell me, didn't you?"

When she didn't reply, he forced her to face him. "Kitten, will you marry me?"

Pursing her lips she shook her head, trying desperately to hold back the tears and failing.

"Why not? I thought you loved me."

"Because you are being forced!" she cried

out, struggling to free herself from his embrace, but Colin kept a tight hold on her.

"You think so?"

"I know so!"

"Chantele, look at me," he said lifting her chin and forcing her to look into his eyes. "Do you really believe your father could force me to marry you if I didn't want to?" When she didn't answer, he insisted, "Well, do you?"

"No," she said, "but you are doing it only because of the child."

"Partly," he admitted, "but mainly because I like the idea of having you as my wife."

Through her tears, hope shone in her amber eyes. "Do you really mean that, Colin?"

He regarded her fondly before he gathered her in his arms and kissed her deeply. Then, he sat on the bed and pulled her down on his lap. "Will you marry me?" he whispered, pressing kisses to the pulse of her throat.

She had never been able to resist his caresses. "Oh, yes!" she breathed, and then, "Colin?"

"Yes, my love?"

"Are you happy about the baby?"

"Of course I am, kitten," he replied running his hand over her belly.

"Oh, Colin, I love you so!" she cried throwing her arms around his neck. Surprised by her exuberance, he lost his balance and they fell on the bed, laughing, but soon their romp led to more intimate caresses, and Chantele traced the contour of his lips with the tip of her tongue before covering his mouth with her own.

"I think I'd better leave," he said, sitting up, "or I'm going to make love to you, and hang your parents!"

She giggled. "I wished you would make love to me now."

"Mademoiselle," he chided mockingly, "you are a very greedy wench."

"Is that a complaint, monsieur?"

"No," he said rubbing his knuckles against her golden cheek. "Don't ever change, kitten. I like you just as you are."

Chantele went through the days as in a dream, waiting for the day when in the eyes of the world she would belong to Colin and he to her. No more hiding their love, she mused happily. Colin continued to be treated with extreme deference by the Daladiers, who had warned Noelle against any outbursts of temper. Chantele knew how she had ranted and raved about the preparations for the elaborate wedding Colin had requested and wondered if she would be able to hold her tongue, but Noelle was shrewd enough to know what was good for her and kept her tantrums in check.

Chantele's mind was now at ease with respect to Juliette, who had been summarily dismissed by her parents without references, a situation which spelled disaster for a serving girl. Juliette was happy now in the position Colin had found for her in the home of his aunt, Mme. Pellisant.

On the morning of her wedding day, Chantele woke to the cries of the water carriers. She was still abed, daydreaming and listening to the muffled street sounds when Rosalyn came in bearing a tray with her breakfast.

"Good morning," Rosalyn chimed, "how are you feeling?"

Chantele stretched luxuriously and replied, "Wonderful!" Last night I was so excited I didn't think I'd be able to sleep a wink, but I must have fallen asleep as soon as my head touched the pillow," she laughed.

"Sometimes I'm sleepy even during the day," she said breaking a croissant and spreading it with butter. "Let's hope I stay awake long enough to enjoy my honeymoon. I don't think Colin would like a bride who sleeps all day."

Rosalyn laughed gaily. "I think he'll understand the needs of a lady in such an interesting condition, as he's fond of calling it."

"You like him, don't you, Rose?"

Rosalyn regarded Chantele fondly. "Yes," she replied candidly, "I really do." She paused before she continued, "For obvious reasons I was very glad when he asked you to marry him, but I must confess I never thought he would go to such lengths. This wedding," she said shaking her head in wonderment. "He knows you'd have agreed to the quiet ceremony your parents suggested and Noelle wished, but that would have been like admitting to them that your marriage was something to be ashamed of. With this wedding he's announcing to the world how proud he is of you and the child."

Chantele took Rosalyn's hand. "I'm glad you understand."

"I do, darling, and I'm no longer afraid for you," Rosalyn said patting her hand. "I know you're going to be very happy."

Chantele hugged her warmly. "Oh, Rose, I love you!" she said in a voice choked with emotion. "I still wish you would come to live with us."

"No, my pet," Rosalyn said shaking her head. "You don't need me now. You'll have many servants to look after you and your child, and Claude still needs me. Perhaps in a year or two, when he's older and goes away to school, I'll come and help you raise the child you are now carrying and others you may have by then. I believe Colin is hoping for a large family," she added, "and from what I've seen, I think he's going to make a wonderful father."

An empty champagne bottle rested in a silver bucket of melted ice by the bed where the lovers lay in each other's arms after a night of passion spent. Drowsy with sleep and languid from love, Chantele rested her head on Colin's chest, following the beats of his heart.

"It's almost morning," she heard him say.

"I wished we could make this night last forever," she said against his chest.

"Everything must come to an end."

"Not my love for you."

"That, too, will come," he said wistfully.

She lifted her head and regarded him curiously. "Why would you say a terrible thing like that?" she said with a frown.

"Because nothing lasts forever," he said soberly. "Everything changes, nothing remains the same. It's the order of life."

"But change doesn't necessarily mean the end."

"*Touche*," he admitted, not wishing to continue their conversation. What was the point? Chantele was too young to understand that love, like everything else, dies in due course. But why fill her pretty head with somber thoughts on their wedding night? Their whole lives lay ahead, and as long as she could maintain the illusion, why spoil it for her? Today he still desired her and she him. How long that would last didn't matter now. They had entered a contract whereby she would bear his name and his children and run his house, and he would provide for her for as long as she lived.

They were just another link in the chain of humanity, nothing more.

"Colin." She was propped on her elbow, regarding him with concern.

"Yes, kitten?"

"Why do you look so sad?"

"I'm not sad."

"Are you sorry?"

"About what?"

"Marrying me."

"You silly goose!" he said, playfully tossing her and pinning her under his weight. "How many times do I have to tell you," he said, kissing her throat, "that," he nibbled the side of her neck, "I'm happy," he pressed his lips to her eyelids, "that I want you," he kissed the tip of her nose, "and that I want that child?" he finished, finding her lips.

With the limitations imposed by life on the ship, and in her new position as Colin's wife, Chantele found that her company was very much in demand by the other ladies aboard the *Mouette*. Most of the passengers were from Louisiana, returning home after visiting relatives in the mother country.

Marguerite and Charles Gerard were a middle-aged couple, but despite the difference in their ages, Chantele felt immediate kinship with the rotund, garrulous woman who had a marvelous propensity for mirth and a strong passion for the bonbons she carried in her reticule. She might have been a beauty in her day, but now her features were distorted by fat, and her heavily ringed fingers resembled little sausages. Her husband was a jolly, beefy man of medium height and great girth who also enjoyed his food and wine. With their children grown and married, their numerous grandchildren were their fondest topic of conversation, and their photographs were shown at the slightest encouragement.

Emma and Gaston Dubreuil were not only husband and wife, they were first cousins, and there was a strong resemblance between them both physically and in their temperaments. Their six-year-old son, Michel, was attended by an old black mammy who exerted over the parents the same tolerant discipline she bestowed on the child.

Therese Vincart's jewels and elegant clothes did little to hide the fact that she was an unattractive woman. Her voice had a plaintive, whining quality which got on one's nerves, and she often appeared to be on the verge of tears. Alfred, her handsome and debonair husband, treated her with great politeness which contained a certain amount of disdain. Chantele could not help but feel sorry for Therese; she was an unhappy woman who tried to find some relief from her frustrations in nervous activity. Even her conversation was punctuated by the constant clicking of her knitting needles. They were accompanied by their nineteen-year-old daughter, Marie France. Even though the girl had inherited some of her father's features, what made a man handsome doesn't necessarily make a woman beautiful. At the onset, Marie France appeared to be a meek, retiring girl, but on closer contact Chantele discovered that her mordant, incisive comments were charged with malice.

The Mortimers were the only Americans in the group, and Chantele observed with a certain amount of curiosity that while the other ladies treated Sally Mortimer with courtesy, her presence was merely tolerated amongst them in spite of the fact that she was a pleasant, if laconic, lady whose sparse conversation was remarkably witty. With her husband, a government official returning from a trading mission in France, the Yankee-born lady made her home in Baton Rouge.

There was also another couple who kept mostly to themselves and were seldom seen. The manner in which they were ignored by the other passengers gave Chantele the impression that, although the man seemed to enjoy wealth and the girl wore elegant clothes and costly jewels, they were socially undesirable. Afraid of committing a *faux pas* that would embarrass Colin, Chantele refrained from exhibiting her curiosity about the pair.

With little to do aboard, the newlyweds spent many hours in their dream world, alone in their luxuriously appointed cabin. Bess continued to pamper her and cluck over her like a mother hen with a new chick, and Colin amusedly narrated that after her first visit to his flat, Bess had been so angry with him that she had accused him of being, among other things, a despoiler of young virgins.

"She's absolutely crazy about you," he confessed. "She and Gideon never had children of their own, and she needs someone to mother. She's given up on me, but now she has you and that makes her very happy. Just wait until the baby is born."

"I wished I had had someone like her when I was a little girl," Chantele replied. "I had no one until Rosalyn became my governess, and I'll never complain of too much love, Colin. Without it, life is so terrible!"

While the men gathered to play cards and other games of chance, the ladies were fond of social amenities. Chantele found their reunions a little tiring, wishing more for Colin's company, but she often accepted their invitations to join them for tea. Colin had spoken so little of their lives in Louisiana, that she found the ladies a fountain of information. But not all of what she learned was pleasant; Marie France made frequent references to a friend named

Marinette Dorleac, obviously expecting a reaction from Chantele and, consequently, arousing her curiosity. Little by little Chantele came to understand what Marie France's insinuations had meant to convey, and she tried to mask her surprise when she realized that Marinette and Colin had been engaged to be married.

She had always known there must have been other women in his past, but she had never suspected anything as serious as an engagement. According to Marie France, the Dorleacs and the Marquandts had looked very favorably upon the match. Why had Colin kept his engagement a secret? Did he still love Marinette? And how would his family react when he appeared with a new bride?

What would she find in L'Esperance?

Four

Chantele remained at the dressing table after Bess had finished brushing her hair and said goodnight. Colin came to stand behind her and regarded her reflection in the mirror.

"Are you all right, princess?" he inquired solicitously. "You've been very quiet all evening."

She wanted to ask him about Marinette

Dorleac, but she did not dare to broach the subject. There was so much she didn't know about him, she mused. He never talked about himself and was very adept at brushing aside her inquiries. What was he hiding from her?

"I'm just a little tired," was all she said.

"Those ladies giving you an earful?" he said in jest. "You don't have to accept all their invitations, you know.

"I find them most informative," she said and inwardly cursed herself for her blunder.

"Is that so?"

"Yes," she said trying to cover her mistake. "They talk about plantation life, and crops, but mostly about their households."

"But that's not all, is it?"

Chantele hesitated before admitting, "No, I guess not."

"You're upset," he said regarding her soberly. "What did they tell you?"

She couldn't keep up her pretense any longer. "Darling, why didn't you tell me you were engaged to Marinette Dorleac?"

Briefly, she felt the pressure of his fingers tighten on her shoulders before he released her.

"I suppose you had to hear about it sooner or later. You might as well know," he said with a frown. "Look, kitten, there was talk about an engagement between us, but I left New Orleans before anything became final."

So it was true, she said inwardly, and aloud,

"Did you love her?"

"No," he laughed, "and if it makes any difference to you, she didn't love me, either."

That, she found harder to believe. "Then, why?"

"L'Esperance and the Dorleac plantations are next to each other," he explained. "A marriage between the two families would one day make the property the largest in the state. It's as simple as that." He regarded her wryly before adding, "Marriages of convenience are not only made in France, kitten. It's done over there, too."

She desperately wanted to believe he had never loved Marinette Dorleac, and she went to him, seeking his reassurance. "Oh, Colin, I thought . . ." She shook her head. "I don't know what I thought."

"I know you're upset, princess," he said gathering her in his arms and kissing her hair, "but there is something you must understand. I'm twenty-seven years old, kitten, and I haven't exactly led the life of a monk. Whatever is in my past should remain there. You are my wife now, and not to be concerned about any affairs I may have had before I met you. Is that clear?"

She assented, but there was something else she had to know.

"Colin, are there . . . I mean," she couldn't bring herself to ask, but he seemed to have an uncanny ability to read her thoughts.

"As far as I know, there have been no children."

She accepted the statement as fact. Colin would never deny a child if he had one, she was sure. Somehow, the words Rosalyn had spoken came to her mind, when she had remarked on what a wonderful father he would make and now this reminded Chantele of Leon Marquandt and his expectations of enlarging his land holdings through his son's marriage.

"And what is troubling you now, princess?"

"Your father," she admitted. "What is he going to say when we arrive already married? Will he resent me?"

"Of course not," he said hugging her. "One look at you and Leon will forget all about the Dorleac property, especially once he learns you're already breeding. My father sets great stock on prolific women, heaven knows the Marquandts have not been very fortunate in that respect, until now. And speaking of little Marquandts," he said placing his hand on her belly, "it's about time this one went to bed."

She let him put her to bed and nestled close to him when he lay next to her. Just before she fell asleep, Chantele uttered a prayer. "Let it be true, please God, that Colin's father will like me."

Chantele had almost forgotten the existence of the two mysterious passengers when one afternoon she almost collided with the girl, who was returning below decks just as Chantele was emerging. Chantele was startled for an instant and then smiled and began to offer an apology. She was even more startled when the girl murmured something unintelligible and rushed away. There had been something in her eyes that Chantele could not recognize and, yet, after the incident, she was unable to put it out of her mind. Suddenly she realized what she had seen in the dark velvet eyes: stark, naked fear. But why? Even if the girl was not socially acceptable, what harm was there in exchanging a few words? Now that she thought of it, several nights before she had seen Alfred Vinçart in animated conversation with the old man.

Sally Mortimer was already having her tea when Chantele arrived, still pondering upon the episode. Today she was glad that, as usual, the other ladies were late. Herself a stranger to Louisiana, Mrs. Mortimer would not condemn her for her ignorance of their social customs, and she was wondering how to broach the subject without appearing a gossip when Sally herself gave her the opening when she remarked, "You seem troubled. Is there anything I can do?"

"I don't know," Chantele replied pensively. "Something happened a few minutes ago that set me to wonder." She paused before she added, "You know that couple, the old man and the girl?"

Mrs. Mortimer assented.

"I almost collided with the girl as I was coming up on deck," Chantele began. "I may be wrong, but she seemed . . . well, frightened."

"Frightened?" Mrs. Mortimer repeated. "Did you speak to her?"

"Not really. As I said, we almost collided on the passageway and I just apologized, but she ran away before I could say anything else."

Mrs. Mortimer gave Chantele a look she didn't know how to interpret and then said, "You really don't know, do you?"

"Know what?" Chantele inquired, puzzled.

"That the girl is the old man's mistress."

"Mistress!" Chantele exclaimed in disbelief. "All along I had thought she was his daughter." Still trying to digest that bit of information, she added, "But that still doesn't explain why she seemed so frightened."

"She had good reason," Mrs. Mortimer replied, "You see, she's the man's . . . well, property."

"His property? You mean . . ."

Sally Mortimer nodded. "The girl is an octoroon," she explained. "Girls with light skin and as beautiful as that one are sold at very high prices in New Orleans. Sometimes by their own families," she added.

"But why?"

"Because no woman in her right mind would have a girl like that in her house as a servant, and there are too many avenues open to them. They either find a protector or, worse yet, end up selling themselves on the streets. The old man is wealthy, he can provide for her. Many of the girls themselves have been fathered by prominent white men. It's quite common for a white man of means to keep a quadroon or octoroon mistress, and as long as they are discreet about it, most wives ignore the situation."

When Chantele appeared unconvinced, Mrs. Mortimer continued, "Not all wives, my dear. Some suffer a great deal, and Therese Vincart is a perfect example. Her husband is a notorious *roue* who for years has kept a string of mistresses on her money."

Seeing Chantele's frown, Mrs. Mortimer added, "It's not idle gossip, believe me, but you are new to their customs and should be aware of what you will find, although you must have seen something similar in Paris. I understand the Emperor's escapades are common knowledge. But in Louisiana, aside from the usual number of conventional affairs, men buy women to keep as mistresses. Some of them stay together for years while others . . . well, they rid themselves of the girls or trade them for others. Alfred Vincart is one of those. But ladies pretend not to see or even be aware that such things happen."

"To be able to understand, at least a little, you must learn more about their customs and traditions. In many ways, the Creoles are like children, craving excitement and luxury like no other people in the world. They are a closely knit group which doesn't allow strangers in its midst. Your situation is different, of course," Mrs. Mortimer added, "but my husband and I have lived in Louisiana for five years and our presence is tolerated only because of his position in the government, but still we are not welcome and never will be. A Creole gentleman is not to be concerned with business, except that of spending money. They love to gamble, and that's the reason many of them live in genteel poverty, having lost all their property," she added, with a shudder of her thrifty Yankee soul. "The father is a venerated figure whose word is law, while the children are raised by their black servants. From the cradle a gentleman is taught that a lady is to be placed on a pedestal; and slavery provides them with a most convenient way to satisfy their more base needs and desires."

"And speaking of their relationships with their slaves," Sally Mortimer continued somewhat amused, "the people on this ship are a good sample of what you'll find. The Gerards are benevolent and, in turn, are pampered by their servants while the Dubreuils are dominated by their black mammy, who probably spanked their bottoms when they were children; and the the Vincarts are petty and intolerant. As for yourself and your husband," she added, "I understand your servants are free, although they were born slaves."

Chantele assented. "My husband is against slavery, Mrs. Mortimer," she said proudly.

"And yet he's heir to a large plantation and a good number of slaves," Sally added wryly. "But as for the girl who seemed so frightened," she continued, "she could be severely punished if she's seen talking to you. As I said, the old man owns her, he can do anything to her and no one would lift a finger to help her."

"But surely there must be laws to protect them," Chantele objected.

"Of course, but they are seldom enforced. For example, by law, slaves should not work on Sundays, but in the five years I've lived in Louisiana, I have yet to see that law enforced. A white man would never bring a complaint against a neighbor for the benefit of a slave. There are, of course, cases of extreme cruelty that do not go unpunished. There was that nefarious Mme. Lalaurie, a doctor's wife who systematically tortured her slaves and was almost lynched when she was found out, but most slave owners do not abuse them, for various reasons. Some are truly good people who would not be unkind to another creature;

others because slaves are valuable property and can't work when they are hurt; and there are even others who are kind simply because they want to present a good image to their peers. But, of course, the most benevolent of masters still can box their ears when he is disgruntled, and many floggings are carried out at the plantations. But I see the ladies coming," Sally Mortimer said, looking past Chantele. "I don't think this is a subject they would care to discuss."

Calm at sea. The sails hung limply from the masts, waiting for winds that refused to keep their appointment. Tempers were short, and several fights broke out among the members of the crew who were busy washing the decks with sea water, scraping and painting and making repairs.

In her condition, and unaccustomed to the tropics, Chantele seemed to suffer more than anyone aboard from temperatures which continued to climb. In vain she sought relief from the heat of her cabin by going on deck, only to find the wet boards steaming under the relentless sun. Her damp clothing clung to her body, increasing her discomfort, and as soon as she entered the cabin Bess stripped her of the sodden layers of clothing and sponged her body with eau de cologne. Wearing only a loose cambric gown, Chantele submitted to the Negress' ministrations, and the old woman applied cold compresses to her forehead, bathed her wrists, and fanned her for hours.

"You feeling better, missy?"

"Ah, yes, Bess, thank you. I never knew it could be so hot! Is it like this in Louisiana?"

Bess bobbed her head. "You'll git used to it, missy. You on'y feel it mo' now beca'se of dat chile you's got growing inside you."

"How long did it take for Colin's mother to get used to it?"

Bess had always been reluctant to talk about Violette, and after a small hesitation said, "Miss Violette was not very strong, missy. She lost many babies, en she was always sad. But when Mistah Colin was born, she was happy, and so was Massah Leon. He always wanted lots of chillen, but Miss Violette took sick ag'in and had no mo' babies."

"But Jacob?" Chantele said, curious now.

"Jacob?"

"Yes, Colin's brother." Was it her imagination, or was Bess frightened? "Bess, why are you afraid to tell me about Jacob?"

"Jacob was jis' a boy dat grew up wid Mastah Colin, missy. His mother was a house nigger."

"But Colin said he was his brother," Chantele said, puzzled, but the look in Bess' eyes cleared the mystery. Of course, if Jacob has been the son of a slave it would explain, but only in part, Colin's reluctance to speak of him. It had been so hot during the night, that she had slept fitfully, and even Colin was thrashing about and talking in his sleep. She could not understand what he was saying, but he seemed very agitated.

"Darling," she called, and he woke with a start, drenched in perspiration. "You were having a nightmare."

He ran a hand over his haggard face. He seemed deeply troubled, but obviously was not going to tell her why. Finally, she asked, "Who is Jacob?"

He gave her a blank look. "Jacob?"

"You were calling his name," she said. "Who is he?"

"My brother," he said after a reluctant pause.

"Your brother? But I thought . . ."

"He's dead," he cut her off.

"Oh, darling, I'm sorry, I didn't know!" She put her arms around him and cradled his head to her bosom, trying to comfort him. Colin's arms went around her waist, and he held on to her as a drowning man clings to a piece of flotsam. Then something happened, something which brought back that violent stranger she had met that night in the garden, but Chantele understood now that what she had taken to be violence was some kind of desperation, as if in taking her he was exorcising a devil from his own private hell.

She wanted so much to be a part of him, to share his sorrows as she shared his joys, but he seemed to have established boundaries beyond which she was not allowed. The only times she felt truly close to him were when they made love, but the night's episode was proof enough that something in his past was still troubling him. Somehow, that something had to do with Jacob. If he would not tell her what it was, she would put aside her scruples and get the answers from Bess, but she had to know if she was going to be able to help him.

Bess was reluctant to talk about Jacob, but when she did, the story she told confirmed what Chantele had suspected.

After almost a week's delay, they would be arriving in New Orleans in less than a fortnight. And the nightmares were back. It had been so long, he had almost believed they would never return. Each dream was different and yet the same; but no matter how they went, they always ended with Jacob dead, his flesh torn, and oh, God, so much blood!

Was his father really ill, or was the letter his way of beckoning him home after the bitter, angry words they had spoken during their last encounter? That argument had ended in his year of self-imposed exile in Europe. But the real confrontation had begun much, much earlier, with Jacob. The years in between had only deepened the hurt on both sides.

Colin's memories of his mother were dim, and yet he could not smell the fragrance of violets without her wraithlike figure coming to mind. Violette had been like the romantic figure in fairy tales, the princess locked in the tower, beautiful and remote. What he had said earlier to Chantele about the luck of the Marquandts with their women had been true: the last three generations had produced one single male to carry on the name, but no other progeny. It had been Leon's dream to fill the big plantation house with the laughter of children, and after a trip to France at the age of twenty-five, he had returned to New Orleans with his young Paris bride. But Violette never adapted to the Louisiana climate. She had hated the heat, the mosquitoes, everything about the plantation and had lived in mortal fear of the hurricanes and of the epidemics which broke out in the summer months. After giving birth to two dead infants, she had become a recluse, and banned from the bed of the wife he loved, the young and virile Leon had turned to a slave named Rachel for solace. A child was conceived, and Jacob was born after Violette had announced a third pregnancy. Happy times had returned to L'Esperance when Violette was delivered of a strong, healthy boy. But when she had been unable to nurse him and Colin had cried with hunger, Rachel took him to her breast and he and Jacob had shared her milk. Rachel cared for the son of the master she loved as she cared for her own, but after Colin was born, Leon never turned to Rachel again.

The boys grew up together, happy and healthy as young pups. It had been Jacob who had been Colin's willing accomplice in his childhood schemes, Jacob who shared his secrets, his experiences, his discoveries. It came as a shock when the difference between them had been brought home, and Colin protested loud and clear when a tutor came and Jacob was banned from the schoolroom. Colin got more than one whipping for refusing his lessons unless Jacob shared them, but had to submit under the threat of losing him to the slave trader unless he returned to the schoolroom. Education was forbidden to slaves, but Colin had taught Jacob what he learned from his tutor. It had been the greatest secret the boys had shared; not even Rachel was taken into their confidence. Jacob was bright and clever, with a passion for the books Colin smuggled out to him.

The Marquandts had always been fair masters, but Colin knew that the threat to sell Jacob had not been an empty one. Even without knowing they were brothers, the love between the boys transcended the difference in color of their skins and their positions of master and slave, and the experience with the tutor only served to strengthen the bond between them.

Colin's affection for Jacob became a source of concern to Leon, but he reasoned that once the boy was sent to school and had other friends of his own class, he would forget Jacob. He had been so sure of it that he let events follow their normal course, and there had been other more pressing problems to worry about. Never strong, Violette's health continued to decline, undermined by her frequent miscarriages. She never left her rooms any more and seldom left her bed.

The boys had been thirteen when the incident which triggered the unbreachable rift between father and son took place. Even the most loving of brothers have their differences, and Colin and Jacob were no exception. Both boys were headstrong and quick of temper, and on many occasions their arguments ended in blows. Even in their anger their secret pact was kept: there was no master and no slave. Colin took as good as he gave. Almost every fight ended in a draw, their anger soon forgotten and both contenders laughing at each other's bruises, but it had been during one of those free-for-alls that Colin's nose was broken. Frightened by the blood and forgetting his own safety, Jacob had run for help before Colin could stop him. The hue and cry that rose when the Marquandt heir was found hurt and bleeding had been so great, that even Violette had emerged from her rooms. Colin insisted it had been an accident; Jacob had been too frightened to answer the questions that were shot at him from every direction; and at that moment of confusion, through someone's indiscretion, Violette had learned that Jacob was her husband's son. Colin had recovered from his injuries, but his nose had never healed properly. Nothing else was said to Jacob and on the surface things seemed to continue as usual; underneath, a huge storm was brewing.

Rachel as dead, but Violette could not bear the thought of Jacob being Leon's son. The boy, who in her mind had disfigured her own child, was a constant reminder of her failure as a wife and as a woman, and nothing would satisfy her but to be rid of Jacob. In spite of being a benevolent master, Leon was not sentimental about his slaves. He was rather fond of Jacob, but he had no place in his heart for the child of a servant, even if he was also his own. Only Colin, his legitimate heir and the son of the woman he loved, mattered to Leon, and Violette's demands to sell Jacob were satisfied when Colin was sent to school in France.

Colin had returned a year later, and the first person he had sought after greeting his parents had been Jacob. No one dared tell him the boy had been sold, and he had looked for his brother in vain. Finally, he had gone to his father, and even to this day Colin remembered the argument during which he had challenged Leon's dictates for the first time.

Colin ran a finger over the bridge of his nose, feeling the injury that had healed so long ago, and remembering Jacob's voice, his laughter when a fish took the bait, and that habit of his to scratch his wooly head whenever he was puzzled. He had looked for Jacob, leaving no stone unturned until he had found him. But he had been too late. Time and time again Jacob had run away from his new master, trying to make his way back to L'Esperance, the only home he knew, and each time he had been caught and whipped until that day when he had not survived his punishment. Only a boy, and he had been whipped to death!

In his anger Colin had cursed his father, the system which allowed such things to happen, and, most of all, himself. Jacob had paid the price for the rules Colin himself had broken by teaching him to read and write and for encouraging him to believe that they were equals— only to leave him behind to discover that the world was not what they wanted it to be. When Colin had returned to L'Esperance for Violette's funeral, he had been barely able to recognize his father. Pain and suffering had left their mark; the tall, proud man he remembered looked much older than his years, his hair had turned to silver, and his face was lined by grief. It had been then that Colin learned that Jacob had been his brother, and he had tried to keep his anger alive, but the love for his father had been stronger. Or was it the guilt they shared?

Colin reflected now on how hard he had tried for years to break away from his father, from L'Esperance and all it represented. If only there had been other children . . . but Leon's second wife had failed to provide the heirs that had become Leon's obsession. Colin had failed to make the complete break just as he had failed to live with Leon's book of rules. If only he could share with Chantele that part of him that he kept locked within himself. But how could she understand his fears? She was so brave, and yet so young, so innocent. Just having her there beside him was a balm to his spirit, but how long would it be until the magic between them began to fade away?

Now that the tradewinds had returned, the heat had abated somewhat and Chantele was feeling better, but Colin was concerned. They would be arriving in L'Esperance at the height of summer. How would she, accustomed to a much cooler climate, bear the heat and humidity which made life miserable even for the natives? He had to see that measures were taken to ensure her comfort. Annette would help. Regardless of her failure to provide him with children, Leon had been fortunate in his second wife. Colin was fond of Annette and especially of her son, Robert, who had been only five years old at the time of their marriage. Leon was the only father the boy had ever known, and Robert adored him.

Colin remembered how during his own childhood, he had admired the man who was his father, and he could easily understand how a fatherless boy like Robert could become so devoted to Leon. Had not he himself been unable to break the ties between them despite their differences? He was also aware of how much Robert had hoped for Leon to adopt him, but Leon had resisted giving the boy his name. Colin had been more than a brother to Robert; it had been he who had taught the boy the marvelous experience of fishing in the river and in the numerous streams crisscrossing the plantation; it had been Colin who had taught Robert to ride, to shoot, and all those things boys love to do as he had done once with Jacob, and in return, he had been rewarded with the affection and admiration of the boy while he had recaptured some of those magic moments of his youth.

The rising sun traced a huge rainbow in the mist of dawn, and flocks of gulls, terns, and cranes disturbed the pervasive quiet as the ship entered the Mississippi delta, that vast spread of tawny marshes veined with waterways where the mighty river makes it rendezvous with the sea. When the sun burned away the mist, Chantele had a glimpse of trees bent into agonizing shapes, their clinging roots holding the land fast against the battering waves. Overhead, white cottony clouds swirled in the gentle breeze of the Gulf.

"It's so peaceful, and yet so strange it's almost frightening," she said in awe. "Like a vision of heaven and hell all rolled into one. Why are those trees so twisted and gnarled?"

"It's the winds that give them such odd shapes," Colin replied.

"The wind?"

"Tornadoes and hurricanes," he explained. "They can be devastating, tearing and destroying everything in their path."

It was almost impossible to imagine such violence, with a feeling of serenity so deep it seemed as though the earth itself had come to a standstill.

Avoiding the sandbars and shallows, the bar pilot cautiously steered the vessel through the narrow channel, and as the ship continued its journey upriver, the land stretched into infinity, flat and abundant with vegetation and wildlife. Poised like a ballet dancer on the branch of a dead cypress, a white-plumed egret watched a flock of brown pelicans dive for their breakfast into the muddy waters of the river. Bright wildflowers provided dots of color amongst a profusion of towering willows and cypresses draped with Spanish moss.

After the tranquility of the bayous, the cacophony of sound and explosion of movement that was the New Orleans levee was almost overwhelming. The river was populated with a wide variety of vessels ranging from pirogues and keelboats to seagoing ships and exotic steamboats gleaming white in the sun. These sported filigree work in fanciful patterns along their triple decks, and their enormous paddle wheels, painted bright red, were poised motionless in the water waiting for the double stacks to belch smoke.

The levee, piled high with bales of cotton, sacks of sugar, and all sorts of cargo, teemed with commotion and clatter. Carts and drays moved along the congested milieu, and roustabouts, their black skin glistening with sweat, moved in rhythm loading cargo while chanting:

> *Working on the dock*
> *bend yo' back*
> *tote it to the lift*
> *white boss hollers*
> *if you ain't swift*

Fearful of exposing Chantele to the dangers of the city in summer, Colin refused to let her disembark, and despite her protest she had to remain aboard while he and Gideon went to secure passage on the next steamboat leaving New Orleans. Chantele was too excited to remain in her cabin as she had been instructed, but she obeyed Bess and carried her parasol to shield her from the burning rays of the sun while she stood at the railing of the *Mouette*, watching with fascination the activity on the levee and enjoying the rich odors of the wharves which seemed to be seasoned with sugar, spices, coffee, and bananas. Steamboats were being packed up to their smokestacks with bales of cotton.

The Gerards came to say their farewells, and Chantele was crushed in Marguerite's affectionate embrace that smelled faintly of vanilla and chocolate. Mme. Gerard made her promise she would visit her when she returned to New Orleans, an invitation Chantele was glad to accept. Marguerite had been a good friend during those long weeks at sea, especially when Marie France Vincart, who had become extremely unpleasant, had made a number of mordant remarks that had left Chantele a little baffled.

She waved goodbye at the departing passengers and noticed the old man leaving the ship alone; the girl who had accompanied him was nowhere to be seen. She emerged later, also alone, as Colin and Gideon were returning. Chantele saw her hesitate briefly and look after them who, apparently, had not noticed her presence. Then, before she boarded a carriage, the girl looked up and saw Chantele standing there. Was it her imagination, Chantele asked herself, or was that look charged with hatred? But the incident was forgotten with Colin's arrival.

"You should have stayed in the cabin," he remonstrated when he found her on deck, but when she began to protest, he added, "Never mind, we're booked on the *Mayflower*, and it's leaving in a couple of hours."

"Two hours!" Chantele explained. "Could we take a quick ride through the city? Oh, please, Colin!"

"Well, all right," he relented. "I suppose you can see something of the Vieux Carre on our way to the levee on Canal Street."

Chantele laughed and almost jumped up and down with glee.

How very young she is, he thought, little more than a child. Aloud, he said, "Darling, in this climate you must try not to excite yourself so much. Please try to remember that."

Gideon was to transfer their luggage to the *Mayflower* while Colin took his wife on the promised jaunt through the city.

"This is the Garden District," Colin said when the carriage entered St. Charles Avenue, a wide street lined with shady trees displaying orchid-like flowers in purple, pink and white. The stately residences were surrounded by lush gardens and sported elaborately ornate wrought iron fences and grill work in their balconies. The air was heavy with the scent of oleander, azalias and jasmine. As they emerged on Royal Street, Colin pointed out the Bank of Louisiana and the numerous shops the majority of which he said belonged to *gens de couleur libres*. "And that's the LeBrance Building," he added pointing out a three-story building blending French and Spanish influence. The balconies were of the most delicate grill iron work ever imagined.

Despite the decline of the Vieux Carre, the cafes and shops were crowded and street sellers hawked their wares, reminding Chantele a little of Paris. The graceful spires of the St. Louis Cathedral were visible from busy Bourbon Street, and as they passed St. Peter Street, Colin pointed out *Le Petit Theatre*, saying that it was probably the oldest one in the country. Finally, they emerged on Jackson Square. "Those buildings on each side of the Cathedral are the Cabildo and the Presbytere," he said, and indicating an equestrian bronze statue in front of the Cathedral, he commented, "And I see they have finally erected the statue of Andrew Jackson."

The Pontalba Apartments, two spectacular structures flanking the square, had been built back in 1849 in an effort to inject new life into the old section of the city, since most new businesses were being built in the American sector.

Across the street was the French Market, located in the same place where the Choctaw Indians had carried their trade before any white man had even heard of Louisiana.

Chantele was sorry they could not continue their exploration, but the elegant and handsome *Mayflower* waited at the levee, ready to cast off. Bess and Gideon were waiting to say their farewells. Their status of freedom made their presence in the plantation undesirable, and they were to remain in New Orleans to care for the Marquandt town house. But Bess was crying copiously when she crushed Chantele against her well-padded frame, and Chantele also had tears in her eyes. Then, a geyser of steam erupted from the half-moon mouth of the whistle announcing departure, and Bess and Gideon left the boat and stood at the levee waving goodbye. A voice boomed, "Hard right! Half ahead!", and the red stern wheel began to churn hillocks of foaming water, increasing to a swifter tempo as the boat entered the mainstream of the river.

Five

The deep-throated whistle blow of the *Mayflower* alerted the residents of L'Esperance to the discharge of passengers, and by the time Chantele and Colin disembarked, an anxious Robert was waiting at the landing. She stood aside while the brothers embraced and heard a note of pride in Colin's voice when he said, "My wife."

Robert seemed to be a likeable youngster, a good-looking boy who in time would grow into a handsome man. His hair was brown and wavy, his eyes a soft brown, and his complexion deeply tanned by the sun.

At the levee, a carpet of buttercups swayed in the gentle breeze, and lush green grass and shrubs went as far as the eye could see on both sides of the gravel driveway leading to the plantation house, hidden from view by the abundance of trees. The luggage was left on the landing to be collected by a servant, and as their coach got under way, Chantele could see a number of female slaves and half-naked children occupied in the maintenance of the grounds. In the distance, she got a glimpse of a gazebo. The gnarled branches of oak trees training their drapes of Spanish moss provided shade along the avenue. There was a lilting, humming sound that seemed to have no particular point of origin but was all around them. She had never heard anything like it before and was about to ask what it was, but with a sharp intake of breath she was left speechless when the house came into view. Set on high ground, its dormers shining like gold in the early afternoon sun, a whitewashed mansion rose amidst the greenery. Moss hung thick over venerable oak trees clustered around the house shading its walls and casting lacy patterns on its tall Tuscan columns and gabled roof. A honeysuckle vine clung to the railings of the galleries above, dispersing the sweet perfume of its creamy flowers, and across the driveway, a white fountain sprayed sparkling jets of water.

Colin helped Chantele alight, and followed by Robert they ascended the marble steps leading up to the porch where a woman and two black servants awaited.

"Colin," the woman said. She embraced him and waited to meet his unexpected companion. Behind her, the two black servants wore expectant smiles.

"Annette," Colin said after returning her embrace, "this is my wife, Chantele. My stepmother."

"Your wife!" Annette exclaimed. She was attractive without being a beauty. Of medium height, her figure was mature, but handsome; her most remarkable feature was her complexion, so smooth and delicate, it was almost translucent. Her thick brown hair, parted in the middle, was coiled in a chignon at the back of her elegant head. It was difficult to determine her age, perhaps in the mid-thirties. Recovering quickly from her surprise, Annette smiled a welcome. "What a pleasant surprise, my dear. Welcome to L'Esperance."

Her voice had a velvet quality, and any misgivings Chantele may have had as to her receptions were dispelled by the obvious pleasure she read in Annette's brown eyes.

"Jossie!" Colin was sweeping the huge black woman in an exuberant embrace. "How's my favorite girl? Did you miss me? I swear, you're more ravishing each time I see you!"

The black woman dissolved into girlish giggles. "Don' 'no noth'n 'bout ravishin', Mistah Colin, but der sho' is mo' of me! she sallied.

Colin greeted the other servant, a small but dignified man he called Simon. Jossie was the cook and Simon the butler, Chantéle learned.

"How is Leon, Annette?" Colin inquired soberly.

Annette's smile began to fade and she shook her head. "He's ill, Colin," she replied and then added, "But let's go inside. Chantele looks as if she could use some rest."

And a bath, Chantele said inwardly. It had been so long since she had had a nice long bath, that the thought of finally being able to soak in a tub was like an invitation to heaven. She had never complained, but the humid heat of Louisiana made her weary and limp, and no matter how often she changed, her damp clothes clung to her body uncomfortably.

In the entrance hall, the oak floor was polished to a high gloss. A large gilt-framed mirror reflected the flowers in an enormous vase on the top of a console of veneered wood. An Empire settee was placed against the wall, which was covered with French paper in white and gold.

113

While the servants rushed to their preparations, Annette led the way into a large, high-ceilinged parlor where purple was the predominant color. A needlepoint firescreen framed in rosewood and placed before the Empire mantel was a work of art that immediately caught Chantele's eye, and while they sat on sofas covered in purple velvet, Simon served ice-cold lemonade in tall, frosty glasses.

"What's wrong with Leon?" Colin inquired as soon as they were seated.

"Shortly after you left he began complaining of pains in his chest," Annette replied. "He kept saying it was indigestion and wouldn't call Dr. Maurais, but when the pains continued, he had no choice."

"What did the doctor say?" Colin inquired with apprehension. "Is it his heart?"

Annette assented.

"Will he recover?"

"He's been confined to his bed for the last two months," Annette replied. "But I'm sure your being here now is the best medicine for him. Especially when he meets Chantele," she added, "You know how much he wanted to see you married."

A servant stood silently at the door and Annette turned to Chantele. "Your rooms are ready, my dear. Justine will show you the way. Do rest a little before supper," she added solicitously, "it takes a while to to get used to this climate of ours."

Colin remained in the parlor with Annette while Chantele followed Justine to the upper level. Halfway up, where the stairs curved, multicolored light filtered through a large stained glass window and spilled over the carpet.

The first meeting with Colin's family had transpired much more easily than she had hoped, Chantele mused, while following the servant. Annette had been surprised, but apparently pleased with the news of their marriage. Judging from Robert's reception, there was a good relationship between the brothers. Chantele was glad Robert was so close to her in age. Perhaps they could be friends.

The bedchamber she entered was of enormous proportions and only a part of a spacious suite complete with sitting room, boudoir, and separate dressing area. There was a circular Aubusson carpet on the polished floor, and every detail proclaimed it a woman's domain, the soft colors of the fabrics, the elegant and delicate furnishings. The shutters at the French windows were left open, allowing a balmy breeze to penetrate the rooms where a large, enameled bathtub had been prepared.

Justine helped her new mistress to discard her clothing, and after all the garments had been removed, she gave a happy cry at the sight of Chantele's rounded belly. "Massah Leon is gwine be happy, Miss Chantele,'' Justine chirped between giggles.

Everyone seemed to take it for granted that Leon would be pleased by the news of Colin's marriage, Chantele mused stepping into the tub. If only it were true, life in L'Esperance would be all she had hoped for, and more. Not that it really mattered, for she would have lived happily in a shack as long as it was shared with Colin, but even though in Paris he had appeared to enjoy a certain amount of wealth, in her wildest imaginings she had never dreamed plantation life could reach such proportions of luxury. But at what cost, she reminded herself. He, who abhorred slavery, was the master of many; a man at war with himself. From what she had seen of the servants, they seemed content enough with their lot. That many of them even felt affection for their white masters was evident if Jossie's and Simon's reception was an indication.

Justine's voice brought her out of her musings. ''You is gwine catch cold, Miss Chantele, stay'n in dat tub so long.'' She held up a towel that she wrapped around Chantele's body when she stood up.

Feeling refreshed and comfortable for the first time in weeks, Chantele brushed aside the robe de chambre Justine had selected and slipped naked between the scented sheets.

The first thing she was aware of when she woke was that lilting, humming sound she had heard upon their arrival. "Justine, what is that noise?"

Justine looked puzzled. "Noise?"

"Yes, can't you hear it?"

Frowning, Justine listened intently and then smiled. "Dat's the cicadas, Miss Chantele."

"Cicadas?"

"Little critters dat live in de trees. Dey sing all night and sometimes all day, too. We pay dem no min' no mo'."

"What do they look like?"

"Dey has big eyes, lots of legs en you kin see right through deir wings."

Insects, Chantele said inwardly.

She had finished dressing when there was a light tap on the door and Colin came in at her invitation. "Good, I'm glad you're ready," he said. "Leon is waiting to meet you."

"Is he angry?" Chantele asked, frightened by the grim expression on her husband's face.

He regarded her absently and then, realizing the cause for her anxiety, smiled and said, "No, kitten, he was very pleased. As the matter of fact, he's been asking for you all evening."

She tried to control her anxiety and he smiled encouragingly. "You have nothing to fear," he said taking her by the hand. "Come along, princess."

Warily, she allowed him to guide her along

the corridor leading into the other wing of the house. He paused briefly before a closed door and without waiting for an invitation admitted them in.

There was a strong odor of medicine in the room, and in a moment of panic, Chantele thought she was going to be ill. The windows were shut tight, and a number of oil lamps dispersed through the room cast their yellow light, leaving some areas in shadow. Colin guided his wife toward the enormous half-tester bed occupying the center of the room. Fighting the feeling of nausea, Chantele forced her attention on the emaciated figure of a white-haired man sitting, propped up by pillows, on the bed. He must have been handsome at one time; there was something left of the masculine beauty in the aristocratic face of sharp, angular features which faintly reminded her of Colin, but the ravages of time, sorrow, and illness had changed all that.

"Father," she heard Colin say, "this is Chantele."

The man on the bed waved a bony hand. "Come closer, child," he said in a raspy voice, "I can't see you."

With her heart hammering in her chest, Chantele obeyed and, aware of her tension, Colin patted her hand and whispered in her ear, "Don't be frightened, princess."

She came to stand by the bed and Leon

could see her features now. His face, filled with anticipation, broke into a smile. "My dear," he said taking her hand and pressing it to his lips that were warm and dry, "I'm so happy to meet you at last."

Chantele felt immense relief flow through her body, as if someone had lifted a great burden from her shoulders. "*Monsieur*," she said feebly.

"No, no, my dear, you must call me Father." He still held her hand in his that was as hot and dry as his lips. "You don't know how long I've wanted a daughter." His smile was as disarming as Colin's. "Chantele," he said testing her name on his tongue, "Very unusual and very beautiful, my dear, as you are."

"Father," Colin interposed, "I believe Chantele has something to tell you. I think you'll be pleased."

Chantele looked at Colin, unable to hide her surprise. She was glad and relieved he had not mentioned to his father the circumstances of their marriage.

"Yes, my dear?" Leon said expectantly.

Chantele found her voice. "I'm with child, Father," she said finally.

Several wordless seconds went by and then Leon raised her hand to his lips and kissed it reverently. When he lifted his eyes to his new daughter, she saw they were brimming with tears.

"Bless you, my child," he said in a voice choked with emotion. "Colin." He extended his other hand to his son and held it. "Thank you, my son."

Annette came in. "I'm sorry," she said apologetically, "but Leon must rest."

"Your news was the best medicine for me," Leon said in a stronger voice. "Annette, I'm going to be a grandfather."

Annette's surprise was apparent, and her eyes turned sharply on Chantele's waist. Then she smiled and said, "My dear, I'm so glad! When is the baby due?"

"Not for a long time yet," Colin replied, and taking his wife by the hand he said, "Let's go, princess. Good night, Father."

"Chantele, will you come and see me tomorrow?" Leon asked expectantly.

Chantele returned to his side and planted a kiss on Leon's parchment-like cheek. "Of course I will, Papa," she said, "and I'll read for you, if you like."

Leon gave her a grateful smile. "Good night, *ma petite.*"

When they stepped out on the corridor, Colin dropped his cheerful pretense and his face was grim again.

"How is he really, Colin?"

Without replying, he walked away.

"Please, wait!" she called rushing after him down the sweeping staircase and out to the front porch. Above the trees, the sunset sky was like an endless canvas, pink, orange, and blue. Without pausing, Colin headed toward the grounds, his long stride making it difficult for Chantele to keep up, but she doggedly followed, sensing he should not be alone with his grief.

The path they took led to the gazebo, set amongst tall magnolia trees spilling their heady scent on the surrounding stillness. Not a leaf moved. Colin slowed down and stood before the gazebo, apparently watching the clinging vines entwined in the lattice work, but she realized he was not looking outwardly, but inside himself. She came to stand beside him and gently touched his arm.

"Darling, don't keep it locked inside you like this. Please let me help you."

His face was fraught with anguish when he said, "I could barely recognize him, he looks so . . . frail!"

She waited, and several wordless seconds went by before he continued. "You should have seen the way he was before, so tall, so strong, so proud. And now . . . I should never have stayed away so long!"

"He will recover," she said trying to soothe his pain. "Don't blame yourself, my love."

"You don't understand," he said, shaking his head with despair.

"Then help me," she said beseechingly.

He was almost tempted to share with her the darkness he carried in his soul, but when he regarded her luminous, eager face and saw her waiting to share his grief, all he saw was how very young she was.

"You're right, he will recover," he said trying to sound cheerful, and Chantele realized that again he had erected that invisible barrier he had built between them.

"Don't shut me out, Colin, please!"

"Don't be silly, darling," he said gently. "Let's get back to the house before the mosquitoes eat you alive. They'll be here in a swarm in a few minutes."

When they entered the drawing room, Robert jumped to his feet.

"Please, Robert, sit down," Chantele said observing him stand awkwardly after she had taken her seat. "Colin tells me that you have been working very hard in his absence. Will you be going to school in France next year?" she added, trying to make conversation.

Robert blushed. "I don't want to go back to school," he said with embarrassment. "No school in France can teach me what I want to learn."

Chantele observed that he was reluctant to discuss the subject. There was time to learn more about her new brother-in-law, she told herself, to win his friendship and his confidence. "Well," she said, "I'm sure you know what you want."

"Don't spoil your appetite for supper," Colin warned her when she reached for the bowl of fruit Simon had placed before her. "If I know Jossie, there'll be a feast tonight."

"She's been fretting all evening preparing all your favorite dishes," Robert said to Colin. He fell silent, and Chantele had the feeling that he had something to say and was having difficulties in broaching the subject. Finally, he seemed to have found his courage. "Colin," he said tentatively, "what you said this evening when you introduced me to Chantele . . ."

"What did I say, little brother?"

"That's what you called me."

"You know I consider you my brother, Robert, even if we don't share the same blood."

"I know," Robert admitted. "What I wanted to tell you is that . . ." he hesitated.

"Yes?" Colin encouraged him.

"My name is now Marquandt," Robert said quickly. "Leon adopted me." He waited expectantly for Colin's reaction, who thumped the young man on the back and said, "I'm glad, Robert. Now when I call you brother, it's really true."

"You are not upset then?"

"Why should I be? I said I was glad, didn't I?"

"I don't think you understand," Robert said with a worried frown. "After Leon adopted me, I was included in his will as heir to a portion of L'Esperance," he finished with dismay.

Colin regarded him with surprise.

"I'm sorry, Colin," Robert said apologetically. "I wanted to be the one to tell you, to explain to you that I always wanted Leon to be my father, but I never meant to take anything away from you," he finished ruefully.

Chantele observed Robert's expectation and the impassiveness of her husband. Colin's attention turned to the wine glass he was holding, and his eyes remained fixed on the amber liquid when he spoke. "I am glad, Robert," he said finally. "I know how much you love L'Esperance. It's right that you should have part of it. I . . . only wished he had done it sooner."

Robert expelled a sigh of relief. "Thank you, Colin."

There were fresh flowers on the Seignouret sideboard and on the long mahogany table set with gleaming crystal and silver and delicate porcelain. There was also enough food to feed an army, and the care of its preparation confirmed that Jossie had indeed been busy. The whole was a new experience for Chantele's palate, a savory soup thick with vegetables they called gumbo; fresh oysters and a variety of

fish and shellfish; a sweet tasting root they
called yams; a dish of saffron rice cooked with
bits of ham and shellfish, and she tasted each
and every course more out of curiosity than appetite. The meal was topped by a cherry dessert
which arrived in its own little inferno of flames.

Although he made Jossie blush at his compliments, Chantele noticed that her husband ate
and spoke little. And after supper, when they
retired to the drawing room and the silence was
bearing heavy on her, she approached a rectan-
gular Empire-style pianoforte occupying a corner.

"Do you play?" inquired Annette, pausing
from her needlepoint.

"A little," Chantele replied. "I haven't
played for a long time."

"Will you play for us?" begged Robert.

Chantele looked to her husband for approval, and Colin nodded. Perhaps a little
music would help cast away some of the gloom,
Chantele said inwardly as she took her seat at
the piano. But she was a little nervous, playing
for her husband and his family for the first
time. She began with *Fur Elise* and was
gratified to see that Colin was listening to her
music.

Robert applauded enthusiastically when she
finished and begged for more. "Can you play
any of the songs of Stephen Foster?" he inquired eagerly.

"I doubt if Chantele has ever heard the music, Robert," Annette interposed, "but look through the sheets, there must be one or two of his songs."

There were several, and Robert selected the new "I Dreamed of Jeannie With the Light Brown Hair," declaring it was his favorite, and encouraging Chantele to sing the lyrics. The lively "Camptown Races" and "Oh, Susannah!" followed, helping disperse the gloom, but at nine o'clock Colin put an end to the evening when he saw Chantele stifle a yawn. He escorted her to her room, and when he gave her a perfunctory kiss at the door, she said, "Aren't you coming to bed?"

"I still have some work to do," he replied, "but you go ahead, princess, it's been a long day."

She watched him descend the stairs and with a sigh went to her suite. Justine came to help her and opened the windows and adjusted a wispy mosquito netting once Chantele got into bed. Chantele was weary and fell asleep almost immediately, only to wake much later, bathed in perspiration. She was alone and wondered how long she had slept. Through the eternal song of the cicadas, she listened to the stillness of the house.

After tossing and turning for what seemed like hours, she pushed the mosquito netting aside, got up, and lit the lamp. Then she stood at the window until the mosquitoes made her retreat under the protection of the netting. She was wide awake now, wondering how long it would be before Colin came to bed. Would he go to his room or share her bed? Since their wedding, she had become accustomed to sharing the same bed with him that now she wished they would continue. It was so good to watch his face in slumber, when he looked so young and vulnerable, to hear his even breathing lulling her to sleep. But the intimacy that had been theirs when they were alone was no longer possible. Everything comes to an end, she mused with a sigh and was reminded of the words he had spoken on their wedding night. Why did he still refuse to let her get closer to him? Had he married her only because of the child she carried? No, it couldn't be! She loved him, needed him desperately. She was debating whether or not to find him when there was a light tap on her door.

"Enter," she bid, hoping to see Colin appear, but it was Annette, in her night clothes, who came in.

"I saw your light," she said apologetically. "Can't sleep?"

"It's too hot," Chantele said shaking her head. And then, "Is Colin still downstairs?"

"He retired hours ago," Annette replied, and seeing Chantele's disappointment, she added, "You'll get used to the heat, but if you like, I can bring you a *tisane* that will relax you and help you sleep.''

''Oh, please, don't trouble yourself,'' Chantele protested.

''Nonsense, my dear,'' Annette said with a wave of her hand. ''You need your sleep after all the excitement you had today. Besides, it will only take a moment. I keep a kettle in my room in case Leon needs something during the night.'' She was gone for only a few moments and returned with a cup of steaming brew.

''I'm sorry to cause you so much trouble,'' Chantele said apologetically, accepting the cup. She didn't want the tisane but took and sip and found it to have a very pleasing taste. ''It's delicious,'' she said taking another sip. ''What is in it?''

''Just some medicinal herbs,'' Annette replied, ''I'm glad you like it.'' She watched while Chantele drained the cup and said, ''If you don't mind, I'll stay until you feel a little drowsy. I've been wanting to have a chat with you, and I know how very trying this day must have been.''

''All of you have been wonderful,'' Chantele said warmly.

''We want you to feel at home, my dear. After all, you will be the mistress of this house one day. I must say,'' she added, ''it will be a relief for me.''

''Oh?''

Annette regarded her thoughtfully before she continued. "It's been different for me than it will be for you. I'm nothing but a glorified housekeeper, and I know it, my dear. Leon married me because he needed someone to run his house, to entertain his friends, and . . . never mind. But he has never loved me. Violette, Colin's mother, was the love of his life."

"But surely he loves you."

Annette shook her head sadly, letting her sorrow pull at Chantele's heart. "No, he does not. But he's fond of me, and we've been relatively happy."

"You love him very much, don't you?" Chantele said taking her hand.

"Oh, yes!" Annette said wistfully, and then seemed to recover quickly, as if embarrassed. "I'm sorry, darling, don't pay any attention to an old woman's ramblings." She stood up and brushed Chantele's brow with her lips. "Good night, my dear. I'd better go now or we'll talk half the night and the tisane won't do its work."

"Good night, Annette. Thank you for everything."

"Sweet dreams, my dear."

Chantele ran through her mind what she had just learned about her step-mother-in-law, and without realizing it, fell into a deep, untroubled sleep.

Back in her room, Annette chuckled to herself while she rinsed the cup used by Chantele and replaced it with her personal set. She examined the contents of the canister before closing its lid and then put it back on the cover, which she locked with the key she carried on a chain around her neck. Even with the new arrival, she had enough to last several months, she congratulated herself.

A dark, furry shadow leaped through the open window and landed on the bare hardwood floor with a soft thud. "Ah, there you are, Minette," Annette said picking up the cat and stroking her silken fur. The animal began to purr softly, watching her mistress through half-veiled yellow eyes while Annette's hand ran absently over the glossy black coat. "What a wonderful day this has been, Minette," Annette said with amusement. Colin's arrival with his new French bride was the greatest stroke of luck she had ever experienced. The girl was so young, so naive; it had been so easy to win her trust and sympathy. All her years of careful planning would soon bear fruit, she could feel it, and it was a heady sensation. She had married Leon Marquandt knowing full well that his desire for children was his only reason for seeking a new wife, but Annette had other ideas on the subject, and the knowledge she had acquired from Dulcie, the old black mammy who had saved her mother from the fury of the slaves during their revolt in Sainte Domingue had helped her avoid conception. Leon had never known that on three occasions she had aborted the children that were his obsession. And that knowledge of herbs and secret rites were the key to unlock the gates of her destiny. It had been easy to administer certain herbs to Leon, and the reason he was still alive today, after his adoption of Robert, was Colin's existence. Only Colin stood between her and the Marquandt fortune. But now he had provided her with the knife to cut his own throat: his wife.

"Soon, Minette," she crooned softly. "Very soon it will all be ours."

Six

Colin had already gone to the fields when Chantele woke the next morning, and in need of exercise after the long voyage, she headed for the stables after breakfast with Annette.

Except for a few old women caring for the very young, half-naked children playing in the yard, the slave cabins appeared deserted as Chantele rode by on the gentle chestnut mare she had selected. The small gardens on which the slaves were allowed to grow vegetables to supplement the staples supplied by the masters appeared well tended and represented a triumph of Colin's efforts to improve their lot. Older children, still too young to be sent to the fields, were occupied in weeding the rows of young plants.

Despite the early hour, Chantele found that her fashionable riding habit tailored in France was too heavy for the sultry Louisiana climate and was gratified to see that the gnarled branches of oaks bordering the path made a shady tunnel that protected her from the sun. To the right, field hands were busy hoeing cotton fields that stretched far into the distance.

Chantele's exhilarating feeling of freedom seemed to communicate itself to her mount, which broke into a gallop when she gave her her head, and venturing farther along the path, Chantele found herself in a portion of the forest not yet yielded to crops, thick with cottonwood. The path bifurcated ahead, and pulling the horse into a walk she wondered if she should continue her exploration or return to the house. Finally, she turned her mount around and headed for home.

Halfway along the way, two riders emerged from the fields and she was delighted to see that Colin was one of them. Happily, she waved at him, but his name died on her lips when she saw that his face was set in anger.

"What do you think you're doing on that horse?" he demanded when he came near her.

"I just . . ."

"You little fool!" he cut her off. "Haven't you any sense at all?"

Her mouth fell open and she was at a loss for words when he took her reins and pulled her horse in tow. Aware of Robert's presence, she held back the angry protests rising to her lips and kept her eyes straight ahead, her back stiff. Colin maintained a sullen silence and when they stopped before the front porch, he gingerly lifted her from the saddle and deposited her on the ground. As soon as her feet touched the ground, Chantele spun around and ran into the house.

She was removing her coat when he came into her room and closed the door behind him. "You fool!" he said barely able to contain his anger, "are you trying to lose that child?"

For the second time that morning her mouth fell open but her fury abated. "How can you say that?"

He gave a sigh of exasperation. "Kitten, a woman in your condition has to be very careful, or she can lose the baby," he said patiently.

"I know, darling, and I've been careful."

"Riding out on your first day here?"

"I didn't go far, and I stayed on the path."

"I don't want you to go riding again, you hear?"

"Oh, damn it all!" she blurted out stamping her foot with indignation. "You're treating me as if I were an invalid. Next thing you'll do is lock me in my room!"

"You continue behaving like a spoiled brat, and I will!"

"I wished I didn't have to have this child!" she screamed with exasperation. She had spoken in anger, without thinking, and was instantly sorry the moment she realized what she had said. Her words seemed to hang in the air between them as they regarded each other and then, without a word, Colin sauntered across the room toward the door.

"I'm sorry you don't want the child, *madame*," he said in frosty tones, "after the great lengths I've gone to give it my name." And before she could react, he was gone.

"Oh, Colin, I didn't mean it!" she cried at the closed door. But *he* had, she thought bitterly. He had never loved her. He had been ready to abandon her until he had learned of the child. What a fool she had been, throwing herself at him, too ready to believe him when he said he loved her when, all along, it had been the child he wanted. Only the child mattered to him, to Leon. And he . . . he was her life. Without his love, she had nothing. But you can't force anyone to love you, she reminded herself. No matter how hard she had tried to win their love, her parents had never accepted her. What's wrong with me, she asked herself despondently.

There was a light tap on the door and she ignored it. She didn't want to see anyone, not now.

The door opened a crack and Annette peeked in. "Are you all right?" she inquired.

Her husband had just told her that he had never loved her, but she was all right. "Yes," she said wryly, slapping the tears that were streaming down her cheeks.

Annette came in and regarded her warily. "What happened?" she inquired. "Colin just left the house as if the devil himself were after him."

"We . . . had a quarrel."

"Don't worry, my dear," Annette said solicitously, "it's not the end of the world."

But it was. The end of *her* world.

"All married people quarrel, my dear," Annette said. "It will pass."

"Oh, I hope so," Chantele said fervently.

"I know it will," Annette said. "Well, you better change, my dear. Dinner will be served shortly and then Leon is waiting to see you."

"I'm not hungry."

"Try to eat something anyway," Annette said persuasively, "even if you're not hungry the child still needs its nourishment. It will only be the two of us, so don't bother to dress." She went to the armoire and sorted through the clothes. "Let's find you something light and cool," she said pulling a lacy robe de chambre. "It's too bad you have to go through your pregnancy during the summer," she said conversationally while helping Chantele into the gown, "the heat can be beastly. There you are," she said taking a step back, "you look beautiful and comfortable."

"You are so kind," Chantele said, moved by the woman's solicitude.

"Nonsense, child," Annette said. "I know how difficult it can be for a new bride, especially in your condition. You are so young," she added with a sigh. "How old are you, my dear?"

"I'll be eighteen in December."

"Almost ten years younger than Colin," Annette reflected. "Really, he should have more patience."

"I'm not a child," Chantele said defensively.

"I know, my dear," Annette said, observing her reaction, "but still you must admit he's a man, not a boy, and should exercise a little more patience with you. I think I'll have a talk with him."

"Please, don't!"

"Someone ought to tell him that women *enceinte* have strange moods and needs," Annette said. "I'm sure he will understand."

"I wish you wouldn't," Chantele still refused. "He might not like it and even think I asked you to interfere on my behalf."

How interesting, Annette said inwardly, the girl seemed uncertain of her husband's affections. Aloud, she said, "Very well, but I think you are making a mountain out of a molehill. Anyway, let's go in to dinner. I'm starved."

Chantele didn't see Colin again until suppertime. Leon's inquisitiveness during her afternoon visit had left her with the feeling that she had been interviewed for a position in their household, but determined to breach the gap that had opened between herself and her husband, she took pains with her toilette, trying to make herself attractive to him. Colin regarded her coolly and was so polite during supper that she wanted to scream. She was grateful when Robert asked her to play the pianoforte after supper and stood by her side, applauding enthusiastically after each performance, but when she looked at Colin for some sign of approval, he only gave her a sardonic smile. The evening wore on interminably, but finally she made her excuses and retired.

After dismissing Justine, Chantele was too restless to sleep and, as she had done before their marriage, she found herself sketching Colin's face over and over until, despairingly, she threw the pad aside and began to pace the floor. No, she could not accept that Colin had married her only for the child. She had to try to win his love—even if she failed. Putting aside her pride, she went to the connecting door and listened for sounds of activity in Colin's room. There was only silence. It was still early, perhaps he was still downstairs. So she waited.

Her nerves were stretched like violin strings when she heard him enter his room, and again she waited until Simon had been dismissed. Then, she touched a bit of perfume to her throat and with a tremulous hand on the knob paused to gather her courage. "Please, Colin," she prayed fervently, "don't turn me away."

She opened the door slowly and entered his room. Oblivious to the decor, her eyes saw only him, sitting on a winged chair by the window. He had removed his coat and his shirt was open at the front, his attention on the book he was holding. She tried to speak and no sound came out, but he seemed to sense her presence and looked up.

"What are you doing here?" he said snapping the book shut.

"Colin, please, listen to me," she pleaded in a tremulous voice. "I didn't mean what I said about the child. I want it just as much as you do, perhaps even more just because it's yours." She waited for a sign from him, and when he didn't say anything, she added, "I love you with all my heart, Colin."

He was at her side in two strides, crushing her in his arms. "Oh, kitten!" he said hoarsely, covering her face with kisses before he found her lips in a searing kiss that made her melt in his arms. Her gown fell at her feet in a silken pool and, effortlessly, he lifted her in his arms and carried her to his bed. Every kiss, every caress she returned with an ardor that matched his own; she was his, his alone, and nothing else mattered at this moment when they were one.

Later, linguid and sated, she took his hand and pressed it to her belly, laughing happily at his wonder when he felt the child move under his hand. "He moved today for the first time," she whispered. "He's saying that all is well."

"I want you to be very careful, kitten. You are new to this country," he said stroking her cheek. "So many things could happen! My God, when I saw you on that horse this morning, I was frightened out of my wits, and so angry I wanted to give you a thrashing!"

"I'm not made of glass, you know," she chided him. "Women have been having babies for centuries without the world coming to a halt on their behalf!"

"That may be so, kitten," he said and she saw the corners of his eyes crinkle with amusement at her vehemence, "but this one happens to be mine."

"And are you going to lock me in my room and hang a sign saying, 'Don't touch'?"

He snorted with laughter. "Kitten, you're *magnifique!*"

"I am serious, Colin. I promise I will be careful, but I want to explore L'Esperance, perhaps help Annette, if she lets me, and do something besides sit around the house all day!"

"All right, kitten, I'll take you around the plantation tomorrow, but as to that 'Don't touch' sign," he added with a mischievous twinkle in his eyes, "I think we just threw it away!" He pulled her into his arms.

Outside, in the corridor, Annette listened to the sounds of their laughter and the murmur of their voices through the closed door. Chantele would not need a tisane to help her sleep tonight. As long as she and Colin were together, the girl was out of her reach. Something had to be done to get them apart.

Chantele began to protest the next morning, when she saw the mount Colin had selected for her. The animal was probably twice her own age and must have been brought out of retirement for the sole purpose of carrying her. But since the choice was between riding the ancient horse and staying home, she had to accept the situation.

They rode to the cotton fields where the

slaves were tending the plants.

"What are they doing?" she inquired.

"Picking worms from the plants," Colin replied. "See the pods?" he said, pulling one off and opening it to reveal soft masses of white fibers growing from the outside skin of the seeds, tightly packed inside the boll. "After the petals fall," he explained, "the fibers begin to develop, and the bolls burst open when they are ready to be picked."

"It's so white," she exclaimed feeling the long, lustrous fibers between her fingers.

"This is Egyptian cotton of the finest quality," he said, "expensive to grow, but bringing the very best prices. After the cotton is harvested," he continued, "the seeds arc separated from the fibers—that's what we call ginning—and packed into bales for shipment."

He paused when a beefy man with a ruddy complexion approached them puffing with exertion, and removed his hat in greeting.

"Good mawning, Mr. Marquandt," he said in English.

"Mr. Graves, the overseer," Colin nodded and presented him to his wife. "This field will be ready in a few more days," he observed.

"Yes, sir, about a week, I'd say," agreed Mr. Graves.

After a brief exchange, Colin touched his heels to the flanks of his mount, and Chantele followed. When she commented on the extent of the field, he said, "It's not very large, since cotton is no longer our main crop. Leon still refuses to abandon it completely, but our best profits are actually in sugar."

Following the path, he guided her to the border of the sugar cane fields, which appeared to be an endless sea of green waves swaying in the sun. "The cane is harvested in the fall," he explained. "Sugar content is at its highest in colder weather, and this allows us to grow both cotton and sugar. After the cane is cut down, the stalks are put through a press in that building over there," he said, indicating a distant structure, "and the juice extracted is boiled down to make the sugar. But," he said, pulling the bandana he wore around his neck and wiping his brow, "this is as far as we can go today, young lady."

He didn't expect a protest from Chantele, who was beginning to show signs of weariness, but as she had insisted on this exploration, she was not about to plead fatigue. Still, she was glad when they headed for home.

"What a beautiful cat!" Chantele exclaimed entering the parlor, where Annette sat holding Minette on her lap.

"Isn't she?" Annette said with pleasure. "Her name is Minette, and I treasure her. Would you like to hold her? She's very friendly, you know."

Minette blinked her yellow eyes when

143

Chantele patted her head and said, "I have a better idea. Stay just as you are, and I'll be right back."

"Where are you going?"

"To fetch my sketching pad," Chantele said rushing out of the room.

She collected her sketching pad and rummaged through her box for a good piece of charcoal. As she did, her fingers touched a soft object and she pulled it out. It was a small, doll-like figure made of coarse cotton cloth. She examined it curiously, wondering where it had come from, and slipped it inside her pocket with the charcoal. She returned to the parlor and began her sketch. When it was finished, she presented it to Annette.

"This is marvelous!" Annette exclaimed with delight. "I didn't know you were so talented."

"I'm not very good at it," Chantele said with a shrug, "but it's fun."

"May I keep it?"

"Of course."

Annette examined the drawing. "It's not signed by the artist," she pointed out and returned it to Chantele, who searched her pocket for the charcoal. Out came the tiny doll and Annette screamed, jumping to her feet and startling Minette, who leaped to the floor, where she arched her back, bristling and baring her fangs with a hiss. Also startled, Chantele dropped the doll.

"Where did you find that?" Annette cried.

"In my box of charcoals," Chantele replied. "I don't know where it came from." She reached for it, but Annette grabbed her arm, crying, "Don't touch it!"

"Why, what is it?"

Annette swallowed hard before she said, "It's a voodoo doll."

"Voodoo?"

"Black magic."

"But what was it doing in my things?"

"I don't know, but someone is trying to harm you."

"Harm me?" Chantele repeated and then laughed, "With a voodoo doll?"

"Don't laugh, Chantele," Annette said in awe, "I've seen what voodoo can do."

"Surely you can't be serious!"

"But I am." And Annette did look frightened, Chantele realized.

"Really, Annette," she said increduously, "it's just superstition!"

"Be that as it may," Annette said, trying to recover her composure, "someone is trying to harm you."

"Who could it be? And why?"

"One of the servants," Annette offered. "Justine?"

"No!" Chantele denied. "Why would she do a thing like that?"

"Who knows!" Annette said with a shrug.

"Have you reprimanded her?"

"No, I've never had reason to," Chantele said defensively. "What are we going to do with the doll?"

"I don't know," confessed Annette. "Let me think. Let's call Simon," she said after a moment and rang for the servant, who appeared almost immediately. "Simon, remove that . . . object," she ordered pointing at the doll.

Simon took one look at the doll lying on the floor and his eyes seemed to bulge out of their sockets. He seemed frozen on the spot.

"Pick it up!" Annette yelled.

Visibly terrified, Simon retreated, shaking his head, "No, mistress."

"Pick it up, I said!" Annette screamed and boxed his ears.

"Stop it!" Chantele cried. "Can't you see he's frightened out of his wits?" And to put an end to the scene, she picked up the doll herself.

"Don't!" Annette cried.

Chantele dropped the doll on the table, at a loss to understand what all the commotion was about. "You are excused, Simon," she said evenly.

"No, wait!" Annette said. "Simon, do not mention any of this to the others, do you understand?" she admonished the frightened servant, who bobbed his head and disappeared as fast as he could. But Annette knew that within the hour every slave in the plantation would know about the incident. Their jungle drum system was highly efficient.

Good. Her plan was now in motion.

Unrest among the slaves had become widespread. Colin could see fear in the eyes of every man, woman and child as he rode his stallion through the fields, feeling more than ever the heavy burden of owning so many human beings. Why had he let himself be caught again in this world he so despised? Rage burned in his heart that a system that reduced human beings to degradation and hopelessness. Floggings were seldom carried out at L'Esperance, but there was a gnawing feeling at the pit of his stomach that warned him that the next few days would bring pain and misery to the blacks as well as shame and sickness of heart to their masters.

"Masters," he said bitterly to himself. What right had a man, regardless of the color of his skin, to proclaim himself the master of another? The old familiar feeling of helplessness flared anew, of his inability to change the system. If only his name was not Marquandt . . . If only he could walk away from this world of misery . . . But he was as hopelessly trapped in it as the slaves. He was bound to carry out his duty at whatever the cost. His father Leon had seen his every dream crushed by the cruel hand of fate; he had lost his children, the woman he loved, and only L'Esperance remained. As his only son, it was Colin's duty to carry on. If there had been others . . . but there was only Robert, who despite his love for L'Esperance, did not have the Marquandt blood.

Leon's health had improved considerably since their arrival. Chantele seemed to have brought new hope to the man who had no longer dared to hope. His recovery had at first seemed nothing short of a miracle, and now he lived for the moment when the new Marquandt would take his place in the sun. Did Chantele realize how important was the life she carried?

It didn't take long for trouble to emerge, as Colin had expected. Unrest brought rebellion, and rebellion brought punishment. The day Leon was allowed to leave his bed, a broad-backed buck named Joshua openly defied the overseer and when Colin had locked the recalcitrant slave in the barn, Mr. Graves had gone to Leon demanding that an example be made of him. Leon wasted no time in ordering the flogging.

"Don't you understand that your weakness is placing all of us in danger, including your wife and your child?" Leon demanded angrily. "If you don't make an example of that one, there'll be no stopping the rest of them, and I don't have to remind you that there are almost three hundred blacks out there. How long do you think it will take them to murder us all?''

"I have agreed to many of the changes you wanted," he continued, "but now fear is the only language they'll understand. If you hesitate to mete out proper punishment, there won't be anything to keep them in line. And it's not only L'Esperance that's at stake. It is our duty . . ." Suddenly his face turned purple and he clutched at his chest, gasping for breath.

"Leon!" Annette cried rushing to his side. "Colin, hurry, fetch his medicine!"

Colin lost no time in doing as he was told and rushed back with a bottle that he gave to Annette. She put the vial to Leon's lips and forced some of the clear liquid down his throat.

"Are you trying to kill your father?" Annette cried angrily at Colin, who stood there with clenched fists watching his father struggle for his life.

After a few minutes, Leon seemed to relax and his respiration became easier. Annette turned to Colin. "I'm sorry, but he must not get overexcited," she said apologetically. "And he's right, you know. My mother was only a little girl when the slaves rebelled in Haiti, but she never forgot how she saw her father tortured and her mother raped and killed by the blacks. They would have done the same to her, if they had found her. You must let Joshua take his punishment, Colin, or there'll be no stopping them. Think of Chantele, of your child. You must protect them,'' she said passionately. ''Now, please go.''

Outside, in the yard, Colin watched with morbid fascination as the lash fell heavily on Joshua's broad back, the black muscles tensing in anticipation of the pain. ''Their skin may be black,'' he mused absently ''but their blood is just as red as ours.''

Every lash that cut through the man's flesh went through his heart. It was a replay of his nightmares, and he was unable to tear his eyes away from the raw, bloody mass of human flesh when at last the punishment was over Joshua was cut down and carried away. Colin crossed the yard, oblivious to the frightened stares of the slaves who made way for him as he went by, entered the deserted house, and locked himself in his father's study. Mechanically, he poured brandy into a snifter and downed the drink in one gulp. Holding the empty glass, he stood on long legs planted firmly apart, staring without seeing the empty grate. Through the smell of blood still clinging to his nostrils, through the torn, bloody flesh still before his eyes, came Leon's accusations. Perhaps his father was right. Perhaps he was weak. Oblivious to the insistent knocking on the door, Colin sank into the leather chair and buried his face in his hands.

''Colin, please, darling, let me in.''

It was Chantele. Oh, God, how he yearned to rest his head on her tender bosom and let her ease the horror from his soul! He was tempted to let her in, but no; twice before, when he had been unable to contain that impotent rage he carried inside him, it had been she who had paid the price for his temporary release. He could not risk hurting her again.

"Go away," he said in a strangled voice.

"Please, Colin."

"I said go away!" he thundered.

Dolefully, Chantele turned away from the closed door. She had witnessed the brutal punishment of the slave with horror, knowing it had all started with the voodoo doll she had found, and she could not shake the heavy burden of guilt she felt. How could she have been so *stupid?* She had seen Colin, standing there in the yard like a man turned to stone, watching what must have been a painful reminder of Jacob's death. She knew the torment he would be suffering now, but again he had rejected the comfort her love could offer.

Annette found her outside the study, crying with despair. "Come along, Chantele."

"He needs me, Annette!" she resisted. "I know he does!"

"He wants to be alone," Annette said, pushing her gently toward the stairs. "You are all wound up, and that's not good for you, my dear. Let me take you to your room," she said persuasively.

Sobbing uncontrollably, Chantele let her guide her to her room, undress her, and put her to bed. Annette was gone for a few moments and returned with a streaming cup of tisane. "Drink this, my dear."

"I don't want to sleep."

"This will only relax you," Annette said. "The state you're in can only hurt the child."

Chantele forced herself to drink and tried to return a half-empty cup.

"All of it," Annette insisted, and too tired to argue Chantele did as she was told. When she finished, Annette watched her close her eyes and instantly fall asleep. The liquid had worked quickly. Everything was going beautifully, she congratulated herself. Very soon, Chantele would begin to show the effects of the fruit of the manchineel tree.

Annette locked the door and pulled an object from the folds of her voluminous skirts. It was an asson, a long-necked calabash rattle with a small bell attached to one end. She stood over Chantele and shook asson, whispering strange words. Then she snipped a strand of hair from the sleeping girl. Back in her room, Annette unlocked the doors of her tall, square armoire, exposing a number of jars and other artifacts, and selected a bowl made from a calabash gourd cut in half. To a small doll very much like the one Chantele had found she pinned the strand of Chantele's hair. Her lips moved in whispered tones as she lit a candle and then burned the doll, letting its ashes drop into the bowl. Then she shook the ashes in the bottom of the bowl and drew a strange diagram, intoning a chant all the while.

Seven

Because of Leon's illness, few callers came to L'Esperance. Colin's views of slavery did not serve to increase his popularity among the planters, but the news of his arrival with a new French bride prompted a number of invitations—which were declined in consideration of Chantele's pregnancy, since the distance involved required elaborate preparations for prolonged visits. Only the Dorleacs, their closest neighbors, had maintained a complete silence, and so it came as a surprise when one morning Simon interrupted breakfast to announce that Marinette Dorleac had arrived.

"It's all right," Chantele said seeing Annette's uneasiness, at the news. "I know about her."

"Did Colin confess to you all the indiscretions of his youth?" Annette said mockingly, rising from the table. "Would you like to meet her?"

"Yes, of course."

Annette led the way to the parlor, and while she effusively greeted the girl, Chantele had occasion to study the woman who would have become Mme. Marquandt had she and Colin never met in Paris.

Marinette Dorleac was beautiful and sophisticated, Chantele noticed with dismay. Her hair, black as a raven's wing, was carefully arranged to accommodate a saucy little hat perched on her glossy thick curls; her eyes were very large and china blue in a perfect oval face. The rosebud mouth curved in a charming smile, and she seemed impervious to the heat. Conscious of her own thickening body, Chantele eyed Marinette's tiny waist and hated her on sight.

"I believe you haven't met Colin's wife," Annette said inoffensively. "This is Chantele."

Marinette eyed her critically and gave her a tight smile. "A pleasure *madame.*"

Chantele simply nodded her greeting.

"Do tell us all about your visit to Natchez," Annette invited while they took their seats. Minette jumped on her lap and Simon came in with a tray of coffee.

"It was divine!" Marinette replied. "There were so many parties, such gaiety! By the way, the Montards send their regards."

"How nice of them," Annette replied noticing that Marinette was pointedly ignoring Chantele. Finally, the girl turned her attention to her rival.

"And how do you find plantation life, *madame?*" she inquired coolly.

"I'm happy wherever my husband takes me *mademoiselle.*"

"But don't you miss the excitement of the court, the balls, the beautiful gowns?"

Chantele shook her head. "I'm afraid the balls and the gowns would serve me no purpose during the coming months, *mademoiselle.*"

Marinette's eyes reflected her surprise and regarded Chantele's body with an appraisal. "It's unfortunate, *madame,*" she said testily.

"On the contrary, *mademoiselle,*" Chantele replied, "I'm very fortunate."

"Indeed," Marinette said with apparent distaste, and immediately turned her attention to Annette, who had enjoyed watching the hostility between the two young women.

Absently stroking Minette's silken fur, Annette drifted into her own musings while apparently listening to Marinette's conversation. Chantele had known about Marinette and was obviously jealous. That Colin had never paid much attention to the girl was beside the point. Pregnant women are very susceptible to jealousy of beautiful rivals.

". . . and he asked me to marry him," Marinette was saying when Annette's attention returned to the conversation.

"And did you accept?" Annette inquired politely.

"Of course not!" Marinette exclaimed with feigned horror. "I don't want to tie myself down to a man and start having his brats! Not yet, anyway. I'm too young to put an end to my life like that!"

Chantele smiled to herself but made no comments. What a fool, she thought. To be married to the man you loved, to have his children, was the greatest joy in the world. Who cared about silly balls and flirtations?

She listened to Marinette's recount of her conquests in Natchez until the girl was ready to take her leave.

"Goodbye, my dear," Annette said kissing Marinette's cheek fondly. "Do come and see us again."

"What did you think of her?" Annette inquired after their visitor had departed.

"She's hateful!"

"My dear, do not be jealous of her," Annette said soothingly. "You are Colin's wife. Whatever was between them is in the past. After all, Colin was quite a ladies' man."

"I know," Chantele said dejectedly.

"But he married you," Annette said. "Don't give it another thought."

Yes, Colin had married her, but only because of the child she carried, Chantele mused. When would he stop treating her like a child, give her a chance to be a real wife, to win his love? She hardly ever saw him any more. After Joshua's flogging, he seemed to avoid her company. He was gone to the fields before dawn and didn't return until after sundown. But what really hurt the most was that when she had gone to him, he had turned her away.

Although unrest still prevailed among the slaves, the flogging of Joshua seemed to have quenched immediate rebellion, and the cotton harvest was proceeding without serious incidents. Depending more and more on Annette's tisanes to help her sleep, Chantele's strength was failing rapidly. Getting up in the mornings was becoming an ordeal. She felt herself grow weaker with each passing day, and now headaches began to plague her.

It was after twelve one night when Colin emerged from the study in a haze of alcohol.

He made his way up the stairs and silently entered Chantele's suite. After the argument that had caused Leon's relapse, he had retreated more and more into himself, but he was in torment and could not spend another night without the tenderness and comfort of his wife. An oil lamp was burning in her room when he stealthily approached her bed and pushed aside the mosquito netting. He gazed upon her sleeping countenance—and was instantly paralyzed by fear. Her face was gaunt, her breathing labored; she was drenched in perspiration and her skin burned to the touch. Her pallor was deepened by the dark circles under her eyes. By God, what was happening to her?

Anxiously, Colin paced the length of the corridor outside Chantele's rooms, waiting for Dr. Maurais to finish his examination. He was out of his mind with worry when the door opened and the doctor stepped outside.

"How is she, doctor?"

"It's nothing serious," the doctor assured him. "Pregnancy during the summer is difficult even for the natives of Louisiana, M. Marquandt. Your wife is new to these parts and it's more difficult for her, that is all."

"Is there anything I can do?"

"Try to keep her as quiet as possible and hope that the weather cools," the doctor said with a shrug.

"Thank you, doctor. Will you see my father also? I'm afraid my wife's difficulties are affecting him very much."

"I'll look in on him."

"May I see my wife now?"

"Of course."

"Colin!" she cried at the sight of him.

"Kitten," he said taking her hands and pressing his lips to her fingers. "How are you feeling?"

"Don't worry so, my love," she said running her finger over his creased brow, "The doctor says I'll be fine."

"Perhaps I should take you away from here, where the weather is cooler."

"No, darling. You can't leave L'Esperance now, and I won't go anywhere without you. And, besides, I'll have to get used to the heat sooner or later. I suppose we'll have to plan our next child more carefully," she added with a tempting grin.

"Let's worry about this one for now."

"I've missed you, Colin," she said taking his hand and kissing each finger. "Oh, darling, I've missed you by my side!"

"I know, kitten," he said, deeply moved, "and I've missed you."

"Lie down with me, Colin."

He stretched out on the bed, careful not to disturb her, and she snuggled close to him with a contented sigh.

"Marinette Dorleac was here again yesterday," she said.

"Yes, I know."

"Were you ever in love with her, Colin?"

"No."

"She's very beautiful," she said, after pause.

"And so are you," he said, stroking her hair. "More so."

"Do you really think so?"

"Kitten, I think you are the most beautiful woman in the world, the sweetest, and the only one for me," he said kissing the tip of her nose.

She smiled happily. "I love you."

"And I love you."

She slipped her hand inside his shirt and caressed his chest.

"Don't do that, kitten," he said alarmed by his response to her touch.

"But I want to touch you."

"Kitten, you are torturing me," he said in a strangled voice.

She kissed the pulse of his throat. "Please make love to me," she said tracing the contour of his lips with the tip of her tongue. His breath was coming in shallow gasps.

"Kitten, you don't know what you're saying!"

"Please, Colin," she pleaded, continuing to torment him with her lips.

"Chantele," he said raggedly, "don't you realize what you're doing?"

"I need you," she said taking his hand and placing it on her breast. He jerked it away, as if he had been burned, and took a deep breath. When he still refused her, she added, "Darling, I'm not ill, truly, I'm not." Her eyes were welling up with tears. "Please, Colin, love me or I'll die!"

Colin hesitated, wrestling with his own yearnings and his fear of hurting her. But at the sight of her tears his resistance crumbled, and holding in check the full power of his desire, he took her gently in his arms. His kiss was passionate, yet tender, and never before had Chantele known such gentle loving in the arms of her husband.

A humid, oppressive heat hung over the plantation like a lid on a kettle. Hardly a leaf moved while a scorching sun beat mercilessly on the bent backs of the slaves working the fields. Colin's temper was short. The house servants went uneasily about their duties, their fear so tangible that Annette had been forced to take charge of Chantele's care because even under threat of punishment Justine would not go near the mistress who she was sure was possessed by the spirit of Damballah, the Snake God. Nothing could suit Annette better; the girl was declining steadily, and it would not be long before she lost the gallant battle she was fighting for her life and that of her child.

And who would be surprised if a bereaved young husband took his own life after losing his beloved wife and child?

The taste of fear was always in Colin's mouth now. He was losing her. Other doctors had been called, but their ministrations had failed to bring Chantele's health back. He was at the end of his rope. "I'm taking her away," he finally declared one night.

Annette panicked for an instant. "But you can't!" she protested.

"If she stays here, she'll die!"

Annette took a moment to collect her wits. "Please, wait a few more days. She's too weak to travel, and besides, Dr. Latour's treatment seems to be working," she said persuasively.

"I can't see any improvement."

"You are too impatient. I can see the treatment is working."

"You really think so?"

"I know it is. I'm sure you'll see it for yourself very soon. And if you take her away now . . . well, I don't know what will happen to your father."

"Don't you think I know that?" Colin said bitterly. "Very well," he relented, "but if she is not better by the end of this week, I'm definitely taking her away."

Annette could not let Chantele out of her

reach. The girl was young and healthy; she would recover quickly, and if she lived to have her child all her efforts would have gone for naught. No, she had to get rid of Chantele before the child was born. There were other ways . . . after all, accidents did happen. "You should give the treatment a little more time," she suggested.

"No, I should not have waited even this long. Unless there's visible improvement, I'm taking her away next week."

Annette gave a sigh of resignation—but she was prepared.

A remarkable recovery took place within days. The antidote was cleansing the poison from Chantele's body, and her youth did the rest. She was pampered by her doting husband, and as she grew stronger, her need for him was renewed. She had been so close to death that now she longed for the comfort of his body against hers, but Colin would not succumb to her pleas. He was tormented by his own need, but he had almost lost her after yielding to her, and he was not about to risk her life again. After Chantele had come to his bed in the night and pleaded in earnest with him, Colin seldom used his room. If only she had known what it cost him to turn her away! He tried to tell her, but she would not understand.

As a boy, he had judged his father ruthlessly

for seeking solace with a slave woman. What had he known then of life, of the needs of a man in love? He himself had been on the brink of committing the act he had so despised in others. The friends of his youth had no qualms in using their female slaves for their pleasure and perhaps, had it not been for Jacob, Colin would have done the same; but every time he saw a yellow-skinned slave in L'Esperance he could not help but wonder if the blood running through the slave's veins was the same as his own.

In the study, Colin was immersed in paperwork. Upon his return to L'Esperance he had discovered that the plantation affairs were in a jumble. During Leon's long illness, many debts had accumulated that had to be settled. Robert had been of invaluable help in the running of the plantation, but he was too young and inexperienced to handle the books. The cotton harvest was nearly over, and the crop was going to be an excellent one in spite of the problems of the past several weeks. Preparations also needed to be made for the coming harvest of the sugar cane.

Suddenly, a scream pierced the silence.

Chantele had been restless. The night was hot, but she was getting used to the heat. It was Colin's indifference she could never accept. No, she corrected herself, it was not indifference. He loves me, she told herself, but does he still want me? She stood before the cheval mirror and studied her bulky body. How could he still find her desirable, she mused, when she looked like a fat cow? And now, Marinette was bothering her more than ever. Since her return from Natchez, the girl had frequently dropped in under the pretense of visiting Annette, but Chantele didn't miss the way she smiled at Colin, brushing against him at every opportunity with a flutter of her long lashes. In her presence he had not given any signs of interest, but he had pretended disinterest in Chantele herself while they were secret lovers. She had gone to Colin time and time again, and he had held her tenderly in his arms and spoken gently to her, treating her as if she were a child. But she was not a child. She was a woman who needed her husband! Marinette was so beautiful, so cool, so perfect, with never a hair out of place, while she herself was as wilted as last week's flowers and just as misshapen. The night before, when she had gone to Colin in the study, she had seen signs of weakening in his eyes even as he had turned her away. Tonight, she would not take no for an answer.

The house was dark and silent when she left her room, holding a candle to light the way. Carefully, she descended the stairs and reached the first landing. The window was open and when the flame flickered in the warm breeze, Chantele had to shield it with her hand so that it would not go out. Suddenly, something dark leaped from the window and bumped against her with a hideous shriek, tangling in her gown and legs. Chantele dropped the candle and reached into space for support. Her own scream seemed to come from far, far away as she felt herself falling into the darkness.

Minette ran up the stairs and along the corridor to Annette's room, where the door opened a crack to let her in. She leaped into Annette's arms and rubbed herself against her bosom, puring contentedly. Annette stroked her coat, a malevolent smile twisting her face.

"Well done, my pet," she said softly, "well done indeed."

Colin rushed out of the study, the hair on the back of his neck still bristling at the sound of the scream he had recognized as his wife's.

"Chantele!" he cried out at the sight of the small heap at the bottom of the stairs. Her beautiful face was still and lifeless. Footsteps were approaching.

"Oh, my God!" Annette had reached them. "Is she . . ."

"She's alive," Colin said more to himself, feeling her pulse. Suddenly he froze; the whiteness of her gown was turning a crimson red. "My God, the child!" he said under his breath.

"I'll go for the doctor," said Robert, who

had also appeared.

"There is not time!" Colin said raggedly, watching the stain of blood grow larger and larger. "Annette, fetch the midwife!"

"But the servants won't go near her," objected Annette.

"Damn it, Annette, fetch her!" Colin shouted, "If she lets Chantele die, I swear I'll break her black neck with my own two hands!"

Chantele whimpered when he lifted her in his arms and carried her upstairs to her bed. "Hold on, darling, please hold on!" he prayed. Where was Annette?

She came back, alone after what seemed an eternity. "She won't come, Colin. No one will."

His face was fraught with anguish and fear. "We can't waste any more time," he said in a tight voice, as he rolled up his sleeves and moved into action. "We'll have to help her ourselves until the doctor gets here. Get some sheets and towels, and sharp knife, and plenty of boiling water. And hurry!" He began stripping Chantele of her clothes, ripping her gown to shreds. Chantele cried out when, torn from the womb before its time, the fetus emerged with a gush of bright red blood. Colin swallowed hard. Not in his worst nightmare had he ever seen so much blood, but he forced himself to take the tiny figure of a human being that was his child. It was a boy, so small that he could not have been more than ten or eleven inches in length. The features of the face were well defined, the nose and lips well formed, the eyelids closed together as in a newborn kitten. The hands and feet were developed to the tiniest nails, and the skin was so translucent that he could see the network of veins. The soft, wooly hair that covered the body was thicker on the head and smeared with a greasy substance and blood. Transfixed, Annette watch as Colin put aside the diminutive figure to direct all his efforts to fight for Chantele's life. He worked like a demon, like a man possessed, but by morning, when the doctor finally arrived, the bleeding was under control.

"Will she live, doctor?"

Dr. Latour removed his glasses and rubbed his tired eyes. He wished he had something encouraging to say to this young man who had fought so desperately to save his wife. "She's very weak, M. Marquandt, but she's holding her own."

"Will she live?"

"I wish I could reassure you," Dr. Latour said, shaking his head, "but I can't. It's in the hands of God now." And seeing the young man's despair, he added, "You did all you could, my son. If you had not stopped the bleeding, she would not have survived. She's young and she wants to live. That's in her favor."

Colin turned his back to the doctor, and regarding his wife's pale face, his hands clenched into fists of impotence. Chantele had been on her way to the study, he knew. If she died . . .

Annette rushed in. "Doctor, please, it's my husband!"

Colin wheeled about. "Does he know?"

Annetted nodded, "He knows."

At the funeral services held for Leon Marquandt and his grandson, Colin stood at the gravesite like a man turned to stone. Deaf to the voices that offered their sympathy, only one thought kept running through his mind: Would there be another grave there tomorrow? Would Chantele lie next to their son in the cold earth? No! She had to live! She must!

Long hours of vigil at her bedside, willing her back to life, seemed to have no effect on him, and when her eyes fluttered open, he was instantly at her side.

"Colin," she said feebly.

"Kitten!" The tightness in his throat made his voice barely audible and he kissed her icy hand.

"Darling, you're crying."

He could not speak, he just held on to her hand.

She remembered then. "The child?" Her eyes misted and a tear rolled down her cheek when he shook his head. "Oh, Colin, I'm so sorry! It was my fault!" she sobbed.

"No, kitten, don't say that!"

"I've been so foolish!"

"No, baby, listen to me. Don't think about it now or you'll make yourself sick again."

"But you wanted that child so much!" she wept.

"There will be others, my love. I want you to live. For me, darling, please!"

"Do you still love me, Colin?"

"Oh, yes, kitten I love you!" He had not realized how much, in fact, until he had almost lost her.

"Chantele closed her eyes and fell asleep, and Colin held on to her hand as if trying to give her some of his strength and his hope.

With Colin constantly at her side, Annette was unable to hinder Chantele's recovery. The news of Leon's death was withheld from her while she made a gallant fight for her own life. A week later, when Dr. Latour pronounced her out of danger, Colin returned to work. Everything had taken second place to Chantele's recovery, but Robert had been doing both his work and Colin's as best he could.

Chantele was saddened by Leon's death when she learned of it, knowing how deeply Colin must have felt the loss of his father and his son at the same time. Added to his old burdens of grief, she wondered at this man she had married, his strength, his self-control. If only she had a small portion of his strength, she thought despondently, their child would not be lying in the ground. But she was too weak, and too afraid of losing his love.

Annette was annoyed by her failure to dispose of Chantele. The girl was recovering slowly but steadily from the accident, but Colin's return to the plantation's business provided her with another chance to begin administering the poison again. Soon the headaches returned to plague Chantele, and Dr. Latour, who had been encouraged by the patient's recovery, became concerned. He warned Colin that another pregnancy before her body had had time enough to heal could carry a death sentence.

Chantele never spoke of the accident, but Colin could see that she continued to blame herself for the loss of their child. "I'm taking her to New Orleans," he announced one day. "She needs the distractions of the city to get her out of her gloom."

"But we're in mourning!" exclaimed Annette, seemingly scandalized by his suggestion.

"I don't need to be reminded," he said tersely, and then, in a gentler tone he added, "In New Orleans she could see other people, go to the theater, perhaps do some shopping. Besides," he added fondly, "you need rest yourself after caring for her and Leon for so long. I don't know what we would have done without you, Annette. You know I'll be forever grateful.''

"My dear Colin," Annette said sweetly, "Chantele is a dear, sweet child that I have come to look upon as my own daughter. I'll always be glad to do anything I can for her, and for you."

"You have always been so kind," Colin said deeply moved by his step-mother's words. "Leon was most fortunate in you, Annette. We all are. But it's time to take some of the burden off your shoulders. Besides, Bess adores Chantele and will take good care of her."

"Perhaps the change will be good for her," Annette said when she realized the futility of an argument, "but it's not right that she should be in the city with only the servants, and with the harvest upon us it will be impossible for you to stay in New Orleans," she said.

"Chantele made a good friend in Marguerite Gerard during our voyage from France. I'm sure she'll help me find a suitable chaperone."

"I won't hear of it!" Annette said firmly. "There is not need to appeal to strangers as long as I can help. I'll go to New Orleans with Chantele. After all, perhaps the change will be good for me, too."

The skies of Louisiana were darkened by the smoke of sugar mills when the Marquandts made the steamboat journey to New Orleans. Chantele was not sorry to leave the house where she had experienced so much unhappiness in such a short period of time and her presence only served to inspire fear. Perhaps after a season in New Orleans things would change, but it would be hard to be away from Colin for so long. She had accepted his decision to send her away without a protest, and she tried to convince herself that he did not blame her for the loss of their child as she did herself. She would be patient, she determined, and she would wait until he came to her and they could start their lives together once again.

Colin remained in the city only long enough to see her settled in her new home, returning immediately to the planation. He had planned on hiring a nurse for Chantele, but Bess would not hear of it, taking the girl under her protective wing and lavishing on her all her maternal love, much to Annette's chagrin.

Leon's death had taken Annette by surprise. She had used her potions to cause his attacks and miraculous recoveries at will in a malevolent gambit to control Colin. She had been so confident of her powers that she had not considered that her manipulations had weakened Leon to the point that he had not been able to survive the shock of losing the child on whom he had centered all his hopes. Colin was now the head of the family. And Chantele the new mistress. Annette gritted her teeth each time she thought of it. Now, more than ever, it was imperative to find a way to dispose of both Colin and Chantele without raising suspicion.

And she found the perfect solution.

Eight

The house on Tolouse Street, a blend of
Spanish and French styles, had been built
shortly after a fire had almost destroyed the entire Vieux Carre back in 1774. Oleanders
displayed a profusion of white and pink flowers
amidst their dark, waxy leaves, and a banana
tree spread its fan-like fronds of shiny green
over the flagstones of the courtyard where

Chantele reflected on how difficult it had been saying goodbye to Colin. Only the knowledge that her presence in L'Esperance would serve just to increase his troubles had made her accept their separation, and she lived for the moment when they could be together again. In the meantime, she wrote long letters filled with passionate yearning and, encouraged by Bess, tried to take as much interest in the running of her home as her health allowed. Conscious of the change in Annette's status, Chantele deferred to her in many ways and sought her advice, but she kept her own counsel by hiring free servants rather than purchasing slaves. Never would she buy another human being; it was bad enough to witness the misery of the poor wretches being sold at the auctions that took place in the most frequented parts of the city, and seeing the numerous notices offering rewards for the return of runaways. Most of the *gens de couleur libres* were artisans and merchants, but then there was an abundance of immigrants seeking employment.

Passage to America was cheap; many of the ships which carried their cargoes of cotton to Liverpool filled their holds with immigrants, using them as ballast on their return trips and, consequently, New Orleans was bursting with immigrants who did the types of work slaves had become too valuable to perform.

Maggie Fitzsimmons was one such person.

With her two young children, who had
miraculously survived the cruel voyage, she had
followed her husband Paddy in his quest for a
better life. But fate had dealt her a stunning
blow when shortly after their arrival in New
Orleans it had been Paddy who had succumbed
to the yellow fever, leaving her to fend for
herself and her children as best she could. Still
a pretty woman, Maggie sought honest employment rather than taking the easy way out, but a
woman living alone in the squalor of the Irish
Channel without a man's protection was easy
prey for the rough characters that inhabited
that slum, and she had been forced to accept
the "attentions" of a boatman named Jack, a
brawny bear of a man who used her and
knocked her about. The only advantage to being Jack's woman was that his reputation was
so fierce it kept other men away from her even
during his frequent trips upriver, but each night
Maggie prayed to the Holy Virgin and St.
Patrick to deliver her and her children from the
boatman's clutches. Being hired as a laundress
in the Marquandt household was a veritable
gift from heaven; the position not only paid a
fair salary but also included living quarters for
her and the children. Once the position was
hers, Maggie jealously guarded her secret from
Jack and waited until he departed. Then, she
packed her meager belongings and she and the
children left behind the nightmare of the Irish

Channel.

Colin encouraged Chantele to take advantage of the distractions of the city, but although he expressed concern for her welfare, his letters were brief and impersonal and a disappointment to her. Through all her life Chantele had found pleasure in her drawing; now she would sit in the courtyard for hours, staring at blank pages that remained untouched. One afternoon, the voices of children brought her out of her reveries. She was aware that Maggie, the laundress, had children living with her, but she had never seen or heard them until this day. Stealthily, she tiptoed across the courtyard and entered the short hallway connecting to the patio that separated the servants' quarters from the main house.

The little girl with hair as red as flame could not have been more than three, and the towheaded boy perhaps a year or two older. Their clothes, mended and patched, were meticulously clean and ironed, but not for long, for the children crawled on the ground following a bright green lizard. The children squealed when the poor reptile managed to evade them and disappeared among the foliage of a clinging vine.

At the sound of their laughter Maggie appeared, drying her hands on her apron and trying to look stern as she told them to keep their

179

voices down. But the children ran to her and she fell to the ground on her knees and enfolded them in a fond embrace. Witnessing the scene from the shadows of the alley, Chantele felt like an intruder and tried to move away unnoticed, but Maggie caught sight of her and paled, clasping her children to her bosom. *"Madame!"* she breathed, "I'm sorry if the children disturbed you. It won't happen again, I promise!"

Chantele heard the fear in her voice. "They were not disturbing me, Maggie," she said with a smile and, stepping out into the patio. "As a matter of fact, I would very much like to meet them."

Maggie rose to her feet and took each child by the hand. Gently, she pushed the boy forward. "This is Paddy, my eldest," she said with pride in her voice.

"Hello, Paddy," Chantele said.

"And this is Molly." The little girl clung to her mother and buried her face in the folds of her skirts. "Come now, Molly," coaxed Maggie, "say hello to the lady."

Molly continued to cling to her mother, refusing to face Chantele.

"I'm sorry, *madame,*" Maggie said apologetically, "she's very shy."

Chantele smiled her understanding. "It's all right, Maggie. You are very fortunate to have such lovely children."

The wistful note in her voice reminded Maggie of the story she had heard about the mistress losing her child, and she didn't know what to say.

From that day on, Chantele looked for the children when she came to the courtyard, and she offered them sweets and treats to gain their confidence. Paddy was friendly and full of mischief, but winning Molly was more difficult. Chantele made no effort to approach her, letting the girl come to her of her own accord. No longer were the pages of her sketching pad empty, but full of individual portraits of the children and scenes of them at play. And what a marvelous experience to see their faces when she showed them her work, Paddy's laughter and delight and Molly's wide-eyed wonder. Her friendship was secured when Chantele gave the children a sketch of themselves as a gift for their mother, and with Molly's chubby little arms around her neck, Chantele felt her eyes mist. Once the ice was broken, Molly showed herself to be a sweet, affectionate girl; ah, but she could also be as mischievous as her brother!

Nothing helped Chantele more out her gloom than the presence of Maggie's children. At last she decided to rejoin the living, and her first call was on Marguerite Gerard. During his brief visit to New Orleans, Colin had gone to Marguerite for help. Beneath that innocuous and rotund exterior lived an intelligent, practical woman who after an initial visit to Chantele understood, as a man never could, that there were wounds that needed time to heal, and that it would be useless to try to force Chantele out of her state of mind. She was confident the girl would recover her spirit in her own time, in her own way, and seeing her now Margueite knew that her young friend was ready to pick up the pieces of her life. The Gerards escorted Chantele on her first appearance in public in New Orleans.

One day, Chantele came home to find that Colin had arrived during her absence. "Colin!" she cried flying into his arms.

"Kitten!" He held her in a tight embrace, and their lips met in a kiss that spoke of their longings.

"Oh, darling, how I've missed you!" she said clinging to him and reclaiming his lips.

It had been so long since he had last held her, tasted the sweetness of her kisses, the soft fragrance of her, that his body responded with a force that frightened him. He held her at arm's length and gazed upon a countenance that was lovelier than ever. The gauntness of her face had disappeared; the eyes that regarded him lovingly were bright and clear, and her skin had recovered its normal golden glow. She had also regained some of the weight she had lost, and her whole appearance belied Annette's reports, but he reminded himself of the doctor's warnings.

"You look wonderful, princess," he said regarding her fondly.

"I feel wonderful, now that you are here," she said searching his face, which was drawn and haggard. "But darling, you look so tired!" she said reprovingly. "You have been working much too hard."

With the mill working around the clock, that was easy; while the slaves' work had been divided into three shifts, Colin spent an average of eighteen hours a day at the mill. But coming home to an empty house after a day of hard, grueling work was like stepping into Purgatory, and he had thrown himself into his work until he was so exhausted that he could barely stand.

"Come, my love," she said taking by the hand as if he were a small child, "Why don't you rest a little before supper."

In her room, she helped him out of his coat, and despite his exhaustion, Colin had to suppress an impulse to take her in his arms when she knelt down before him to take off his boots. Without removing the rest of his clothes, Colin stretched out on her bed and immediately fell asleep.

He woke with a start. Chantele lay next to him, and for a moment of panic he could not remember how they had come together. He

remembered then his hasty trip to New
Orleans, when he could not spent another day
without the sound of her voice, the light of her
eyes. Her letters only served to increase his
yearnings and now, feeling the warmth of her
body against his and the caress of her breath on
his skin he felt as if he had been granted ab-
solution. Once he had made no distinctions between love and passion; if someone had told
him then that he would travel miles for just a
kiss and a smile, he would have laughed. Today, he was much wiser.

Realizing that Chantele was awake and looking at him, he kissed the tip of her nose and
held her close. She could hear the wild thump-
ing of his heart, and propping herself on an
elbow gazed into the eyes that betrayed his
longings.

"Darling," she whispered against his lips,
"don't be afraid to touch me. I'm well now,
truly I am."

God, how he wanted her!

"I just want to hold you," he said enfolding
her soft and yielding body in a tight embrace.
She could feel the pressure of his erect hardness
against her and kissed the pulse of his throat,
making him groan as if he were in agony.

"Stop it, Chantele!" he said, pushing her
away.

The hurt look on her face made him pause,
and he tried to explain the situation without

frightening her. "Kitten, there is something you ought to know," he began. "I didn't tell you before because I didn't want to frighten you, but we . . . er . . . must control our . . . our need for each other for some time."

"But, Colin," she began to protest, but he didn't let her finish.

"It's too soon, darling," he said gently caressing her cheek. "We must give your body time to heal, to recover all its strength."

"But I am well now," she said stubbornly.

He was reluctant to mention the threat to her life if she got with child again; God knew how much they both had felt the presence of death.

"You are much better, kitten, I can see it," he said trying to summon his patience. "But until you are completely recovered, we can't run the risk of another pregnancy. Do you understand?"

She regarded him soberly, trying to sort his words in her own mind. She bowed her head and Colin saw two tears run down her cheeks, and he gathered her in his arms. "Don't cry, kitten," he said kissing away the salty tears, "we must be patient, darling. It won't last forever," and added wryly, "It only seems that way."

Chantele clung to him in desperation. His words had frightened her. "I need you so, Colin!" she sobbed against his chest. "Hold me, darling, please hold me!"

185

Knowing her the way he did, he realized that it was as rough for her as it was for him, and he decided that he would try to give her the relief that he denied himself. Chantele was surprised when he began making love to her after all he had said, and in the pitch of her passion she cried out for him, but he refused to take her, and when it was over, she saw that his desire was still intact and unfulfilled.

He groaned when she touched him and tried to ease his need. Colin almost went out of his mind when her lips traced his fevered skin and and she took him in her mouth and played havoc with his senses. All his pent-up passions finally exploded and the pleasure was almost agonizing.

"I love you," she said kissing his damp chest.

Their passion was temporarily spent, but the contentment they had known before was missing. Even so, he was still stunned by this beautiful woman that was his wife.

Deep-seated traditions and upbringing are hard to shake, and for all his disagreements with many phases of the system, Colin was very much a Creole. His struggle with his father had been more the bitter because of his deep devotion to him; his protectiveness of his young wife stemmed from the quixotic tendency to put "good women" on pedestals; and what Chantele had done to ease his need had left him with an unshakable feeling of desecration. She represented all that was good and pure in his life. She was to be cherished and protected; and he loved her too much to let her play the whore again.

Meanwhile, like a spider spinning her web, Annette was setting her plans in motion. Soon after their arrival in New Orleans she had sent a message to Marinette Dorleac, whose visits to L'Esperance she had encouraged to stir Chantele's jealousy. She had never been truly fond of Marinette, but since the time Leon had proposed a match between her and Colin, Annette had cultivated her friendship with an eye to the future. Now that Colin and Chantele were married, Annette did not discard the value of that friendship to undermine the marriage. Marinette hated Chantele for taking what she had believed to be rightfully hers. Their efforts, so far, had been fruitless; Chantele's jealousy had not provoked any conflicts between her and Colin. But men are different; if the tables were turned and it was Chantele who became involved with another man . . . A real involvement was not necessary; it would be enough to make Colin believe there was one. Chantele's devotion to her husband was a problem; the girl appeared blind to the admiring glances from the youngbloods Annette had collected to frequent their salon, especially Lucas DeCouer, a handsome young man whose brown eyes did nothing to conceal the admiration he felt for Chantele. Colin's absence from New Orleans was an incentive to pay homage to the lonely beauty, and Lucas never missed a chance to be close to her. There must be a way to make Chantele susceptible to another man's attention, Annette mused, and it was Marie France Vincart who gave her the key.

With the harvest soon to be over, it would not be long before Colin returned to New Orleans. Chantele wanted to be ready for him, and she also wanted to put her stamp on the home they would share. She let the exotic magic of New Orleans possess her in the crowded streets that were a melange of languages and sounds and thriving with people of all colors and stations; where elegant ladies and gentlemen mingled with colored people and Indians in their native garb. The quadroon women she saw, easily distinguished by the bright tignons they wore, were beauties of dark liquid eyes and coral lips very much like the girl who had been aboard the ship that had brought her from France.

The many shops of the Vieux Carre offered a wide variety of merchandise, from the most delicate ladies' wear to exotic goods such as the Kermanshah rug she purchased for the main hallway. A set of standing candelabra she saw in a window were perfect on each side of the archway leading to the staircase, and a Sheraton sofa and other pieces of English furniture blended beautifully with the Louis XV settee and dove-colored Aubusson rug in the drawing room. A pair of exotic Hindu dancers carved from ivory found a home in the empty niches on each side of the doorway leading to the dining room, and Chantele was unable to resist the Italian watercolor she found in the small shop of M. Galvez.

"I'm terribly sorry, *madame,*" the shopkeeper said apologetically, "but Mr. Garrett has already indicated his desire to buy the painting." He gestured toward a tall man who was standing at the other end of the shop examining other articles. "Perhaps you will find something else . . ." M. Galvez added solicitously.

Chantele tried to hide her disappointment and examined other paintings just to please the shopkeeper, but, involuntarily, her eyes returned to the watercolor time and time again. She noticed Mr. Garrett in conversation with the shopkeeper, and then the man approached her and Annette, who was not as scandalized as she pretended to be when he introduced himself.

"I beg your pardon, Mme. Marquandt," he said politely, "but M. Galez tells me that you are interested in the watercolor."

His French was flawless except for a slight

accent. His manner, although perhaps a little forward, was polite and respectful, but his dark blue eyes had an appraising look as he addressed Chantele.

"That is correct, Mr. Garrett," she replied. "I will ask M. Galvez to let me know if you have a change of heart about the painting."

"Madame," he said with a gallantry Annette had not expected from an *Americaine,* "I would not dream of depriving a beautiful lady of something her heart desires. The watercolor is yours, if you want it."

"Mr. Garrett!" Chantele exclaimed taken by surprise. "It is very kind of you, but I can't possibly accept your generosity. You found it before I did, therefore, it is rightfully yours."

Paul Garrett was fascinated by the charming smile, devoid of conscious coquetry, that accompanied the refusal. The girl seemed completely unaware of the devastating effect she could have on a man.

Witnessing the exchange, Annette tried to look disapproving while all the time she was bursting with exhilaration. Paul Garrett's manners could not have been more urbane, but that he felt a strong attraction for Chantele was plain to see. Who was the man? It would be easy to find out, so this would not be the last meeting between he and Chantele. She herself would see to it, if he did not.

When they returned from their shopping expedition, Gideon informed them that the parcel from M. Galvez' shop had been delivered.

"But I was not expecting anything," Chantele said with a frown, "Where is it?"

"In the drawing room, *madame*."

Annette followed her into the drawing room, already knowing the contents before Chantele opened the package. Bravo! Paul Garrett had not disappointed her.

Chantele exclaimed in surprise when she found the watercolor and read out loud the small card inserted in a corner of the frame. "With my compliments to a very beautiful and gracious lady, P.G." She wanted to be angry and somehow could not. "I'll have to return it, of course, but it really is perfect for this room," she said wryly.

"The man doesn't take no for an answer," Annette said trying not to sound smug. She liked Paul Garrett more and more.

Chantele looked at Annette and burst out laughing, "I'm afraid this time he'll have to," she said, "I couldn't possibly accept it."

"There is no address on the card," Annette pointed out, "How will you contact Mr. Garrett?"

"I suppose I'll have to return it to M. Galvez," Chantele said with a shrug, and with one last look at the painting, she added with a sigh, "I'll send it back tomorrow."

She was going to the theater with the Gerards

that evening and had just enough time to get ready.

Lucas DeCouer came to their box and lingered longer than necessary hoping for an invitation to join their party, but he finally took his leave with resignation as the invitation never came. Marguerite Gerard took her role of chaperone seriously. She cared a great deal for Chantele and was aware of several unfavorable comments made as to her appearance in public without her husband so soon after the death of her father-in-law. The fools did not realize or care that the seclusion of mourning was the last thing the girl needed after the tragedy she had endured. Colin had given evidence of remarkable perception and understanding when he had sent his wife to New Orleans. Too bad his obligations kept him at the plantation; a beautiful girl like Chantele was to men like honey to flies, and her husband's absence was too conspicuous.

During intermission, when groups of friends gathered in the lobby for refreshments, Lucas again sought Chantele. Many acquaintances were also there, Marie France Vincart with her parents, and Marinette Dorleac with Henri Dumont as her escort. At the other end of the lobby Chantele spotted Paul Garrett, who raised his glass to her in a discreet and silent toast. She was tempted to speak to him and desisted when he did not approach her, but Lucas had seen the exchange and was seething with fury.

"The nerve!" he said angrily, "I have a mind to call him out!"

Chantele was alarmed by his vehemence. "Please, Lucas, don't!" she whispered. "You'll only create a scene."

"The man is a gambler, an adventurer not worthy of being in the same room with you!" Lucas said passionately.

"A gambler?"

"Riff-raff from the river boats who lately has become a regular at the Crescent," he elaborated. Obviously, Lucas was also a regular at that particular gambling hall.

"Listen to me, Lucas," she said persuasively, placing a restraining hand on his arm, "the man did nothing to compromise my reputation, but you will if you call him out." Chantele was not as unaware of Lucas's admiration as she pretended to be, and she thought this the perfect time to cash in her chips, "If you care for me at all, Lucas, you will do as I ask."

"I'd do anything for you, my lady!" Lucas said vehemently. "Anything at all!"

"Then put the incident out of your mind," she said softly, gazing into his eyes.

Chantele realized that, unconsciously, she had been playing a very dangerous game. Lucas DeCouer could have created a scandal over nothing. Oh, what a fool she had been, pretending not to see his ardent glances, his gallantries, his admiration. It had been just a silly way to satisfy her vanity when all she had ever wanted was for Colin to love her and be with her. She had managed, momentarily at least, to stop Lucas from challenging Paul Garrett to a duel, but Lucas was too impetuous to be trusted to keep his word if confronted with the gambler. Despite his skill with the rapier, somehow Chantele felt the young man would be no match for Paul Garrett, and she didn't want to see either of them hurt on her account. She was rather fond of Lucas, and despite their short acquaintance, she also liked Paul Garrett. There was something incredibly romantic in his gesture of sending her the watercolor. An adventurer? Perhaps. But also a man with excellent taste in art.

She made up her mind to contact Paul Garrett as soon as possible. She had to warn him to keep clear of Lucas. Would he comply? Perhaps not, but she had to try. If her name became involved in a scandal, her reputation would be ruined, and any chance she and Colin had would be lost.

Why do I get myself involved in such situations, she chided herself. God, how she missed Colin! It had been too long since he had come from L'Esperance and they had been in each other's arms for just one night before he had returned to the plantation. Other men found her desirable: Lucas, Paul Garrett. Why not her husband, who was the only one she had ever wanted?

The patter of rain against the window brought memories of that afternoon, so long ago, when she had visited his flat in Paris. It had been raining then, too, when she gave herself to him for the very first time.

In her bedchamber, Annette crossed the room to close the shutters when the rain began to fall. A movement in the shadows of the doorway across the street betrayed the presence of a man. Annette turned down the lamps and returned to the window. The man was still there and could only be spying on the house. Then, he stepped into the circle of light from the street lamp and Annette could see that he was a huge, corpulent man dressed in the garb of the boatmen who plied the river. Then a woman came from the house. The stole she wore over her head concealed her features. There was what seemed an angry exchange between them before the man hit the woman on the face and the stole fell away, exposing her features.

Why, it was Maggie, the laundress!

The Italian watercolor hung on the wall in the drawing room between the framed sketch Edouard Manet had presented to Chantele and a painted Oriental silk screen. Paul Garrett had agreed to her request only after Chantele had accepted the painting. He had promised to avoid Lucas DeCouer's provocations, and her mind was more at ease. An adventurer he might be, but she trusted him to keep his word. It was a pity they could not be friends, she mused, but a man of his reputation could only damage hers.

Colin was in New Orleans now and life was good again, even though he still refrained from being a real husband to her. He had been back for almost a week and they had not yet made love, but on her birthday, Chantele was bound and determined to bring him to her bed. She had planned a late supper at Antoine's for just the two of them after a night at the opera, and then, when they came home, he would not be able to say no to her.

"You should always wear white," he said encircling her waist, "the color of purity."

"Only virgins are pure and innocent, *monsieur,*" she sallied, "and I am a married lady." She turned in the circle of his arms and brought his head down to meet her lips. Her tongue tantalizingly traced the contours of his lips before it explored his mouth in a deep, passionate kiss that had not an ounce of innocence in it, and pressing her body to the length of his she could feel his response even through her voluminous crinolines.

She released him with a throaty, provocative laughter and offered him the diamond necklace he had given her for her birthday to put around her throat. His hands were shaking, but he finally managed to secure the clasp.

Colin wasn't even aware of which opera they were watching. In the darkness of the theater he was only conscious of Chantele's nearness, of her hand occasionally brushing his thigh, of the invitation in her amber eyes each time they met his. He broke into a cold sweat trying to focus his attention on the stage and failing miserably. He knew himself well enough to know that with Chantele bent on seduction, he didn't stand a chance. How he endured their late supper he didn't know, and in the carriage that took them home he tried to avert his eyes from the sultry lips that invited his kiss, the soft curves that beckoned his touch.

There had been no one else for him since that first moment when Chantele had danced by in the arms of another man and set her tawny eyes on him. She had fanned the flame of his desire until it had seared his heart with love. What a fool he had been to believe he could just walk away from her after possessing her beauty! He had scorned love only to be consumed by it. His body tensed at the touch of her hand.

"Chantele . . ." he began.

"Yes, my love?"

"Please, kitten, don't."

Chantele ignored his plea and nibbled at his earlobe.

"It's too soon, kitten."

"No, it's not." She felt the tremor of his hand as she took it to her lips and lovingly and temptingly kissed each finger. "Kiss me, darling," she said pressing his hand to her breast.

Only their arrival saved him from succumbing to her temptation. He sought the refuge of the study while she went to her room, selected a pretty white robe de chambre and brushed her hair until it gleamed. Then, she touched perfume to her throat and went in search of her husband. Gideon was snuffing out the lamps when she appeared at the top of the stairs.

"Is my husband in his study, Gideon?" she inquired.

"No, *madame*."

"Where is he?"

Gideon hesitated. "Mistah Colin went out, *madame*," he finally said reluctantly.

Colin had taken to the streets as if pursued by demons, determined to stay away all night if necessary. He had to ease the torment in his loins; and when he found himself standing across the street from the Orleans Ballroom, where a quadroon ball was in full swing, without a second thought he went in.

Nine

Under the crystal chandeliers of the Orleans Ballroom, Simone Vaillant stood between two aging admirers who were trying to outdo each other to gain her favors. How different it was now she was free to pick and choose her lovers. It was exhilarating to have men beg for what they once had demanded as their right. But now all that had changed, and the house, the elegant clothes filling her armoires, and the beautiful jewelry were hers alone and no one could take them away.

Simone fingered the ruby pendant that hung on a gold chain between the mounds of her full breasts, temptingly displayed by the deep decolletage of her scarlet satin gown. The ruby was her latest acquisition, her reward for the few hours of pleasure enjoyed by a besotted admirer much like the two standing by her side. Her glossy black curls were artistically coiffed under the matching tignon she was forced to wear, the badge that proclaimed her blood. How she hated that symbol that marked her as a possession to be bought and sold! But not any longer, she reminded herself; all that was in the past. Now men could buy a few hours of pleasure, but never her person, and all because of that fateful voyage from France.

Her aunt had meant well, she knew, when she had selected Maurice Duval as her protector. He was a rich old man who pampered his young quadroon mistress and didn't beat her often, but Simone had hated the sight of his flabby body, its stale odor, his grasping, trembling hands upon her flesh fondling the most intimate recesses of her young body.

She had enjoyed the trip to France, where for once she had discarded the odious tignon and walked in the Tuileries Gardens with her head up high, as any other woman free to chose her destiny. Even the return voyage had been somewhat bearable in spite of the haughty Creole ladies aboard, until that awful Alfred Vincart had walked into her life. To dispel his boredom, he had shown the old man perversed ways to enjoy a young mistress. With his ability to perform as a man on the wane, Maurice Duval had welcomed the novelty of seeing the young woman who was his property taken by another man before his eyes. The other man being Alfred Vincart, of course, who was clever in devising new ways to debase her while the old man drooled and panted and made her perform hideous acts upon his body. She had wanted to die then; had almost thrown herself overboard when Colin Marquandt had saved her life.

He was like no other white man she had ever encountered. He had listened to her tale of woe and dried her tears and changed her life. How he had delivered from the evil of Vincart and Duval she did not know, but he had freed her before the voyage had ended. Simone would have done anything for him, and had offered herself only to be turned down by him.

His wife was aboard. It was the same girl who had tried to speak to her once. Simone thought of the girl, tall and blond even though the color of her skin was slightly lighter than her own. She had eluded Colin's wife the times she had seen her on board, but the girl never

tried to speak to her again. Someone must have
told her what she was. But Simone could not
forget the last time she had seen the young
woman standing at the rail of the *Mouette* in
the New Orleans levee. Marquandt was returning to the ship then, and with eyes only for his
wife had not seen that Simone had been there,
too. She had never hated anyone as much as
she had hated Chantele Marquandt, who had
the only man Simone had ever loved.

Once in New Orleans, Simone had received a
note from Marquandt's banker and been
pleasantly surprised to learn of the provisions
Colin had made for her. The banker had also
given her a letter from his client. Simone still
kept that letter and had read it so many times
that she had memorized each word. She was
free. The funds deposited in her name would
help her start a new life. He wished her well
and said goodbye.

But she had not believed his farewell; no
man would give a quadroon woman a sum as
respectable as he had given her without making
any demands. She had waited for a long time
before she realized that he had never meant to
seek her out, and finally, she had ceased
waiting.

As the mistress of an old man she had learned
tricks that could arouse the passions in any
man unless he was dead, and in no time at all
her skills had made her a popular and highly

paid courtesan. Now she had her choice of lovers.

Suddenly, the voices around her grew dim and the presence of the men by her side seemed to recede into the background. She had waited so long for this moment, that she thought her eyes were playing tricks on her; but no, Colin Marquandt was standing at the entrance of the ballroom, looking about as if searching for someone. Their eyes met and held, and her heart beat faster as he crossed the room, advancing toward her. Wordlessly, he offered her his hand and her companions were left speechless when she took it and walked away with him.

At the entrance she said, "I have my own carriage," and was disappointed when he was not impressed. Her heart was racing now; for the first time in her life she would lie with a man she loved, and for an instant her confidence deserted her. She looked up at the man at her side. His face was set and drawn, and she felt her heart brim with love and a tenderness she had never known before. He had come to her at last, and she would see that he would never leave her again.

"Coal man, coal man!" cried the vendor, and Maggie Fitzsimmons's heart skipped a beat. How different her life was now from what it had been only last summer! In the space of a few months she had lost her Paddy and spent her time in hell, but the Holy Virgin and St. Patrick had heard her prayers and saved her from the clutches of the devil. Her children no longer went hungry or played in the stagnant water of filthy narrow streets, but in a lovely patio with trees and flowers and birds, and where an angel of a lady looked upon them as they played. Their quarters were clean and comfortable; she had her savings, and her children had all the food they could eat for the first time in their lives, not to mention the treats the lady of the house and her Negro housekeeper gave them. Even *monsieur* was kind to the children, and Molly, who had always been wary of strangers, had gone to him without reluctance the first time she had set her green eyes upon him. Maggie had been astonished when she had found her daughter sitting on his knee, listening intently to some story he was telling.

Her children needed a father, and Maggie needed a husband. There had been no other man for her but Paddy, so sweet and loving that she could not stop the tears each time she thought of him and of their little cottage in Ireland where they had so little of everything but love. It broke Paddy's heart to hear the children cry with hunger, and since the day his cousin and only relative had sent that letter from America, Paddy had dreamed only of saving enough money to pay their fare to the New World. But there had never been enough for the whole family, and Maggie would not let him go alone. She had always feared their farewell would be forever. Then, someone had told him of the ships that carried immigrants in their holds for only a small fare. Their meager savings had barely covered the price, but they were on their way. Like other desperate people, they were packed in the hold, and Maggie remembered the stench of urine and feces and vomit and sweat that clung to her nostrils even after they had left that nightmare of a ship. All their illusions had been crushed in New Orleans, a city filled with immigrants like themselves who fought over the meanest jobs, just to survive. Paddy had paved streets, drained canals, doing anything that would put bread in their mouths, and Maggie had helped by taking in laundry. When he had failed to return one night, Maggie had known that something terrible must have happened. Unlike others who spent their hard-earned money on drink, Paddy always turned all his earnings over to her, keeping only a few pennies to himself when she pressed them into his hand. She had almost gone out of her mind with grief when two days later someone had told her that Paddy was dead. He had fallen victim to the dreaded yellow fever and died alone in a hospital because no one had told her where he was. He had been buried in a pauper's grave, and she had fallen on her knees upon the earth and smashed her fists on the grave, crying out and blaming God for taking her Paddy away.

After the grief came the fear, when she realized that without Paddy, it was up to her to feed her children. One of her patrons ran a fancy house and told her that she could make more money during a night on her back than washing other people's dirty laundry for a month of Sundays. She had been tempted by so much money, until she had seen some of the girls parading almost naked, showing off the bodies they sold for coin, and Maggie knew that she could never be one of them. She had already sinned terribly when she had blamed God for her misfortunes, and she prayed with all her heart for forgiveness. And forgiveness finally came, but not before she had paid her dues to the devil in the person of Jack the boatman.

But now he could not hurt her or the children any more. She had been frightened when he appeared again to take her away, but somehow she had found the courage to tell him that she was under the protection of the Marquandts. He had not been completely convinced and said he would be back, but he had not hurt her.

Maggie had been terrified. If the Marquandts knew of Jack, would they protect her or would she lose her job, the only security Molly and Paddy had known in their short lives? Mme. Marquandt was kind, but a fine lady like her would never keep a harlot in her house, as she was sure to think of Maggie when she learned she had been Jack's woman.

The summons from the Widow, as Annette was referred to among the servants, came the day after Maggie had met Jack. Maggie had been surprised, since the Widow had never addressed her in all the time she had been employed there. Without a preamble, Annette had asked who was the man she had met on the street the night before and, caught off guard, Maggie had broken down and poured out the whole story together with a fountain of tears. When she finished, Maggie threw herself on her knees before Annette and begged her not to turn her out and, surprisingly, the Widow had been kind and understanding. She had asked many questions about Jack, and once she had her answers, the Widow had promised Maggie that her secret was safe and that she had nothing to fear. When Jack came back, the Widow herself would send him away. Maggie had covered her hand with kisses mingled with tears of gratitude.

That had been weeks ago, and Jack had never again bothered Maggie, who now preened at the sound of the cries of the coal man. But no ordinary coal man was he, but

Sean O'Malley, whom she had met at church one Sunday and since then had taken the place of his regular driver when the coal delivery was to the Marquandt household. Maggie knew that very soon now Mr. O'Malley would have gathered enough courage to ask to be allowed to keep company with her, and she would say yes, for Mr. O'Malley was a darling man. Not as sweet at Paddy, perhaps, but a darling man indeed.

Everything was falling into place with perfect precision, and like a puppet master, Annette pulled the strings from behind the scenes. It had taken time and patience and cunning to gather all the pieces, but now they were all there: Lucas, Paul Garrett, Simone Vaillant, the pawns; and Jack, her insurance.

Even Annette had been frightened by his ferocious appearance the night Maggie had alerted her to his presence. Annette had met him in the shadows of the night, and the bargain had been made. Jack could have Maggie back, plus a good bonus in coin, in exchange for his services.

And now that everything was ready, all she had to do was sit back and watch the play unfold, with perhaps a little cue on her part every now and then to accelerate the action. That was the beauty of the plan: no suspicion would ever fall upon her, and there would be no Marquandt left to defy her claim to L'Esperance and the fortune. Everything would be hers. And of course, Robert's.

Chantele had her pride; Colin had rejected her for the last time. She had ceased in her efforts to bring him to her bed, and all through the madness which possessed the city dressed for carnival, she had lived as in suspended animation. Colin continued to be as affectionate and attentive as ever, but he had changed. Perhaps his new calm and renewed patience were the result of her own behavior now that she did not make any wifely demands, she tried to reason. If only she could believe it. She tried and failed to push away her suspicions of another woman, and as never before she prayed that she was wrong.

Annette realized that Chantele was so in love with her husband that she was willing to close her eyes to his infidelity, and this would never do. She wondered if seeing Colin with Simone Vaillant would prompt her into action, and never a believer of the direct approach, Annette found the way to convey the knowledge to Chantele. In this, Marie France's viperous tongue was her weapon.

"My dear, you should never pay attention to what Marie France says," Annette said sweetly after the guests had departed. Chantele was visibly shaken by Marie France's insiduous remarks about Colin and a quadroon girl. "The girl is envious of your happiness," she finished, trying not to smirk.

"My happiness!" Chantele said bitterly.

"Don't despair, my dear," Annette said, "You have so much! Your beauty, your youth, a magnificent home and a husband who loves you."

"Does he?"

Realizing that everything depended on her reply, Annette chose her words with care. "Of course he does. And even if what Marie France said were true, it could only be passing fancy. Men are men, my dear, and on occasion they . . . indulge themselves. But remember," she added, "you are his wife."

Chantele shut her eyes tight and clenched her fists until the knuckles turned white. She wanted to scream. No, she could never share Colin's love! If it was true and there was another woman in his life, she had to know. She could not live for another minute with this uncertainty that was destroying her. She had tried, and failed. "I must know, Annette."

"Don't, my dear," Annette said, putting her arm around her shoulder, "Don't torture yourself like this."

"I have to know!" Chantele sobbed.

"Very well, my dear," Annette said with a sigh of satisfaction, "if you insist. But what will you do? I hope you are not planning to confront Colin," she said, suddenly alarmed. The girl was too direct in her dealings. "That won't do, my dear," she rushed to add, "If there's no truth to the rumor, he will be very hurt."

"So there are rumors!" Chantele said.

"Well . . . yes," Annette said, feigning reluctance. "But perhaps they are wrong. They must be."

"How long, Annette?"

"How long?"

"How long have you known?"

"My dear, I don't wish to upset you."

"I have to know!"

Annette weighed her answer carefully. "You are placing me in a very difficult position, Chantele," she said warily, "Colin is my son by marriage."

"He's my husband!"

"Please, dear, try and collect yourself," Annette said persuasively. This was going very well, she congratulated herself. Chantele was almost hysterical. "After all, they are only rumors. I'm not sure Colin has betrayed you, and neither are you."

"Then I must see for myself," Chantele said firmly. "Will you help me?"

"I . . ."

"I'm sorry, Annette, I have no right to ask a thing from you," Chantele said. "Only tell me one more thing. Who is the woman?"

Annette examined her hands thoughtfully, taking her time before replying, as if deciding whether or not to answer. Then, she gazed into the girl's drawn face and said, "Her name is Simone Vaillant."

Chantele remained silent.

"Just promise me one thing," Annette implored, and this time her tone was sincere. "Don't confront Colin. If he has been true to you, he'll never forgive you."

An enclosed carriage was stationed across the street from the briquete entre porteaux cottage where Simone Vaillant made her home. Inside, behind the heavy veil that covered her features, a woman alone intently watched the house. The coachman dozed on his perch, his frayed collar upturned against the wind. A jealous wife spying on her husband, he catalogued his passenger. The small cottages on the ramparts were occupied by fancy quadroons kept by prosperous white men. Why should the woman care if her husband had a little sport with a hot-blooded quadroon woman he smirked, as long as she had the benefits of his name and his station?

Hours dwindled slowly and dusk had fallen when Simone Vaillant drove away in her carriage. Recognizing her immediately, Chantele realized what Marie France had tried to tell her at the end of the voyage. Even then, Colin and the quadroon had been lovers. With a sinking heart, Chantele ordered the cabby to drive away.

"Where to, lady?"

She could not go home, not yet. If she met Colin now, she didn't know what she would do. "Just drive."

Chantele didn't know how long they had roamed aimlessly when she saw that they were in front of Jackson Square. "Stop!" she called.

Pocketing his fare, the cabby watched the crazy woman cross the square in the direction of the cathedral. "Women!" he muttered and popped the reins.

The flickering flames of the candles at the foot of the altars were like glowing fireflies in the quiet gloom of the deserted cathedral. Chantele fell to her knees before the image of the Virgin and raised her eyes to the sweet, immobile face tried to pray. But she could not. A raging tide of grief washed over her and she chocked in her own tears, her body racked by heart-rending sobs.

The voice was as gentle as the hand that touched her shoulder, "My child, let me help you."

She raised her gaze to meet the owner of the voice, a white-haired priest standing at her side. "Father." She could not control her sobs, and the priest helped her to her feet and gently guided her into the vestry, where he poured a glass of wine and offered it to her.

"Drink it, my child," he said when she shook her head, "it will settle your nerves so we can talk."

The priest masked his surprise to see such a young face behind the veil Chantele was forced to lift to drain the glass. Several wordless seconds went by as Father Murphy waited for the girl to regain her composure.

"Now, my child," he said when her sobs had subsided, "tell me what grieves you so. If you prefer," he added, "I can accept your confession."

His gentleness was a welcome balm on her bruised spirit. "Thank you, Father," she said, and then, trying to collect herself, "Bless me, Father, for I have sinned." A sob punctuated her words.

Father Murphy listened as the girl poured out her story in a tremulous voice. She held nothing back, from her first lie to Rosalyn when she had fallen in love with Colin and ending with her vigil of Simone Vaillant's house.

"But you don't know for certain that your husband has committed adultery," Father Murphy said when she had finished. "You say he is gentle and loving and, yet, in the same breath you accuse him of a mortal sin based only on malicious gossip."

Chantele didn't answer.

"My child, in your wedding vows you promised to honor your husband. Trust is a very important part of honoring the man you married. Trust him, child."

"But I want to, Father, so very much!"

"In His infinite wisdom Our Father forgives the sins of His children," the priest said. "Pray, my child, and He will give you strength."

In the days that followed, Chantele gave much thought to Father Murphy's advice. More than anything in the world she wanted to believe in Colin. And yet, the doubts were still there.

With their first wedding anniversary almost upon them, Colin encouraged his wife to arrange a ball to celebrate the occasion. She had been undecided; even though she had attended the theater with the Gerards, after his return to New Orleans they had refrained from accepting invitations in consideration to Leon's death; but there had been enough grief, Colin said, and to put an end to their mourning they would at least attend the Charmont ball.

He only wants my happiness, Chantele thought guiltily. How can I doubt him? And to please him, she went ahead with the preparations. Annette helped her prepare a guest list.

"I shall need a new gown," Annette pointed out the day when they were to attend the Charmont party, "and I'd like to try a new shop on Royal Street I've heard is excellent. Will you help me make a selection?"

Chantele readily agreed, but nothing was further from Annette's mind than a new gown. She had waited for Chantele to do something drastic during the past few days, and watching her renewed trust in Colin had sent her into a frenzy. As a desperate maneuver, she had to create a confrontation, and what better place for two women to meet than a dressmaker's shop? Annette herself had seen the gown Simone Vaillant was to collect that very afternoon. She only hoped the girl would be punctual.

She was, and dark velvet eyes met amber ones in surprise that immediately became hostility. And then, without taking her eyes off Chantele, Simone addressed the shopkeeper. "Be sure that M. Colin Marquandt gets the bill," she said, and with a sardonic smile playing on her coral lips, she added, "as usual."

Accustomed to sending Mle. Vaillant's bills to different men, the shopkeeper simply nodded her assent.

Chantele's face was drained of color, and she stood there, frozen on the spot while Simone Vaillant walked out of the shop with a proud toss of her head.

"*Mesdames,*" said the shopkeeper, "May I be of service?"

"We changed our minds," Annette replied, and taking Chantele by the arm led her to the street. "I'm sorry," she said contritely, "I never dreamed this could happen."

Chantele gazed at Annette with eyes that seemed to look right through her. "Don't trouble yourself," she said in an empty voice. "It's of no consequence."

Let's hope it is, Annette said inwardly.

There was no pain, there was no sorrow; there wasn't even anger. And she could not even cry. All there was was a terrible emptiness inside her, as if she were hollow. And cold. She was so cold!

With bated breath Annette watched her, knowing that it would not be long.

The gown she was to wear to the Charmont ball was white. Colin liked her in white, she mused absently. "I've changed my mind, Bess," she said to the Negress, "I don't want that gown."

"But, missy . . ." Bess tried to argue.

"Please, Bess, do as I say." Her tone, albeit quiet, left no room for argument, and shaking her head, Bess put the gown aside. "Which one do you want, missy?"

"It doesn't matter."

Miss Chantele was acting mighty peculiar, Bess mused going through the gowns hanging in the armoire. The collection Chantele had

brought from Paris remained almost untouched. The black feathers trimming an amber dress
made it Bess's favorite. The vivid color of the
gown accentuated her pallor, and Chantele applied rouge to her cheeks while Bess secured the
feathers in her hair.

Always an affluent city, New Orleans was
now at the height of its golden era, and the
splendid mansions of the Garden District were
eloquent exponents of the great fortunes whose
foundations rested on sugar cane and king cotton. The Charmonts lived in such a mansion,
gleaming white in the moonlight as carriage after carriage traveled the circular driveway to
discharge passengers. Elegance and taste were
displayed in the salons where the guests had assembled and, in the minstrels' gallery above, an
orchestra played inobtrusively before the beginning of the dance. French windows opened to
terraces softly lit, and torches illuminated por-
tions of the lush gardens, surrounded by
fences of elaborate cast iron.

Annette joined a group of matrons who
readily received her in their midst, and as the
evening wore on, she wondered if Dumas *fils*,
Moliere, and other famous playwrights felt the
same kind of excitement watching their plays
being performed on the stage as she was feeling
now, waiting for the last act of her creation.
But how could they? They dealt with fictional

characters and situations, while her own involved real lives.

What was wrong, Colin asked himself, watching his wife with alarm. He had never seen her so cold, so remote as she had been during their first dance. His immediate concern had been for her health, but no, it was something else. He was well aware his flight had hurt her pride and had been tempted to smooth her ruffled feathers, but then he had reflected on how her current behavior was making his abstinence so much easier to bear. If it could ever be easy, that is.

He was sure that very soon, if not already, her health would be completely restored. It was the fear of another pregnancy that was keeping him away from her. The memory of last summer was still too painfully fresh in his mind. He had seen a healthy young girl teeter on the brink of death because of the seed he had planted in her womb. Of the would-be son he had buried he could not even bear to think. He would never turn Chantele into another Violette, suffering miscarriage after miscarriage until the woman had turned into a ghost. He wanted children, her children, but he wanted her even more, healthy and vibrant as she had been in Paris, as she had been the night she had tried to seduce him and he had escaped because he had known that he could not resist her. He had been in torment then, and he had found release.

The first time Simone Vaillant had offered herself to him he had not even been tempted, in spite of her beauty and the illusion that his feeling for Chantele was mere physical attraction. But now that he knew of love, he was aware that what Simone had given him during their night together was much more than any man receives from a courtesan. It had been there, in her dark liquid eyes, in her quivering flesh, and after the initial release of the passion inspired by Chantele that he had tried to be a lover to Simone.

He had been deeply touched by this girl who, dropping all her defenses, had wept in his arms as Chantele had cried when he had taken her innocence. She had told him then that she loved him, that she had waited for him long after their return to New Orleans, and listening to her velvet voice in the dark, Colin had felt ashamed that he had used her to vent his need without giving a thought to her feelings. Because for him it had been a mere physical release, nothing more, and what would have satisfied him before knowing Chantele's love, now left him unfulfilled, unsatisfied. Because, without love, that most intimate and special act between two people was pleasurable but meaningless; but when love was there, no other experience could match it. It was much more than the blending of two bodies, it was the meeting of two souls, two hearts, of two complete beings, and for one beautiful and magical moment, those two separate people become one heart, one soul, one dream.

What a romantic he had become, he mused, shaking his head wryly. Live and learn. Right now, he didn't like the ardent glances Chantele was getting from her dancing partner.

But Henri Duval's gallantries were falling on deaf ears. All night long Chantele had been as in a trance, unable to distinguish one dancing partner from another, a fixed smile on her face. But suddenly it was Colin whose arms were around her.

"Kitten, what's wrong?" he said gently. "Are you feeling all right?"

She could not feel at all. It was as if she were dead. She moved, and talked, and breathed, but there was no feeling inside her.

He stopped dancing, and taking her hand led her to the terrace, where he put his arms around her and held her close.

"I love you, kitten."

When she didn't answer, a feeling of dread invaded his soul. Was he losing her? He lifted her chin and tried to kiss her, but she seemed to come back to life.

"Don't!" she cried pushing him away.

"Chantele, I love you."

She regarded him with eyes that were too

bright, and throwing her head back emitted a shrill laughter that chilled him on the spot. Without a word, she turned on her heel and left him standing there, unable to move.

The next time he saw her, she was dancing with Lucas DeCouer.

The world was closing in about her when Chantele walked back to the ballroom. She couldn't bear Colin's kisses. Why did he continue to torment her? His love was a lie!

"Where are you, my beautiful lady?"

Chantele realized that Lucas had spoken, gazing deeply into her eyes. "Here in your arms, my gallant knight," she replied, making herself smile.

"If only that were true, my lady," he said huskily. "You know I love you, Chantele."

Why didn't it thrill her to hear this handsome young man confessing his love? Were all her feelings as dead as her child? She had known no other man but Colin, no other kisses, no other love. But Colin had betrayed her and pretended to love her while all the time . . .

"Will you give me at least one shred of hope that you feel something for me?" Lucas implored passionately.

Why not, she said inwardly. What did it matter any more? Her eyes spoke of promises, and she smiled mysteriously. "Perhaps . . ." she said.

"Oh, my lady, how you torment me!" Lucas said hoarsely. "Please tell me that you love me!"

She laughed softly. "But your lady is not free, sir knight," she said. "There's a dragon at her door."

"Then I shall slay him, my lady, just for a smile of your sweet lips!"

Colin had said something similar, eons ago, she mused. Lucas's eyes were fixed on her lips. "One kiss, my lady, and I'll be your slave."

Her eyes sparkled when she said, "It's too warm in the salon. Perhaps it will be cooler in the gardens."

Annette watched them disappear through the French windows, and when Colin followed, she knew the curtain was about to fall.

Lucas could hardly believe that at last he was tasting the lips he had for so long yearned to kiss, holding the yeilding body that had robbed him of his will. Chantele clung to him desperately, pressing her body to his, but his kisses did nothing to fill the emptiness inside her. Suddenly he was torn away from her and she realized that he was sitting on the ground, shaking his head, and that Colin was looming over him, fists clenched.

Lucas rose and confronted him. Their voices were loud, yet she could not understand what they were saying. Only a word here and there penetrated the vacuum that seemed to surround her. "Pistols . . . dawn . . . oaks."

Lucas was walking away and Colin was advancing toward her. His lips were moving and his face was fraught with rage.

"I could kill you!" he said through teeth clenched with fury. The blank look she gave him only served to increase his rage, and his hands went around her throat and he was squeezing until her temples were pounding and everything was growing dim. The notes of a waltz drifted in through the fog that was enveloping her brain, and she closed her eyes. She was cold, so cold . . .

The pressure on her throat was released, and she fell on her knees to the ground. Excited voices were coming closer.

Annette was disappointed Chantele was still alive, there had been enough witnesses to see Colin trying to strangle his wife, it was too bad he had not finished what he had started. But then, she had been prepared for this eventuality. Jack was still waiting.

Ten

Colin seemed to have vanished in the ensuing confusion. Brushing aside many offers of help, Annette took charge of Chantele, who, still dazed by the events of the evening, was unaware that the route they took did not lead to the Marquandt house on Tolouse Street. When the carriage came to a halt, she did not even question why they were at the levee at that hour in the morning.

A man stepped out of the shadows. "Any problems?"

"None," Annette replied.

Chantele was shaken out of her apathy when a gag was stuffed into her mouth and she was stripped of her dress and petticoats. The man twisted her arms behind her back and quickly bound her wrists. A heavy sack was pulled over her head.

"Have you a safe place to keep her?" Annette inquired.

"The boat is half empty. There are plenty of cabins."

"Good. Remember, wait until you are far enough away before you dump her into the river. The body must never be found."

"Don't worry, lady, no one will ever find her."

Chantele was flung on a soft surface and the sack removed from her head. It was dark, but when a lamp was lit she saw they were in what appeared to be the stateroom of a steamboat.

"Well, well, well . . ." the man said, "what a nice surprise."

Chantele cowered when he advanced toward her. He was huge and grimy, and a glint of malice shone in his dark, porcine eyes. His face, swarthy and pockmarked, twisted into a malevolent grin, showing a row of rotten teeth.

Clad only in her chemise and pantalettes,

Chantele twisted away when he placed a big paw on her bosom. The man laughed, grabbed the chemise, and ripped it down. His huge hand closed on her breast, testing its fullness.

"Now, me beauty, don't get unfriendly," he sneered. "We're gonna be spending the next few days together." She kicked him when he began to pull at her pantalettes, but he didn't even seem to feel it.

"A live one, ain't you!" he said, amused by her struggles. Her pantalettes came off, and she felt his rough hand on her naked flesh.

"Nice piece of fluff, I'd say," Jack said running his eyes over her body with a leer. "You'll have to wait a bit for Jack, me luv," he smirked, "we're casting off in a few minutes. But I'll be back to show you what a real man feels like," he said, stroking the bulge in his pants.

He grabbed a handful of her hair and looked menacingly into her eyes. "I don't want to hear a sound out of you, me beauty, you hear?"

He tied her ankles together with a rope he pulled from his pocket, and then tied the end to the bedpost. "That's so that you won't be running, looking for Jack," he said with a sinister laugh. He turned down the lamp and Chantele was left in darkness.

What had happened? She had gone through the night in a haze and suddenly she was here with this monster. Then, she remembered Colin trying to kill her. Did he want her dead and dumped into the river? This could not be happening, she told herself. It had to be a nightmare.

An eternity passed. She had almost dozed off when the door opened and moments later the lamp was lit again.

"Now, me beauty, old Jack is back," he said, loosening his belt and pulling his filthy shirt over his head. She stared in horror at the barrel of his chest covered with a thick mat of dark hair. Leering at her, he shed his pants; his shaft was thick, stiff, and menacing. "Look at it, me beauty," he said proudly. "Like I promised, you're gonna find out what a real man feels like between your legs."

He climbed onto the bed with her, and straining against her bounds she writhed and twisted away from his grasp, but she could not get far.

"Be nice, me beauty, and I'll go easy on you," he said. "Your friend in New Orleans wants you dumped into the river in a sack, but I'm sure she don't mind if I have me bit of fun with you first."

"It's always better without a stitch on, ain't it, me beauty," he said tearing away the shreds of her chemise. "Nice," he added, kneading her breasts.

He smelled of rum and of stale sweat, and nausea rose in her throat when his hands ravished her body and his mouth slobbered and sucked her flesh. Straddling her, he tried to pull her legs apart, but she locked her knees together.

"Now, me luv, don't be so stubborn." Again he spread her legs apart and forced them down with his own. Her cries of pain and horror when his stiff hardness impaled her were drowned by the gag in her mouth. Her struggles only increased his pleasure. The man was pumping savagely into her, his ragged breath grating her ears. With an animal grunt he sank his teeth into her neck as his body shook violently. The pain in her arms, still bound behind her back, was excruciating. He collapsed on top of her.

"That was good, me luv," he said, rolling off her. "We're gonna have a jolly good time." He gave her breast a squeeze. "Look, me beauty, you know I'm suppose to kill you, but you be real nice to old Jack and I'll let you go when we get to St. Louie. Is it a deal?"

Chantele stared at him through eyes wide with terror.

"I'm gonna take that gag off now, and no screams, you hear? If you do, I'm gonna let you have it," he said, pressing his huge fist against her cheek. "You understand, me beauty?"

He loosened the gag and she opened her mouth to scream, but he quickly covered it with his own. Chantele gagged when his thick

229

tongue went into her mouth and desperately tried to clench her teeth, but he held her by the throat and squeezed until she was suffocating. Then he released her and she took gulps of air, filling her lungs. "Now you learn to obey Jack, won't you, me beauty?"

Chantele began to cry, sobbing raggedly. "Please, let me go," she pleaded.

"Now, now, me luv, that's no way to behave," he said, lifting her chin and trying to kiss her, but she squirmed out of his grasp. Her scream was cut by a stunning blow that landed her flat on her back.

"I warned you, me luv, no screams. Or you'll get more of the same."

She tried to hold back her screams when he mounted her again, but could not, and he hit her again and again until she finally became quiet.

How many days and nights she was kept in that stateroom she didn't know, drifting in and out of consciousness. No longer did she struggle or resist Jack. He had beaten her into submission. Her face was swollen and discolored; she could barely see out of one eye. Every inch of her body screamed with pain. It would soon be over, she said to herself in moments of awareness; she was going to die and didn't care. Anything would be better than this.

Jack had already been paid for killing the

girl. But what was the profit in it, he asked himself. The girl would be just as lost in a crib in St. Louis, and he could get a few dollars for her. Her face was a bloody mess, but she would heal.

It was well past midnight and the dock in St. Louis was deserted when Jack left the ship carrying a heavy sack slung over his shoulder. He was watched by two derelicts hiding among the bales and crates, sharing a bottle of rum.

"What do you think he's got in there, mate?" said one to the other.

"Dunno, but it looks heavy."

The same idea crossed their minds. "He's big, mate," Billy pointed out.

"But there's two of us, and I've got Betsie here," Mickey said, stroking the handle of his bowie knife. "All right, here's what we'll do."

Stealthily, Jack advanced among the cargo crowding the dock and almost tripped over a fallen drunk. The man was blocking his path, and he was forced to step over the body. As he did, a hand shot out and grabbed his foot. Jack fell headlong on the dock, and his sack went flying through the air, hitting a large crate before it landed with a thud.

Jack began to rise to his feet but never made it; out of the darkness a knife was plunged into his back.

The two derelicts scrambled for the sack, and in a fever of excitement pulled at the rope tied to one end. Billy reached into the sack and promptly jerked back his hand.

"What is it, mate?" Mickey asked.

"It's a body," Billy said, bewildered.

"A body?" Mickey asked in disbelief. "Let me see."

He pulled at the sack and uncovered the naked body of a woman. Her blond hair was matted with blood.

"Is she dead?" Billy inquired warily.

"Dunno," Mickey replied and touched the body. "She's still warm."

Chantele groaned against her gag. The two men jumped to their feet.

"She's alive!" Billy exclaimed.

"Let's get out of here," Mickey said warily. He turned and began to walk away. Billy started to follow and then stopped. "What about her?" he said, vacillating.

"She'll be dead soon," Mickey said with a shrug. "Let's go."

Billy started to leave, but something pulled him back. In another life, before his affair with the bottle, there had been a wife and a little girl with golden hair. Somehow, he could not bring himself to abandon the woman.

"Wait!" he called after Mickey. "I'm not leaving her."

"Have you gone loco, mate?" Mickey exclaimed. "If we're caught with her we'll hang!"

"You can have the whole bottle if you help me."

Mickey hesitated. "Where will you take her?" he finally asked.

"There's a doctor not too far from here. We can take her there."

"And what will the doctor say when he sees us with her?" Mickey argued. "We'll be hanged, I tell you."

"No, he won't see us. We'll just leave her at the door."

Mickey took a moment to think. The thought of the bottle of rum was too tempting to resist. "All right, mate," he finally agreed, "I'll go ahead to make sure the coast is clear."

Billy pulled the sack over Chantele's head and carried her in his arms. Keeping to the shadows, they made their way to the doctor's house. They were almost there when, across the street, a man opened a window and stood there, scratching his belly with gusto and looking out, sending the two derelicts to the protection of a doorway.

"He'll see us!" Mickey said. "I'm getting out of here."

"No, wait!"

The man across the street turned and moved away from the window. Mickey stepped out of their hiding place and, after making sure no one was about, signaled his companion to follow. Finally they reached their destination, a two-story house with a doctor's shingle in front. Gingerly, Billy deposited Chantele on the doorstep, yanked at the bell three times, and ran across the street, where he hid in the shadows and watched. He saw a light go on in a room on the upper floor. A minute later, the front door opened.

Meanwhile, in New Orleans, Colin paced the length of his jail cell like a caged tiger while trying to sort out what had happened after he had stopped short of killing his wife—who had disappeared without a trace. At first, when the police arrested him for her murder, Colin believed he had actually killed Chantele in the garden until they showed him the bloodstained gown they had found hidden in his room. It was the same gown Chantele had worn that evening.

During the interrogation, he had been unable to tell the police where he had gone. So shaken had he been that he only remembered roaming aimlessly until dawn, when he had faced Lucas' pistol under the Dueling Oaks. He had seen Lucas fall to his bullet, still alive, but with blood covering the front of his white shirt. And he could not erase from his mind Chantele's eyes, open, without fear, while he was choking the life out of her. She had not even tried to defend herself against his fury.

"You have a visitor, Marquandt," the jailer

said, interrupting his thoughts, and Colin saw Annette standing behind the man. "Five minutes, lady."

"Has she been found?" Colin asked anxiously.

"No," Annette replied shaking her head. "I'm afraid she's . . . gone, Colin."

"Gone? What do you mean gone?"

Annette took her time in replying. "After you disappeared and I took her home, Chantele was acting very . . . strange," she began. "I've never seen her like that."

"In what way?"

"Very cold, aloof, and yet I could feel her anger. I was very concerned and asked her if I should stay with her, but she said she wanted to be left alone. Next thing I knew, she had disappeared and the police were in the house."

"Have you spoken to Marguerite Gerard?"

"Yes, and she hasn't heard from Chantele, either. But . . ." and she let him see her hesitation, "Colin, I'm afraid there's more that you don't know. I feel terrible for not telling you before, but I just didn't know what to do."

"What are you trying to tell me, Annette?"

"That there was . . . a man," Annette began warily and was gratified by the expression on his face. "Chantele and I met him while we were shopping one day. She was interested in a watercolor he had just purchased. You know, the one hanging in the drawing room." She paused, letting her words sink in. "You were in L'Esperance then, and I knew she missed you terribly . . ."

"Did she see him again?"

"He came to the house once," she admitted with a flush. "I tried to warn her that her reputation would be ruined by associating with a man like Paul Garrett, a professional gambler, but she told me to mind my own business." Annette paused before she added, "I'm afraid they met again after that. I saw them together once, quite by accident."

"And you didn't tell me?"

"Colin, please, try to understand my position!" she said with anguish. "Both you and Chantele are very dear to me. I didn't want to hurt either of you. I tried to tell her that she was courting disaster by encouraging Lucas's attentions, by associating with Garrett, but she was too young and too impetuous to see the danger. I hoped she would come to her senses after she managed to avoid a duel between them," Annette said and paused to let a tear fall. "I always believed that she did love you, Colin, that her affair with Garrett would be over once you were back together again, but after what's happened, I feel so responsible . . ." she wept.

"This man, Garrett, where is he?"

"No one knows, Colin. I'm afraid he's disappeared, too." She paused for effect before she added, "There is one more thing you should know, Colin. Chantele knew about you and Simone Vaillant."

It was a moment of triumph. When she saw that he believed her, Annette had to make a supreme effort to maintain the grim expression on her face.

Chantele had images of blurry faces and faint voices followed by darkness. It happened again and again, but now something cool was being pressed to her lips, and she drank avidly.

"Easy now," a voice said, "not too fast."

She could not see very well even though her eyes were open. The light shadow before her began to come into focus, a man in a white coat who was giving her another spoonful of water. She could see him better now. She tried to speak, but no sound came out. She accepted another spoonful of water and then another.

"I'm thirsty," she croaked.

"Here, let me help you," the man said lifting her head gently. "Drink it slowly," he said holding the glass to her swollen lips. When she finished, the man observed her closely. "Better now?"

"Yes, thank you."

He took her hand and felt for her pulse. "You are going to be alright," he said.

She became aware of her strange surroundings. "Where am I?" she asked feebly.

"You're in my house," the man replied, "I'm Dr. Spinner."

Chantele was silent for a moment before she said, "How . . . did I get here?"

"We'll talk about that later," Dr. Spinner replied, "how do you feel?"

Her entire body was a mass of pain. There was a dull ache in her head, and when she touched it, her fingers found it bandaged.

"You got a nasty bump on your head," Dr. Spinner said. "I expect you'll have a headache for a while yet."

"What happened?"

"Don't you know?"

She tried to remember, but her mind was a blank. "I can't remember," she admitted.

"It's all right," Dr. Spinner assured her, "it'll come to you. Is there anyone we should notify?"

Again, nothing. "I don't know, doctor."

"What is your name?"

Try as she might, nothing came to her. "I don't know," she said with dismay. "Doctor, what's wrong?"

Dr. Spinner regarded her with a frown. He had heard of cases like this but never actually seen one. Amnesia, it was called. "You suffered a severe blow to the head," he said gently, "that may have caused a temporary loss of memory. But don't worry, my dear, I'm sure everything will be all right. Also, you have bruises on your face and body and a broken rib, but you will heal with proper rest. How is your vision?''

Chantele looked around, examining her surroundings. The room was small; the paper on the walls had a pattern of yellow roses. There was a dresser with a beveled mirror above it, on the dresser a ewer and a basin. Lacy curtains billowed at the window, and there was a chair beside them.

''Can you see clearly?''

''Yes.''

''Good. Are you hungry?''

''Yes.''

''That's a good sign,'' Dr. Spinner said with a smile.

''Doctor . . . how long have I been here?''

''Ten days.''

''That long!'' she said, aghast.

''Sleep was the best thing for you,'' Dr. Spinner said gently. ''We have been feeding you broth, but now you need something more substantial. Miss Pruitt, my housekeeper, will bring you a tray.''

''Thank you, doctor.''

Miss Pruitt was a plain woman in her early thirties. Her brown hair was parted in the middle and coiled at the back of her head, and her light blue eyes looked kind. Chantele tried to sit up, but pain stabbed through her like a knife, reminding her of her broken rib. Even after the many days without food, the smell of the clear soup, roast chicken, and boiled carrots made her a little nauseous. A small plate of custard was more appetizing.

"Thank you, Miss Pruitt," Chantele said when the woman helped her sit up and plumped a pillow behind her back. Chantele tried to eat while Miss Pruitt occupied herself in the room, but she had no appetite. Seeing this, Miss Pruitt remarked, "Please try to eat a little more, my dear, you need your strength."

"The food is delicious," Chantele said, "but I'm afraid I'm not very hungry."

"Do try a few more bites," Miss Pruitt coaxed. "And drink your milk . . . oh, dear," she said with a flush.

"What is it, Miss Pruitt?"

"Dr. Spinner said you can't remember your name."

"I'm afraid so."

"Perhaps we should give you a name until you remember your own," Miss Pruitt suggested.

Chantele tried to smile, but her face felt stiff and sore. "That's a good idea," she said, "have you any suggestions?"

"Let me think," Miss Pruitt said pensively, and in the meantime, Chantele noticed a little girl peeking into the room from the doorway.

"We have a visitor," she indicated, and Miss Pruitt turned to the door.

"Melissa, your father told you to stay out of this room and not disturb this lady," Miss Pruitt said, trying to be stern, but Chantele could see the woman was very fond of the girl.

"She won't disturb me," Chantele said. "May she come in?"

"Very well, Miss," Miss Pruitt agreed, and then she called to the girl, who had hidden behind the door. "Come in, Melissa, and say hello to the lady."

The girl looked seven or eight years old. Her long russet hair was parted in the middle and hung in two thick braids tied with yellow ribbons. Her gamine face was covered with golden freckles, and her brown eyes were filled with curiosity as she slowly entered the room and came to stand at the foot of the bed.

"This is Melissa, the doctor's daughter," Miss Pruitt said.

"Hello, Melissa," Chantele greeted.

The girl continued to stare at Chantele curiously and then asked, "Is it true, Miss?"

"What is, Melissa?"

"That you don't know your name?"

"Melissa!" cried Miss Pruitt, and Melissa colored under her freckles.

"It's all right, Miss Pruitt," Chantele interposed. "It's natural for Melissa to be curious." Addressing the girl, she said, "Yes, Melissa, it's true. What is your dolly's name?" she inquired, noticing the rag doll the girl carried under her arm.

"Clara," Melissa replied, holding up her doll.

"That is a very pretty name," Chantele said pleasantly. "Perhaps you can help choose one for me until I can remember my own. Will you?"

"Oh, yes, miss!" she said eagerly, and when she smiled, Chantele saw that a front tooth was missing.

Dr. Spinner walked in. "I see you have met my daughter," he said to Chantele. "I hope she has not disturbed you."

"Not at all, doctor," Chantele replied. "As a matter of fact, she is going to help us chose a new name for me."

"Is she now?"

"Yes, Daddy."

Dr. Spinner regarded his daughter absently and then said, "Very well, but run along now. I have to examine my patient."

Dr. Spinner was too busy to notice his daughter's disappointment at being dismissed so unceremoniously, but Chantele did. "Bye, Melissa," she said, "I hope you come and visit with me later."

Melissa turned and gave her a smile. "Yes, miss," she replied, dragging her feet toward the door.

When Miss Pruitt retrieved the lunch tray, Dr. Spinner noticed the food had barely been touched. "You'll have to do better than that," he said reprovingly.

"I'm sorry, Doctor, I just couldn't."

"Any nausea?"

"A little."

"Dizziness?"

"Yes."

"Hmmm," he said, examining her face. Then, he removed the pillows that supported her and helped her lie flat on her back. Adjusting his stethoscope, he indicated to Chantele to loosen her gown. He appeared satisfied with her heartbeat and then proceeded to examine her broken rib. Chantele whimpered when he pressed his fingers to her abdomen, and when he finished, she waited for him to speak.

"Have you been able to remember anything?"

Chantele shook her throbbing head. "What's wrong with me, Doctor?"

Dr. Spinner regarded her with a concerned frown. "Perhaps it's better you don't remember," he began, and when Chantele opened her mouth to protest, he added quickly, "for now."

"Why, Doctor?" she said with growing apprehension.

He seemed to be considering his answer. "You must have suffered a great deal," he began. "When I found you at my doorstep you were more dead than alive." He paused. "The blow to the head may account for your loss of memory, but . . . there is so much about the mind that we do not know!"

"What do you mean, doctor?"

"It's too soon to tell," he said evasively.

"Doctor, there is something else you are not telling me, but I must know. Please!"

Dr. Spinner regarded her with compassion and then shook his head before he reluctantly added, "Yes, perhaps it's best that you do." He sat on the edge of the bed and took Chantele's hand in his. "Your bruises are not the result of an accident," he began. "You were beaten very badly. I'm afraid, my dear, that you have been . . . raped."

Chantele's eyes widened and she shook her head. "Oh, no!"

"I'm afraid so," he said, and increasing the pressure on her hand. "Repeatedly." He paused. "You must have suffered a great deal at the hands of your captor or captors, my dear. Perhaps it is best that, at least for now, you don't remember what truly happened."

Chantele was crying softly.

"You have been through a terrible ordeal," Dr. Spinner said gently, "but you are young and your body will heal itself in time and with proper care."

"Will I remember who I am, Doctor?"

He paused before he replied, "I don't know.

Perhaps the loss of memory will only be temporary."

"But you can't be sure."

"As I said, there is a great deal about the human mind that we don't know, my dear. We'll just have to wait and see, and concentrate on healing your body. Time will take care of the rest," he finished, patting her hand. "What you need now is plenty of rest and nourishment, and you are welcome to stay here with us until you are well again."

"I'll never be able to repay your kindness," she said deeply moved.

Dr. Spinner made a gesture of dismissal. "The best way to repay me is by getting well. I hope you do justice to your supper. Try and get some sleep and don't let Melissa disturb you with her curiosity, and that's an order," he admonished.

"She didn't, Doctor," Chantele protested. "Will you let her visit? She was very pleased when I asked her to choose a name for me."

"About that . . ." he began hesitantly and then paused.

"Yes, Doctor?"

He shook his head and smiled. "I would like to call you Victoria, if you don't mind."

"Victoria?"

"It fits you well," he said. "From your speech I can tell you are English," he added with a shrug trying to hide some embarrassment.

"I like it, Doctor, I like it very much."

When she was left alone, Chantele ran through her mind everything she had learned. Who had attacked her so savagely? Why? And who was she? Where did she come from? She searched her mind desperately and could not even summon her own image. She had a new name, but she didn't even know what she looked like.

Slowly, painfully, she pushed the covers aside and sat on the edge of the bed. Her body screamed in protest when she managed to stand on wobbly legs. The room was spinning around her and she steadied herself against the bedpost. In her weakened condition, the few steps to the dresser seemed like a hundred miles, which she covered more by force of will than by strength. Leaning on the dresser, she hesitated before looking into the mirror. When she did, the image she saw made her quail. Her head was fully bandaged, her face a mass of purple bruises; one eye was still badly swollen. Overwhelmed by her efforts and the shock of her appearance, Chantele sank slowly onto her knees and into darkness.

Eleven

It had been early spring when Chantele was left on Dr. Spinner's doorstep, a time when people from many parts of the country and the world passed through St. Louis on their way West. California was their goal; the journey was long and arduous and many would never get there, but the crowds Chantele saw from her window were cheerful and noisy, their wagons filled with all their worldly possessions, their hearts filled with hopes and dreams.

Two months had elapsed since she had awakened not even knowing her name, and her injuries had healed as Dr. Spinner had promised. When she was able to look at herself in the mirror, the image she saw was that of a stranger. There were no scars on her face, but her memory was blank.

Through the open window of his office came the murmur of Chantele's voice reading aloud to Melissa, and Dr. Spinner could not concentrate on the papers he was trying to study, a problem he was having more and more since the woman he called Victoria had entered his life.

A tall and lanky but pleasant-looking man, George Spinner, M.D., was in his late thirties, with dark brown hair sprinkled with gray. He removed the wire-rimmed spectacles he wore for reading, pushed aside his papers, and listened. Victoria, he mused. Melissa had readily accepted his suggestion of the name, but his reasons for it were different than those he had given. Victoria, his victory over death after the painful defeat that had cost him the life of his wife, Lucy. He had told himself over and over it was just that which made Victoria so special to him, but at this moment, he finally admitted the truth to himself. He was in love with the girl who in so many ways reminded him of

Lucy. Their physical resemblance stopped at Victoria's honey-colored hair, but their tenderness, their gentleness and grace were the same.

The cholera epidemic of '53 had claimed more lives than any other, and Dr. Spinner had been so busy caring for strangers that he had not been there when Lucy had fallen victim to it. It was a memory that had never ceased to torment him. There had never been enough time; a young doctor had to establish his practice and they had their whole lives ahead, he had believed. Suddenly, time had run out; Lucy was gone, gone forever, and he had tried to bury his grief in his work.

But now there was Victoria, and for the first time in years, George Spinner, the man, was alive again. The notes of Lucy's piano had beckoned him to the parlor one afternoon after all his patients had gone. The young woman at the keyboard wore Lucy's dress, and for an instant he had believed that Lucy was back. But it was Victoria, and he could never look at her again as a mere patient but as a woman, a young and very beautiful and desirable woman who occupied his thoughts constantly.

Chantele was growing restless as week after week passed and no replies came to their inquiries. There had been a few days of hope when a couple had arrived searching for their missing daughter only to go away in disappointment. There seemed to be no one to claim her.

Melissa was a bright child, and helping her with her homework afforded Chantele some relief from her own troubles. One afternoon, after school, their attention was beckoned to the street by a commotion outside. Chantele opened the front door and, followed by Melissa, saw the people running in the direction of the levee.

"What's going on?" she inquired from a passing stranger.

"It's a showboat, miss," the young man replied, pausing only to touch his cap. "The circus is coming to town!"

"The circus!" Melissa exclaimed clapping her hands with glee. "Oh, Vicky, let's go see the circus!"

Chantele hesitated. "Shouldn't we ask your father first, or Miss Pruitt?"

"Daddy is busy and Miss Pruitt went shopping," Melissa replied. "Oh, please, Vicky, let's go or we'll miss the parade!"

Chantele regarded the pleading child and hesitated only briefly. "Let's go," she finally said to Melissa's delight.

Hand in hand they joined the crowds running down toward the river, Melissa skipping jubilantly at Chantele's side. Soon the magnificent showboat came into view, a steamboat of enormous proportions painted in gleaming white and red, pulled in tow by another steamer. Bells on its hurricane deck chimed their merry tunes while on the towboat a brass band played loudly and enthusiastically.

"Look, Vicky!" Melissa cried in her excitement. "Look at the clowns!"

The crowd roared at the antics of three clowns struggling to juggle enormous balloons and ending up in a tangle with each other. A man in coattails and tall hat stood at the prow, megaphone in hand.

"Ladies and gentlemen!" his voice rose over the din. "Welcome to the Circus Magnificus! Tonight you will see the greatest show on the face of the earth. The most daring acrobats will defy death before your very eyes!" He pointed at the performers poised on the texas deck in their colorful costumes, who saluted the crowd to a roll of drums. "Hector the Fearless will astound you with his ferocious wild jungle beasts!" A rumble of excitement ran through the crowd when a man, apparently the fearless Hector, cracked a long whip over his head with a loud report. "Ladies and gentlemen!" the man with the megaphone continued, "the performance begins at eight!"

While some of the performers distributed handbills, the brass band left the towboat and began forming on the dock. The crowd parted, allowing the band to lead the boisterous parade on to the streets. Caught in the excitement, Chantele and Melissa followed. When they reached Dr. Spinner, he was standing at the door with some of his patients.

"Daddy!" Melissa cried running toward him. "Could we go to the circus tonight? Could we, please?"

Chantele reached them in time to hear the doctor say, "Of course, Melissa," and then he added, "and perhaps Victoria would also like to go."

"And Miss Pruitt," added Melissa.

Dr. Spinner blushed. "Yes, of course, Miss Pruitt, too."

"Vicky, we're going to the circus!" cried Melissa, bubbling with excitement. "I'll go tell Miss Pruitt!" She ran into the house, leaving Chantele with the doctor.

"Quite a parade, isn't it?" he said self-consciously, and Chantele nodded, her eyes following the parade. "Have you ever been to the circus, Victoria?"

Chantele made to reply and then turned to face him. "I don't know," she admitted.

Dr. Spinner took her hand and squeezed it warmly. "Don't worry," he said gently. "You'll see it tonight. Perhaps you will remember."

"Will I, doctor?"

"My name is George," he said, blushing.

A large pipe organ played its rousing tunes as the equestrian act delighted the spectators

gathered in the enormous amphitheater, and
the crowd applauded and cheered when fifteen
performers dressed in dainty plumed costumes
and riding atop beautiful chestnut mares made
their mounts waltz in formation. The audience
held its breath when a female acrobat performed her daring act on a tightrope while the
throaty voice of the pipe organ punctuated
each one of her steps; and they were held in
awe by the ferocious lions which growled
menacingly while obeying the whip of Hector
the Fearless.

And there were other curiosities to see:
stuffed tigers and figures in wax, puppet
dancers, a man with no arms, and an invisible
lady who attracted a large crowd. The concert
hall on the towboat offered comedy sketches
and minstrel acts.

It was an evening to remember and it was
midnight when the group returned home, tired
but happy. Melissa had fallen asleep during the
minstrel act, and her father carried her in his
arms to her room, where Miss Pruitt put the
girl to bed.

Chantele was also ready to retire, but the
doctor appeared to be in the mood for company and she accepted his invitation to a glass
of sherry.

"It was a lovely evening," she said. "Thank
you."

"I can't recall when I had such fun," he admitted. "It's been a long time."

"You work too hard, doctor, you need some relaxation, too." She was tempted to add, "And Melissa needs a father."

"I suppose you're right, but there never seems to be enough time."

Chantele was very conscious of the time that had elapsed since her arrival. She felt well enough now; she could not stay much longer. "Yes, it's been over two months since I came here, doctor," she said.

"You can't be thinking of leaving us yet, can you, Victoria?"

"I owe you, Miss Pruitt, and Melissa more than I can say," she said tentatively, "but I can't stay here for ever. I must earn a living, try to find my way . . ."

"But where will you go?" he interrupted vehemently. "What will you do?"

Chantele turned the glass in her hands and said, "I don't know. I don't even know if I'm prepared to do anything that will earn me a living, but I must find employment of some sort."

"You are not strong enough yet!" George Spinner said firmly. "You still can't remember anything about your past."

"I'm beginning to wonder if I ever will," she said quietly.

"You can't leave us just yet. Your progress has been excellent, but only because you've had plenty of rest and good care." He paused. "I will examine you again tomorrow, and then we'll see. Right now, I want you to stop thinking about going away before you are fully recovered. Besides," he added, "we may still hear from your family."

"I'm beginning to doubt that, too," she said. "I'm very grateful for all you've done, but I can't depend on your generosity forever."

He seemed about to say something and then changed his mind. "It's late," he said. "There's plenty of time to discuss this matter."

Chantele gathered the glasses and took them into the kitchen. She was about to rinse them when he stopped her. "Leave them, you must get to bed now. It's been a long day for you."

"I'm a little tired," she admitted.

Together, they climbed the stairs to the second floor, and he paused uncertainly at her door.

"Good night, doctor."

"Is it so difficult to call me George?" he asked. "Good night, Victoria."

For Chantele, the change in Dr. Spinner's attitude toward her was a cause of concern. She owed him her life, and even more, the care and comfort she had received during her convalescence. She was deeply grateful. But she could not return his affection. And it had not taken her long to notice that the ubiquitous

Miss Pruitt was in love with her employer, a fact Dr. Spinner seemed to be completely unaware of, and that Melissa needed much more than the casual attention she got from her father.

Tonight, Dr. Spinner had been twice on the brink of saying something to Chantele about his feelings, and she was glad that he had not. Her hopes of being claimed by her family were fading more and more each day, and she had to find a way to make a living. There were many affluent families in a thriving city like St. Louis, but would any of them employ her as a governess, take into their homes a woman without a past? And if she stayed in St. Louis, what were the chances of learning her identity? No, she could not sit still waiting for fate to find her. She had to leave St. Louis, visit other cities, try to find a familiar place that might help her remember or even find someone who had known her. But she was destitute; even the clothes she wore had belonged to the late Mrs. Spinner. What kind of work would allow her to travel and support herself? She discarded one idea after another as impractical. She was tired. Perhaps Dr. Spinner was right, the day's activities had left her exhausted.

This had been the most exciting day of her new life, the parade and the circus a welcome distraction from her predicament. She laughed, thinking of the serious Miss Pruitt looking younger than ever and laughing and clapping her hands at the antics of the clowns, just like Melissa. And even the sober Dr. Spinner had forgotten, momentarily at least, the heavy burdens of his profession and his personal grief.

Chantele drifted into sleep, thinking of the exciting life of the circus, the nomadic existence of the performers, and she sat up with a start. That was her answer!

Dr. Spinner came early to her room. "I thought I would examine you before my other patients begin to arrive," he said apologetically.

She stood aside to let him in. For the first time, she felt embarrassed when she had to undress for his examination, and was it her imagination, or did his hands linger on her body a little longer than usual? His touch was different, as if his professional detachment had begun to desert him.

"The infection has cleared," he said clearing his throat. He regarded her before he said, "You may dress now."

"Thank you, doctor."

"George," he reminded her.

She was alarmed by his strange behavior this morning. She owed this man her life, and didn't want to offend him.

"George," she said in a small voice and saw that he was pleased.

"Today you must rest," he said. "Don't overexert yourself."

He seemed reluctant to leave her room, and Chantele let go a sigh of relief when he finally did. She had hoped she had been mistaken, but all the signs were there. He's a wonderful man, she said to herself, but I can't entertain any romantic ideas about him. Or anyone else, for that matter, at least not now.

She had no recollection of the rape and yet she had the instinctive feeling that somehow she knew the meaning of love. Had there been someone she had loved, who had loved her in return?

There were nothing but questions in her mind, and she had to find the answers. She thought of the plan she had half-formulated before falling asleep. Could she do it? Many showboats stopped in St. Louis. Not all of them were as large and as opulent as the Circus Magnificus; there were other, smaller ones which might hire her. Could she sing, could she dance, could she act? Those were the questions she would have to answer when seeking employment.

She dressed, running questions and possible answers through her mind, and in the kitchen she found Miss Pruitt vigorously kneading dough on a table, her sleeves rolled up to her elbows and a smudge of flour on her cheek. Behind her, the Negro cook was slamming around pots, obviously displeased at Miss

Pruitt's invasion of her domain. The aroma of freshly baked bread permeated the kitchen, and there were two loaves on the table.

"Can I help?" Chantele offered after her greeting.

Eleanor Pruitt shook her head. "No, I'm almost done," she said shortly. "Your breakfast is on the stove."

"Thank you," Chantele said and began to fill her plate. "Has Melissa left for school?"

"A few minutes ago."

Chantele ate her breakfast while she discreetly observed Miss Pruitt, who seemed to be venting her anger on the dough. "It was fun going to the circus last night," she said casually.

"Yes, it was."

"Melissa was very excited."

Eleanor nodded, intent on her work.

"Even Dr. Spinner seemed to have enjoyed it." Chantele ventured. "Did you know his wife?" she inquired after a pause.

When Eleanor nodded, she ventured further. "What was she like?"

"A fine lady," Eleanor replied. "Young, pretty . . . like you." Her voice broke into a sob, and Chantele rushed to her side and put her arms around her, trying to comfort her friend.

"You love him, don't you?"

Eleanor redoubled her tears. "He doesn't

even know I'm alive!''

"He's been grieving over the past," Chantele said gently, "you must give him time."

Eleanor dabbed at her tears with a corner of her apron. "He was not, last night, the way he was acting toward you," she said dejectedly.

"Perhaps I remind him of his wife, wearing her clothes and all," Chantele said. "I should never have accepted them."

"It's more than that," Miss Pruitt said shaking her head. "You are very much like her and I . . . I was never pretty, and I'm not young any more."

"That's nonsense!"

"I thought if I gave him a chance to get to know me, he would come to love me. But it's been almost three years and I don't think he knows my first name."

"You're far from being old, and you can make him notice you," Chantele said encouragingly.

"How? All he has to do is look at you, and I don't stand a chance."

"I will be leaving soon, Eleanor."

Eleanor regarded her through her tears. "Where will you go? You have no family, no money, how would you live?" Her concern was real.

"I'll find a job," Chantele replied. "I need to travel, and the circus last night gave me an idea. I'll try to find employment on a showboat."

"Showboats!" Eleanor cried, horrified at the suggestion. "Oh, Victoria, you don't know what you're saying! Those people . . ." she shook her head in disapproval.

"But I must," Chantele said. "I don't know what else I can do and travel at the same time. Can't you see? Perhaps I'll find someone who knows me. Besides, Dr. Spinner is now coming out of his period of grief. When that happens, I'll be gone and you'll be here. He's bound to discover how right you are for him."

"You really think so?"

"If he doesn't, he's a fool," Chantele said. "And besides, Melissa loves you."

"I love her."

"You see?"

Eleanor sighed. "I hope you're right," she said.

And so do I, Chantele said inwardly. She cared deeply for these people. Perhaps one day soon, George Spinner would look around and see that a new life and a new love were there, just waiting for him.

After the circus was gone, days passed one after another without much change in their lives. Chantele practiced the piano while Dr. Spinner saw his patients and made his house-calls, and both Eleanor and Melissa told her that she had a fine singing voice. They all roared with laughter when she danced around the house, much to the surprise of the Negro servant who shook her head muttering to herself about the white folks gone out of their heads. A new feeling of friendship had developed between the women, and Chantele knew how much she would miss these people. But leave she must.

The opportunity finally presented itself when a small showboat, a far cry from the opulent floating palaces, stopped in St. Louis seeking Dr. Spinner's professional help. One of the members of the troupe, the young leading lady, had suffered a broken leg during a fall. The boat was run by an English family who had sought new audiences playing in small hamlets and villages along the river. It was all rather an adventure to them, and recognizing Chantele as one of their own, they accepted her services without much ado.

"You can't do it, Victoria," Dr. Spinner protested when she told him.

"George," she said gently, "you know I must."

"But a showboat!" he said in despair. "Granted the Talbots seem to be nice people, but you are so young and so vulnerable. No," he said flatly, "it's just too dangerous."

"I must work, George."

"Then at least stay here in St. Louis, where I can help you if anything happens."

"I can't, George, you know I have to find out who I am."

"I don't care who you are!" he cried passionately. "Victoria you must know that I love you! Please, stay here, let me take care of you!"

Chantele felt her eyes mist. This was the moment she had so dreaded. "No, George," she said gently. "I care too much for you to accept your offer. I'm very grateful to you for my life, for all you've done, but you deserve much more than I can give you. I'm not a whole person now; until I know more about myself, I can't give my love to any man." She paused. "You do understand, don't you?"

He nodded, sadly.

"You'll find your own way, George, just as I must find mine. But I will never forget you."

Everything about Earl Talbot was dramatic: his thick, graying mane of hair, his eloquent dark eyes, the gandeur of his gestures even offstage; but most of all, his deep, resonant voice. But in spite of all this, it didn't take long for Chantele to realize that the real force behind the family and the troupe was Mrs. Talbot. On or off stage, no one questioned her authority, which she exercised over them with tolerance and good judgment.

Almost the entire cast was related by blood or marriage. There were the children: Laurel, the ingenue, whose misfortune had opened the way for Chantele; the boys, Edwin, Monte, and Barney, a rowdy ten-year-old whose antics only ceased when he was holding a fishing line in his hands.

Thadeus Metcalf, Mrs. Talbot's brother, accentuated his dark looks to play his specialty, villainous characters capable of such evil that he made audiences hiss with hatred—and yet he was a gentle man with a wonderful sense of humor. His wife Sarah was occasionally called upon to appear on the stage, but her favorite occupation was taking charge of their wardrobe. Their two children were also in the cast, Caroline, a pretty girl who had inherited her father's dark looks, and Casey, as fair as his mother.

But what was an Irishman like Jim Madigan, who did not hide his fear of the river, doing on a showboat with an English troupe? He played the romantic lead to Laurel's ingenues, and it didn't take much intelligence to discover that he had hopes of carrying the role into real life. There was no mistaking the way his sea-green eyes lit up in Laurel's presence or whenever he spoke of her. That Laurel was not as impervious to his charm as she pretended to be was obvious to everyone but poor Jim. Born in New York of Irish parents, Jim Madigan had spent most of his life in the theater, and in addition to playing romantic roles he was also an excellent song-and-dance man who drilled

Chantele in the routines they would perform. With two of the Talbot boys, Jim was rehearsing a minstrel act they wanted to include in the bill that consisted of farces, light comedy sketches, melodramas, and scenes from Shakespeare. In spite of the excitement the arrival of a showboat inspired in the small communities where they played, it was not unusual to encounter some resistance to their performances by the local puritans, but Shakespeare was readily accepted by all. And Earl Talbot was at his magnificent best as Petrucchio, Hamlet, or Othello.

In a small company like the Talbots', every member was involved in all aspects of putting on the show, and even though she had no acting experience, Chantele discovered that she had other talents to draw upon which she had not known she possessed. She took pleasure in painting scenery, sewing costumes, and playing the organ.

Although she had gone through the rehearsals without a problem, the night of her debut she was sick with dread as she awaited her cue.

"I can't do it, Jim!" she said in awe, eyeing the audience of farmers in their Sunday best. She couldn't remember her simple lines, and her hands were shaking so that the rattle of the cups on the tray she was to carry could be heard on the stage.

"You'll be fine," Jim said gently. "We all

265

feel the same before we go on. That's your cue."

She turned eyes wide with fear on his face painted black. "I can't!"

Jim gave her a gentle push and she stumbled on the stage, where she stood paralyzed with fear, clutching the tray and staring at the audience who stared back in surprise and then began to chuckle with amusement.

Improvising, and without apparent concern, Mrs. Talbot addressed the vicar played by her husband. "Yes, Vicar," she said evenly as if it were part of the dialogue, "I'm afraid the new maid is not yet well trained." She attempted to take the tray from Chantele, but the girl would not let go. Mrs. Talbot tried again, and when Chantele still hung on, Mrs. Talbot put her arm around her shoulder and guided her out off stage staying, "You may take the tea back to the kitchen, Mathilda, the vicar would prefer some sherry," and the play continued without a hitch.

Backstage, Jim Madigan was trying to console a Chantele who had gone to pieces.

"It's all right," he said holding her gently. "It's perfectly all right."

"No, it isn't!" she sobbed, "I ruined everything!"

"No, you did not. The audience didn't even notice."

"Of course they did. They laughed at me!"

266

"They are suppose to laugh. It's a comedy, not a tragedy."

"Oh, Jim, what am I going to do? I couldn't blame the Talbots if they let me go after this, but what am I going to do?"

"They are old troupers, Vicky. They know something like this can happen to any of us. Don't be so hard on yourself. You should have seen what happened just before you joined us." He paused, inviting her curiosity.

"What happened?"

"Well, you know how Barney is about fishing," he began, and when she nodded, he continued, "on this particular night, he did not appear on cue, so it was repeated a second time. Nothing. Then, about thirty seconds later, he comes running in with the biggest catfish you ever saw. He stands in the middle of the stage as big as you please and raising the catfish, which by the way is still twitching its tail, he yells, "I've got one!" Jim laughed, shaking his head. "Needless to say, the audience was laughing so hard some of them were in tears."

He was pleased to see that Chantele was also laughing. "Don't worry, Vicky, you'll be fine."

At that moment, Monte and Barney came rushing in, almost out of breath. "Got all your fishing done for tonight, Barney?" Jim asked with a wink.

Fishing was everyone's favorite pastime. It not only provided relaxation, but also supplied the table, and Chantele took to it with as much gusto as the others.

Along with the steamboat, the Talbots had acquired the services of old Capt. Nesbitt, a pilot whose knowledge of the river made their journeys as safe as they could be. He was also a gifted storyteller who entertained the entertainers with a rich collection of legends of the river.

Late one evening, when they had tied the boat up for the night, Chantele watched as Capt. Nesbitt lit his pipe after dropping a pinch of tobacco into the river. She had seen him do this before, and this aroused her curiosity. "Why does he always do that?" she asked Barney, who sat next to her with a fishing line in his hands.

"That's tobacco for Big Al's pipe," the boy replied.

"Who is Big Al?"

"It's a huge alligator that lives in the river. He's so big that when he moves his tail he can change the courses of the river, and when he smokes his pipe the fog is so thick that all the river traffic has to stop." He continued rambling on about the legend, but her attention had wandered to the two figures standing close together on the afterdeck. Laurel Talbot had become more receptive to Jim Madigan's courtship since Chantele had joined the troupe, and she wondered if spending so much time with him herself had anything to do with the girl's new attitude toward her beau. To Chantele, Jim was a good friend and a marvelous teacher, and Laurel had nothing to fear, for his heart still belonged to her.

With a sigh, Chantele looked around to see the Talbots holding hands as they went into their stateroom; the Metcalfs sitting close together in quiet conversation. Love was all around her. But she was alone.

Twelve

Her earnings were small, her loneliness great, and at times she wondered if it was worth it; and yet, she knew she would do it all over again if she had to. During the months she had spent with the Talbots, she had gained a new name and a new career, and when the time came to say goodbye, it had been truly hard. How she missed them all! It seemed like the

last eighteen months had been a series of farewells without having found what she was
searching for; for her past was still a blank.

Under the name of Victoria Page she had
joined other showboats and other theatrical
companies, where she had found friendship
and kindness, but also jealousy and hostility
and many unwelcome advances by actors and
stage managers who promised employment in
exchange for favors she was not inclined to
grant. There had been lean times when she had
seen her meager savings dwindle almost to
nothing without prospects of work. And stage
fright remained her constant companion. No
matter how small the part, she felt ill before
each performance; but at last she had learned
to conquer her fears and there had been no
other failures on stage.

One thing she discovered about actors: in ad-
versity, they were all brothers. She had made
friends among them, but none like Marietta
Long. They were as different as two women
could possibly be: while Chantele avoided the
overtures of the many wealthy admirers in each
town they played, Marietta made the most of
these opportunities. She was pretty and viva-
cious and, from humble origins, impressed by
the generous gifts she received. A special
friendship had developed between them, and
Marietta was the only person to whom
Chantele had confided her secret.

For three consecutive nights the Raines Theatrical Company had played successfully to a full house at the elegant Losantivile Theater in Cincinnati as they had played to audiences in other towns along the river. Even though she was cast only in small parts, it was the best job Chantele had had since she left the Talbots.

"Are you sure you won't join us?" Marietta inquired after the performance. As usual she had already latched on to a local youngblood, Willy Braun, whose father owned the largest brewery in Cincinnati. "Willy has a friend who is very interested in meeting you."

Chantele finished shedding her costume and stepped into her dressing gown. "Thank you, no, but do enjoy yourself."

"That I will," Marietta said airily, "but what are you going to do? Sit by yourself in that ghastly hotel room like you did last night and the night before?"

When Chantele didn't bother to reply, Marietta continued, "It's been well over a year, and you don't know any more now than you did then," she said with exasperation. "Don't be a fool, Vicky. You're not going to be young and pretty forever. If you don't make use of your chances now, one of these days you'll find that you're old and alone, and still playing bit parts."

Chantele, who had heard it all before, ignored her.

Marietta let out a sigh. "Suit yourself," she said, slipping into her dress, a costly creation that was a little too daring for Chantele's taste, although she had to admit that Marietta looked stunning in it. The green satin contrasted vividly with her creamy complexion and flaming red hair. "Help me with this, won't you?" Marietta said, turning her back to her friend.

Chantele fastened the back of the gown while Marietta put on her jewelry. "You could be wearing beautiful clothes and trinkets like these," she said showing off her new diamond bracelet.

"We've been through all this before, Marietta," Chantele reminded her. "Don't worry about me, I'll be fine."

"Oh, sure."

"You go out with your Willy and enjoy yourself."

"And what should I tell his friend?"

"That I hope he has a wonderful time, too."

"You're impossible, Vicky!"

"I know."

Marietta left in a flurry, and remaining at the dressing table, Chantele asked herself once again, while she removed her makeup, if she was really being a fool, hoping against hope to find her identity. No, she could not allow herself to be discouraged. Hundreds of people saw her on stage every night; one day, sitting in that

273

audience would be the one person who would recognize her, perhaps even someone who had been searching for her all this time. She refused to believe, as Marietta had suggested, that perhaps her family, wherever they were, believed her dead.

She dressed in her worn but serviceable dark woolen dress and collected her cloak, which would never see another winter. Perhaps her share of the benefit performance would provide her with enough funds to replace it. It would be nice to have beautiful clothes and jewels, she mused, but not at the price Marietta paid.

Stepping into the darkened alley, where some of the girls were met by their escorts for the evening, Chantele wondered what Willy's friend looked like. It didn't matter; one of many men who thought any actress was fair game.

She didn't like walking alone at this late hour, but she made her way to the cheap hotel where several members of the cast were staying. Marietta was right, the room was ghastly. So small that it was filled up by a few pieces of furniture that had seen better days; paint was peeling off the walls, and moisture had stained the mirror above the scarred dresser. But her worst enemy was loneliness. There were times when she was almost in physical pain, longing for arms to hold her, for someone who cared if she lived or died, someone to whom she could give all the love that was inside her and crying out for release.

There you go feeling sorry for yourself again, she berated herself. It had been a long day. Perhaps tomorrow something would happen.

Another successful performance was over, and Marietta and Chantele were back in the small dressing room they shared when there was a tap on the door. Marietta answered; it was one of the stage hands.

"I have a package for Miss Page," the boy said.

"I'll take it," Marietta offered.

"I was told to hand it personally to Miss Page and wait for a reply."

Chantele heard the message and went to the door. After a cursory glance at the note, she returned the case to the boy. "Please give it back to the gentleman, Johnny. He'll understand."

"Aren't you even going to open it?" exclaimed Marietta, dying of curiosity.

Chantele shrugged and Johnny hesitated.

"Well, if you are not even curious, I am," Marietta said taking the case from Johnny's hand. She opened it and drew a sharp intake of breath at the sight of a diamond bracelet sparkling in its dark velvet nest. "Who sent it?" she inquired avidly.

Chantele read the signature on the card again. "Michael Lawrence," she said, and taking the case she snapped it shut and handed it back to Johnny, who gave her a puzzled look.

"Lawrence is Willy's friend," Marietta said. "The one I told you about." When Chantele made no response, she added, "He was very disappointed when you did not join us last night."

"You little fool!" she cried, exasperated with Chantele's indifference. "The man is really interested in you. You saw the bracelet he sent you. He would cover you with diamonds!"

"Just for the pleasure of my company at dinner?" Chantele said raising a mocking brow.

Marietta had the grace to blush. "Of course not," she admitted, "but you would like him, Vicky. He's a very attractive man. He could have any woman he wants."

"Then let him find someone else."

"He wants you."

"That is his misfortune," Chantele said with a shrug. "I'll pass. Really, Marietta, we've been over this too many times already. You do as you please, but do me a favor and leave me out of your plans."

Each night, after the performance, Michael Lawrence sent an invitation accompanied by a gift of jewelry, each more impressive than the last, and each night Chantele sent them back with the same reply. Marietta was having hysterics, and by now even Chantele was curious as to how far her persistent admirer would go.

Johnny, who had taken upon himself to deliver the presents, waited expectantly for Chantele's reply while the girl examined the jewels. Gossip had spread, and by the third night several performers had gathered to admire the presents.

Marietta was beside herself; it was sheer torture for her to see the magnificent jewels Chantele was rejecting. "I wish you would reconsider," she urged her friend after Johnny had departed with a diamond and ruby necklace. "The man will tire of your rejections."

"I hope he does," Chantele said with a sigh. "Everyone is expecting me to capitulate at any moment and, frankly, Marietta, the situation is getting on my nerves. Even Horace has been impossible about it."

"Oh, he's just frustrated," Marietta said with a shrug. "But that's another thing, Vicky, he'll keep you in bit parts as long as you act so uppity with him."

"Are you suggesting that I sleep with him to get better roles?"

"Of course not, but at least keep him hoping."

"Really, Marietta," Chantele protested, "I admit he's not as pushy as other stage managers I've encountered, but if I give him any encouragement he'll expect more than I can deliver. And then I'll find myself in the street. No, it's a chance I can't take. You know

I really need this job."

"You wouldn't, with a man like Michael Lawrence to take care of you."

"Marietta . . ."

"Listen, Vicky, the man is crazy about you, and he's in a position to make life very pleasant for you," Marietta said, undaunted by Chantele's displeasure. "I asked Willy about him."

"I don't want to hear . . ."

"Oh, but you will!" Marietta interrupted. "Michael Lawrence is not only a very wealthy man, Vicky, he is also very powerful. And you would never believe how handsome he is, a real dream. He's asked me a lot of questions about you."

"You didn't tell him . . ." Chantele exclaimed, alarmed.

"Of course not!" Marietta denied indignantly. "Your secret is safe with me, you know that! You are my friend," she continued, "and I want you to be happy. Lawrence can make you very happy, Vicky, give you all the nice things you deserve."

"I don't need luxuries, Marietta."

"Vicky, you're not like any of us. Whoever you are, I can tell you are different, a real lady. Don't tell me you are happy with this life, because I know you're not. Forget about finding your past; live for today, for tomorrow. A man like Lawrence can make a world of difference, believe me. You don't say anything to me, but I know you disapprove of what I do . . ."

"But I don't . . ." Chantele protested, but Marietta didn't let her finish.

"I'm your friend and I know you love me, but I also know that you do disapprove. But, please, Vicky, don't judge me too harshly. I saw my mother turn into an old woman well before her time, alone and poor after my father ran out on us. I don't want that for myself, Vicky, nor for you."

There were tears in Marietta's eyes and Chantele embraced her fondly. "I don't disapprove of you, Marietta," she said with emotion, "Truly, I don't. You're the best friend I've ever had, and I do love you."

Marietta returned the embrace and then pulled away, embarrassed for letting herself be carried away by emotion. "There!" she said looking at herself in the mirror. "Now my eyes are all red and puffy and so is my nose!"

Chantele watched her friend dry her eyes and apply more powder to her nose.

"Oh, I hate to cry!" Marietta said with annoyance, "it makes me look positively horrible!" She whirled about and gathered her fur wrap. "I hope Willy doesn't notice I've been crying."

"He won't, and you look beautiful," Chantele said.

Marietta gave her a quick smile and rushed out the door.

There was no present for Chantele after the performance the following night, and the group gathered at her door dispersed mumbling that the "Ice Maiden," as they sometimes called her behind her back, had lost her admirer.

"I told you he would get tired and turn to someone else," Marietta said reproachfully.

"I do hope so," Chantele shrugged.

They finished changing in silence, Marietta in a daringly low-cut gown of black lace, a new diamond necklace sparkling at her throat. Willy Braun was a generous lover.

"Willy is waiting, but I'll walk you to the street," Marietta said seeing that her friend was also ready.

They had taken a few steps into the darkened alley behind the theater when a tall figure stepped out of the shadows, frightening them.

"Good evening, ladies," a pleasant voice, deep and virile.

"Oh, it's you!" Marietta exclaimed, pressing her hand to her bosom.

"I'm sorry I startled you, ladies," the voice said. "Will you introduce me to your charming friend, Miss Long?"

Marietta recovered her composure and smiled, "Of course," she said breathlessly, "Vicky, this is Michael Lawrence. Victoria

Page.''

Chantele saw no graceful way out of the situation and offered her hand. His was warm despite the chill of the night, as were the lips he pressed against her hand.

A pleasure, Miss Page,'' he said and turned to Marietta, "I believe Willy is waiting in front of the theater, Miss Long.''

"Y-yes,'' Marietta stammered, "of course. Good night, Vicky, Mr. Lawrence.'' She turned and rushed away.

"Marietta, wait!'' Chantele called after her, but her friend was already gone. Her heart was pounding, and she was getting very angry. "Good night, Mr. Lawrence,'' she said tersely and began to walk away.

"Miss Page, please wait!''

"I do not like to be tricked, Mr. Lawrence. I have made it plain I have no wish of your company.'' Again she turned away.

"Miss Page,'' he said, "will you accept this with my apologies?''

She stopped and with a sigh of exasperation turned to face him. "If it's another one of your presents, Mr. Lawrence, I . . .'' Her words died on her lips at the sight of the long-stemmed rose he was offering.

"Do not be angry with your friend, Miss Page. She didn't know I'd be here.''

Chantele's anger abated, and she took the rose. "Apologies accepted, Mr. Lawrence.''

"Michael, please. Truce?"

She smiled and nodded, "Truce."

"Will you let me drive you to your hotel, Miss Page?" he offered. "The streets are not safe for a woman alone at this hour of the night."

"Thank you, but that won't be necessary. My hotel is not far."

"Please, my carriage is just over there," he said indicating a carriage stationed nearby.

She did not trust him. "Thank you, but I prefer to walk."

"Very well, then," he agreed pleasantly, undaunted by her refusal. "May I walk with you?"

"If you wish."

She could see him better under the street lights. Marietta's appraisal had not been exaggerated; Michael Lawrence was a very attractive man. He appeared to be in his thirties and carried himself with elegant ease. Chantele found herself wondering about the color of his eyes and wishing she could see him more clearly. He was very tall; she only reached his shoulder as they walked side by side, his carriage following at a discreet distance behind.

"I have offended you and I am sorry," he said taking her arm to help her skirt a puddle, "but I wanted very much to meet you. Will you forgive me?"

"No offense taken, Mr. Lawrence."

He let several wordless seconds go by before he said, "I enjoyed your performances very much. You have a lovely voice."

"Thank you," she said, and couldn't resist adding, "Is it the theater you like, Mr. Lawrence, or the actresses?"

He threw back his head and laughed heartily. "Touche!" he said, and answered, "Both."

They stopped in front of the hotel and she could see it cost him an effort not to comment on its shabby exterior.

"Will you dine with me tomorrow?"

"No, Mr. Lawrence."

"I thought we had a truce."

"A truce is not an alliance."

"Am I so distasteful to you that you won't even have an innocent supper with me?"

"Do not play games with me, Mr. Lawrence," she said drily. "You are wealthy, young, and attractive, and you know it."

"You mean if I were poor, old, and ugly you would accept my invitation?" he asked, feigning pain.

His expression was so amusing that she had to laugh.

"Ah, you can laugh," he said, pleased by the success of his acting. "It becomes you. You should do it more often."

"Good night, Mr. Lawrence," she said offering her hand. "Thank you for walking me home."

He kept her hand in his. "You haven't accepted my invitation."

"It's late, Mr. Lawrence, and you already have my answer."

"I insist."

He would not release her hand. "Oh, very well," she said, feeling very foolish.

"I'll collect you tomorrow at one o'clock," he said, and kissed her hand slowly and deliberately. He stood on the sidewalk watching through the foggy window as she disappeared up the stairs. Then, smiling to himself, he turned and signaled for his carriage.

Up close, and without her stage makeup, she was younger and much more beautiful than he had expected. Individually, and in a conventional way, her features were irregular, yet they combined to give her face a rather exotic, compelling beauty. And of one thing he was now sure; she was not merely being coy by refusing his invitations. She had meant it. But why? And as the carriage crossed the deserted streets of Cincinnati, Michael pondered on the engima the girl represented. Why would a beautiful woman like her, obviously a lady, be satisfied to exist as she did? What was she really after? Like everyone else, she had her price; he had to discover what it was. Whatever the price, he could pay it; his influence reached into every part of the city.

Michael Lawrence was not an idle young

millionaire like his friend Willy Braun, whose only pursuits in life were fun and games. Money alone was not enough for him; it was the combination of money and power that counted, and he had both. By hook or by crook, Michael Lawrence always got what he wanted. And he wanted Victoria Page.

The exhilaration she felt was mingled with apprehension, and Chantele wished she had not accepted Michael Lawrence's invitation. Tonight had seen only a change in his tactics. But he was all the things Marietta had said, handsome, young, and very, very charming. She could also see that he was a man accustomed to being obeyed, to having his own way, getting what he wanted. And he had made it very plain that he wanted her. Perhaps it was the sense of danger about him that appealed to her because she realized that yes, she wanted to see him again. Marietta had accused her of hiding from life, rejecting it, fearing it, and she was right. She had made the theater her life with room for nothing else, but there was still that emptiness inside her that nothing and no one could fill. She was only an actress, a half-person. It had been too long since she had allowed herself to think along these lines. Perhaps it was meeting a man like Lawrence that made her loneliness seem heavier than ever. Like the links of a chain one month had followed another since that day in St. Louis when she had looked into a mirror to see an unknown face staring back at her.

The light from the street fell across her bed, and she heard a carriage rattling down the quiet street and fading into the distance. Tomorrow, not yesterday, was what she should worry about. And tomorrow would bring Michael Lawrence.

He was already waiting in the lobby when she appeared promptly at one o'clock. "I hope you're hungry," he said after the greeting.

"I am famished," she admitted.

"Good," he said, pinning a small bouquet of tiny roses to her cloak, "because I'm treating you to an excellent German dinner."

Vine Street was teeming with traffic, boys peddling their candles, and farmers heading their pigs to the slaughterhouses. At the levee, roustabouts sang their doleful songs as they unloaded cargo.

"Bustling city, isn't it?" she commented.

"Indeed," he replied. "Cincinnati has more industries than any other city in these parts. Foundries, factories, breweries, and, of course, the packing houses."

"Those I can smell," she said wrinkling her nose, and he laughed.

"One gets used to it. After a while, it's hardly noticeable."

"I find that hard to believe," she replied, and suddenly they heard screams emanating from a large building. Her eyes widened. "What was that?"

"Absalom Death," he said with a frown. "Actually, it's the Commercial Hospital, a combination of a hospital, medical college, orphanage, and insane asylum. I told the coachman I wanted to show you some sights, but this was not what I had in mind. Raymond," he called, "take us 'Over the Rhine'."

They heard a steamboat whistle for a landing as they crossed the canal, leaving behind the cries of vendors and the din of snorting horses and rattling wagon chains. Beyond the canal was "Over the Rhine," the German community where little streets were lined with neat red-brick houses and shops, and the signs were all in German.

"This is a lively place in the evening," he said, once they were inside the restaurant, where they followed an obsequious waiter to a table set in a cool, quiet grove. "I must bring you some time."

Chantele had time to examine him discreetly while he ordered their meal in fluent German. Everything about his presence proclaimed good breeding; his finely chiseled features; his powerful hands, with long, aristocratic fingers; his hazel eyes which at times looked more green;

and his light brown hair worn a bit shorter than was the fashion. There was an air of confidence and unaffected elegance about him that pleased her, and she realized that she found him more attractive than she had been ready to admit.

Sliced bratwurst whetted their appetites for a delicious sauerbraten accompanied by potato pancakes that seemed to have been made of lace, and red cabbage sprinkled with caraway seeds. The whole was washed down with a dry, delicate wine, the most delicious Chantele thought she had ever tasted.

"Catawba wine," he identified it, "a local product, but I think it's better than any imported champagne."

Chantele had thought that she had eaten her fill, but when a slice of apple strudel was placed before her, she was unable to resist.

"It was delicious," she said, feeling wonderfully drowsy. Not often did she have the opportuniy of eating so well. Suddenly, she was embarrassed. "I usually eat a small dinner before the show," she began, and then was annoyed with herself. She owed him no explanations.

"I must confess you are a puzzlement to me, Victoria," he said suddenly. It had taken him a while to realize that the mysterious quality that had baffled him about her was a certain combination of innocence and sensuality that he had never encountered in any other woman before. The girl didn't fit any known pattern. She was like a nightingale in a nest of sparrows. Even in her old dress and devoid of jewels, she was every inch a lady. But what was a lady like her doing in the theater?

"There is no mystery, Mr. Lawrence," she replied with apparent ease, but he noticed he had upset her. "I have to earn a living, and I choose the theater."

"Forgive me," he apologized. "I didn't mean to pry. I seem to always say the wrong thing to you."

She made a gesture of dismissal. "It's not important, Mr. Lawrence, but it is getting late. I have a rehearsal at four. Shall we go?"

"Of course," he said signaling the waiter. "Will you have supper with me tonight, after the show?"

She shook her head. "I don't think that would be wise."

"I thought you enjoyed our outing today."

"I have," she conceded, "but I also know what you want of me, and I must tell you I have no intentions of becoming your paramour, Mr. Lawrence. I'm sure there are other women who would be more . . . amenable to your wishes."

"You certainly don't mince words, do you?"

"I just wanted to make it perfectly clear to you that you would only be wasting your time with me."

"It's my time to waste," he said with a

shrug. "Look, Victoria, you'll be in Cincinnati for only a few weeks. I'll accept any terms you offer."

She seemed to be weighing her answer. "No," she said shaking her head. "It's impossible."

"What are you afraid of?"

"I'm not afraid."

"I won't press you, Victoria. It will be strictly on your terms."

Why did he have to make things so difficult, she mused wryly. She wanted to believe him. She was tired of being lonely. She needed a friend.

"Friendship, Michael," she said finally. "Only that."

"If that's what you wish."

"I do."

"Very well, then, it will be as you say," he said, taking her hand, and the touch of his lips made her wonder if she had made a mistake. But she could not hide from life any more.

"Well?" Marietta inquired avidly as soon as she stepped into the dressing room.

"He's as handsome and as charming as you said he was," Chantele admitted.

Marietta let out her breath, "You're not angry with me then?"

"I ought to be for running out on me last night."

"I swear I didn't know he was waiting outside," Marietta claimed.

"I know," Chantele said, "he was kind enough to exonerate you."

"You do like him, don't you?"

Chantele smiled. "Very much."

Marietta threw her head back and laughed with a mixture of relief and joy.

"But wait," Chantele warned her. "Don't jump to any conclusions."

"What do you mean?"

"I have accepted his friendship, nothing more."

"You mean to tell me . . ."

Chantele didn't let her finish. "That's right," she said, "nothing happened."

"Are you seeing him again?"

"We're having supper after the show."

"Good," Marietta nodded approvingly and immediately turned to more practical matters, "What will you wear?"

"I haven't thought of it," Chantele confessed. Her wardrobe was very limited. "The blue faille, I suppose."

Marietta was scandalized. "Oh, no, you're not!" she cried visibly horrified. "You'll wear one of my gowns."

"I appreciate your offer, but I can't accept it. The blue faille will do just fine."

"Oh, I give up!" Marietta exclaimed throwing her hands up. "Any woman would turn her armoires inside out looking for a beautiful gown to wear for Michael Lawrence, and what do you do? You find the oldest, drabbiest dress you own!''

"I don't think it's so drab," Chantele protested. "It's true it is old, but of good quality."

"What are you trying to do? Discourage the man?''

"I told you we're friends, that's all."

"In a pig's eye!"

"Marietta!"

"Oh, I'm sorry, Vicky, I just can't understand you at times like this," Marietta said shaking her head. "I suppose he agreed."

"As a matter of fact, he did."

"Even you can't be that naive, Vicky."

Chantele paused. "I don't know what will happen, Marietta," she confessed. "I'm not rushing into anything. All I know right now is that I like him. Today, for the first time since I can remember, I felt so . . . oh, I don't know what to call it. Young, perhaps. Yes, that's it, young and carefree. And happy. For a little while, it didn't matter that I don't know who I am."

Marietta regarded her friend warily. "Well, then, be careful, Vicky," she warned.

"Careful?"

Marietta nodded. "Yes," she said. "Enjoy Michael's company and the comforts his money can give you, but don't fall in love with him, Vicky. He'll only break your heart if you do."

Chantele turned and facing the mirror smiled wryly at Marietta's reflection. "I suppose you're right," she said, "but at least for a little while I'm going to live my life as it is now."

Thirteen

Heads turned when they entered the restaurant. Marietta and Willy were there, but Michael ignored their invitation to join them.

"I don't want to share you with anyone tonight," he said. "Or are you afraid they'll think I finally succeeded in my pursuit of you?"

"It doesn't matter. I stopped worrying about

what people think a long time ago," she said with a shrug, and then added, "Did you like the show tonight?"

"I was too busy watching you. You were absolutely fantastic."

She laughed merrily. "You mean you liked my costume." Again she had been cast in the role of a page. Her long legs, encased in beige tights, always created a stir.

"That's true," he admitted with a chuckle. "You looked absolutely delicious."

"Well, I didn't forget my lines, not that they required a long memory," she said wryly. "Sometimes it's frustrating, when I think I'll get a better part and end up playing a page because of the way I look in tights."

"What happened?"

"Oh, nothing, really."

He could see that she was annoyed. "I see. Patrons are not the only ones pursuing pretty young actresses, are they?"

When she made no comment, he asked, "Why do you stay in the theater, Victoria?"

"It's honest work, and there's not much else I can do."

"A woman as beautiful as you could have anything she wants."

"Becoming a star by favoring the right people?" she said bitterly, "or perhaps the mistress of someone like you? No thank you, Michael. I have to live with myself, and I don't think I could if I did that.''

"How long have you been on the stage?''

"Almost two years,'' she replied warily. "I don't pretend to be a great actress, but I like it, it can be fun. It keeps me busy, and I travel a lot.''

"But you don't stay long anywhere,'' he pointed out. "Is that what you want?''

She shrugged. "It suits me. But enough of me, tell me about yourself.''

"There's not much to tell,'' he said evasively. "I came to Cincinnati a few years ago, got involved in some business ventures, and here I stayed.''

She wanted to know more about him but did not want to pry; after all, she had her own secrets to keep, and to avoid further inquiries on his part she turned the conversation to general topics like the theater, books they had read, and music. And he was pleasantly surprised to find her so well read.

Who was this woman who fascinated him so? She had deftly avoided his inquiries about herself. Her speech was not the product of training but that of a woman born to the upper classes; yet she was an actress, a profession hardly suitable for a lady. But a lady she was, more so than many others he knew. Everything about her bespoke breeding: the way she moved, her innate grace, her delicate and uncommon beauty, her hands with their long, tapering fingers. Even her dress, showing traces of long wear, was elegant in its simplicity. She had rejected his gifts of jewelry yet accepted his flowers with disarming grace. Did she really believe he would be satisfied with a friendship? Was she really that naive, or was it a calculated ploy?

If it was, he was willing to play her game. There was no doubt in his mind as to who the victor would be; in business or in love, Michael Lawrence always got what he went after, and he wanted this woman more than any other he had ever met. His mind drifted from her conversation and he could almost feel the texture of her silken skin under his fingers, the taste of those sultry lips, and his loins stirred as he imagined the moment of possession.

Michael was biding his time. Somehow he knew that this was a woman worth waiting for, one who would make the most delightful mistress, and gradually holding hands, an occasional kiss, a casual caress became a part of their relationship. There were visits to the beer gardens of the Rhineland where they joined in the Teutonic singing and laughter; midnight suppers in private dining rooms, sometimes in the company of Marietta and Willy Braun; and finally their gatherings moved to the elegant suite Michael occupied at the Burnet House.

This was perhaps the happiest time Chantele

had known, and with less than two weeks remaining of their engagement in Cincinnati, it was coming to an end. After Marietta and Willy had gone, Chantele remained in Michael's suite. She did not evade the arms that encircled her waist or the lips that traced the nape of her neck or the hands that cupped and fondled her breasts. She let out a sigh, abandoning herself to his caresses, and when he turned her in his arms, her kiss told him that the waiting was over.

"Hold me, Michael," she whispered, and he felt her trembling in his arms, like a frightened rabbit.

Michael was a man of discriminating tastes, and Victoria Page was nature's work of art; not a cold, marble statue, but a warm, passionate woman whose flesh tingled with anticipation at his touch. Not a single word was spoken as he caressed every inch of her ivory flesh, savoring the moment he had waited for for so long. She was silk and satin and honey and fire, and never before had the possession of a woman filled Michael with the thrill of victory he experienced when he made her his, when he plunged deep into her as if trying to reach the innermost core of her being, when she cried out her surrender and then wept in his arms.

Propping himself up on one elbow, Michael

regarded the lovely profile with a wonderful sense of pride and possession. She was entirely his now, this beautiful woman whom so many desired.

Her eyes fluttered open when he chuckled with amusement.

"Do you know what they call you?" he said running a finger over the curve of her breast.

"The Ice Maiden?"

He threw back his head and laughed heartily. "You knew about that?"

"Of course."

There was nothing cold or hard about her, he thought framing her face with his hands. It would take a long time to tire of her. "The fools," he said, seeking her lips. Then, he released her and ambled naked across the room, returning with a number of small parcels which he dropped on the bed. "I've been saving these for you," he said, and Chantele recognized all the jewelry she had rejected.

"Michael, I told you I don't want them."

"But you'll wear them for me," he said undaunted by her protest. "Now."

"Now?" she raised a delicate brow. "But, Michael, what are you doing?"

He was emptying the cases on the bed. "Lie back," he said.

She obeyed, and he began placing the jewelry on her naked body. "I bought these for you," he said, "I want to see them on you."

He fondled her as he placed each piece of jewelry on her bare flesh and she shivered with pleasure when his caresses became more and more urgent until she could not bear to be without him.

"Now, Michael, now!" she urged.

Still, he continued the bittersweet torment. "What do you want, Victoria?"

"You, Michael, I want you!"

"What do you want me to do, my darling?"

"Take me, Michael," she said hoarsely, "Please take me now!"

"And if I don't?" he asked continuing his maddening caresses.

"Please!" she cried.

He laughed and touched his pulsating hardness to her quivering flesh. "Is this what you want, my sweet?"

"Oh, yes!" she sobbed thrusting her hips upwards, seeking him, "Oh, yes!"

He penetrated her partially and then withdrew.

"Michael, please!" she cried.

She was almost out of her mind when he finally drove into her and moved slowly and deliberately within her.

"Faster, Michael, faster!" she urged him, but he kept the slow, maddening rhythm of his thrusts. Frantically, Chantele dug her fingernails into his back, drawing blood, and she clasped him to her with her legs. Her moans mingled with sobs as he accelerated his tempo and only when her climax came did he allow himself the release of his own passion.

Panting, Chantele lay back on the pillows, a thin veil of perspiration glistening on her skin in the glow of gaslight. Michael watched the rise and fall of her heaving breast.

"Happy, my sweet?" he asked, running a possessive hand over her body. "Tell me what you felt, darling."

Without opening her eyes, she took his hand and pressed it to her breast. "I felt as if my whole body was on fire," she began.

"And . . ."

"It was a mixture of excrutiating pain and yet intense pleasure," she continued. "I thought I'd die if you didn't take me quickly."

"But you didn't die, did you, Victoria?"

"Oh, yes, my love," she said and pressed his hand to her lips. "I died a little before you gave me life again." She looked into his eyes, that looked greener than ever. "And you, Michael? How did it feel to you?"

He took a moment before he replied, "Like I had conquered the world."

She touched his face gently. "You conquered me," she said and kissed him softly on the lips. "I love you, Michael."

For the first time in memory, Chantele was happy. No more lonely nights staring at the four walls of some obscure hotel room, trying to unravel the enigma of her life so that her misery would not choke her. She had allowed herself to dream, at least for a little while, putting aside that mysterious past that she could not remember. She relished every moment in Michael's arms, his consuming passion, knowing that the end was near, but neither spoke of parting. When the time came to say goodbye, she would take with her the memory of this time when she had been able to pour out the love she had kept locked within her heart. One lovely memory to carry with her in the future when loneliness became again her only companion. She cast away any thoughts that Michael only desired her as he had other women before her and would again after she had gone. She had learned to live one day at a time. It was enough that he made her feel alive again, warm and loved, and even more, that she could love him in return.

The rehearsals for the opening in Chicago began on the last day of their engagement in Cincinnati, and Chantele, who had been assigned a small role, was appalled when Horace Ralston, the stage manager, called another girl to replace her.

"But why, Mr. Ralston?" she inquired. "I already know the part."

"There is no point in your rehearsing a role

you won't be playing, is there?" he replied.

"What do you mean?" she said with dread. "Have I been dismissed?"

"Dismissed?" Horace Ralston laughed without humor and looked around at the performers who were watching the scene with smirks on their faces. "Come now, Miss Page, you have not been dismissed. "Your *friend,*" and he spat out the words, "has compensated us very handsomely for the loss of your artistic talents in the middle of the tour. But I would not worry if I were you," he added with malice. "You won't go hungry. After all, it seems he's willing to pay even better for your other talents."

Chantele felt as if she had been slapped in the face. Tears welled up in her eyes as she saw the smirks and the malice on the faces staring back at her. Marietta, who had turned deadly pale, took a step in her direction.

So Michael had bought her way out, without consulting her and even after she had made her feelings known to him. Did he think he could keep her as his mistress, and buy her? Anger flared within her and she didn't want to see him ever again, or any of these people who where supposed to be her friends. Holding back her tears of outrage and shame, Chantele stretched to her full height. "If I no longer work for you, then you must find someone to replace me tonight," she said with dignity to a startled Horace Ralston. Then, she turned her back on him and slowly walked away.

Marietta went into their dressing room to find her cramming her few belongings into her carpetbag. "Oh, Vicky, I'm so sorry!" she said with anguish. "Horace had no right to do that to you! He's hateful!"

"It doesn't matter," Chantele said quietly, but her face belied her words.

"Of course it does!" Marietta cried. "But don't worry, darling, Michael will set everything right for you."

"I don't ever want to see Michael again," Chantele said in the same quiet, but angry voice. She removed the ring she wore, the only jewel she had accepted from Michael, and put it in Marietta's hand. "Will you see that he gets this back?" she said, and snapped her bag shut.

"But, where are you going?"

"As far as my money will take me."

"Have you lost your mind?" Marietta said, horrified. "You can't just walk away from Michael like this, Vicky! The man is crazy about you! He'll do anything for you!"

"To be his mistress, his kept woman, his whore? No thank you. Goodbye, Marietta," Chantele said hugging her friend, "You've been the best friend I've ever had." Her eyes misted when she added, "I only hope we'll see each other again some day."

"What shall I tell Michael?" Marietta said, realizing that her friend was not going to change her mind.

"Just return the ring to him, he'll understand."

"Oh, Vicky, what will become of you alone, penniless?" Marietta sobbed.

"I have been able to save a little."

"It won't be enough," Marietta said, and taking the bills she carried in her purse, she pressed them into her friend's hand. "Take this at least, Victoria," and when Chantele tried to refuse the money she said, "for me, please. I won't know a moment's peace worrying about you. I wish it were more."

Chantele saw the anxiety in Marietta's face and accepted the money. "Thank you, Marietta," she said hugging her friend. "I'll return this to you some day."

"Oh, go on!" Marietta said, slapping away the tears that were running down her cheeks. "Don't worry about it. All I want to know is that you're safe."

"I'll be all right, Marietta," Chantele smiled wryly. "Don't worry about me. I'm a survivor."

Her money took her as far as Pittsburgh, where she rented a room in a boarding house run by a widow who allowed her to pay part of her board by working. Each day Chantele pounded the streets in search of other work, auditioning and waiting, waiting and auditioning, and after three weeks and with only a few pennies left in her purse, she had to reject the only offer she got because the job entailed duties of a more intimate nature than acting on the stage. It was a problem she had faced before and would again as any other woman alone, and that was why the job with the Raines Theatrical Company had been so good. Horace Ralston had made an occasional play for her but had never forced his hand. Now, she was back to the beginning: no job, no prospects, and an empty purse. She had to find something soon.

Coming home after a day of fruitless search, Chantele was too involved in her own musings to notice the carriage stationed a distance away from the boarding house. She did not see the two men until they were upon her.

"Miss Page?"

"Yes," she replied, and there was no time for more. Before she knew it, she was being forced into the carriage with the two strangers who warned her not to scream, and then maintained a forbidding silence.

Her inquiries received no reply. She was frightened. Where were these men taking her? What would they do to her? There were stories of women who were abducted and forced into a life of prostitution. Even though she had no recollection of the rape she had endured, the thought of a similar fate terrified her. She could not stop trembling.

"Not a sound, Miss Page, or it will be your last," one of her captors warned her when the carriage stopped by the side entrance of what appeared to be a large hotel. She was caught in the grip of icy fear when the hard barrel of a gun was pressed against her ribs and she wished she had the courage to run away even if it meant her death.

She was taken up back stairs and along deserted corridors before they stopped before a door on the top floor. One of the men unlocked the door and propelled her into the room without using force. One man stood guard beside her while the other knocked on an interior door and was bid to enter. After a few minutes that seemed more like hours, the man came out and beckoned her to the room. When she didn't obey, her guard took her by the arm and forced her into motion. The door was closed behind her and all she saw was an unmade bed before she was flung forcibly upon it. She tried to scramble to her feet but was frozen in mid-action when she took one look at her captor's face.

"Michael!" she said with a mixture of surprise and relief.

He seemed to have recently risen and his face was white with rage when he took her hand and forced on her finger a ring he had taken out of the pocket of his robe. It was the same ring she had left with Marietta. "You left this behind," he said tersely.

Anger brought back her courage, and she stretched herself to her full height when she said, "It doesn't belong to me any more. It never did."

He seized her violently by the shoulders and his fingers dug into her flesh. "No woman walks out on Michael Lawrence, Victoria," he said through clenched teeth before his mouth descended upon hers in a savage, brutal kiss. She did not struggle, and when she remained passive he released her angrily.

"Did you think you could buy me, Michael?" she said bitterly. "After you made me lose my job?"

"Good grief, Victoria, why do you insist on keeping that damn little job when I can give you anything you want?"

"By becoming your mistress until you tire of me?"

"I don't understand you!" he said pacing the floor impatiently. "You've given yourself to me countless of times and yet you refuse to become my mistress? For heaven's sake, what's the difference?"

Chantele bit her lip and tears welled up in her eyes when she said, very quietly, "We were lovers, Michael. I thought you knew the difference."

He saw a tear roll down her cheek before she turned her back to him. Her shoulders were drooping and her sorrow was almost tangible. Michael regarded her not knowing what to say. She had given herself to him, but not for the rewards he could give her. She had never sold herself to him.

"I want you back, Victoria."

"No," she said shaking her head without facing him. "The dream is over."

No, he would not give her up. She was like a drug, she was in his blood. "No, it's not over," he said, turning her to face him, and lifting her chin up he added, "I've been out of my mind, searching for you, since you left me, Vicky. I can't let you go, I need you, my darling."

"Oh, Michael, please don't!" she sobbed.

But Michael silenced her protests with his kisses, repeating, "I need you," over and over, weakening her resistance. Sensing her surrender, he held her and possessed her and when she gave herself to him he knew that he would do and promise anything to keep her. She was weeping quietly in his arms when he said, "Marry me, Victoria," and was surprised at his own words.

She lifted her face and regarded him with eyes that were softened with tears when she said, "I love you, Michael, but I can't."

He had never expected a rejection, and when Chantele saw his face blanch, she added, "I can't marry you, Michael, or anyone else."

"Why?"

She seemed to be searching for the words to tell him. "Almost two years ago I woke up in St. Louis," she began, "not knowing my name, where I came from, or even what I looked like until I saw my face in the mirror." Shuddering at the memory, she heard his sharp intake of breath.

"What happened?"

"I don't know," she confessed. "I had been badly beaten; I had taken a blow to my head and the doctor said perhaps my memory would return one day." She turned haunted eyes to him when she said, "After all this time, Michael, my memory is still a blank."

"Who found you?"

"I was left at the doctor's doorstep in the middle of the night."

"Were the police called?"

"Yes, and inquiries were made, but it all happened in early spring, when so many thousands of people go through Missouri on their way West."

"Did you ever hire an investigator?"

"I tried to but could never afford it. All I could do was try to find someone who might have known me, or some familiar place that would help me remember."

"That's why you went into show business."

"Yes." And when she hesitated, he knew there was more to tell. "Michael, there is something else you should know," she said tentatively, trying to gather her courage. "I . . . the doctor told me that I had been raped."

Michael's mind was working furiously. He had almost felt cheated when after she had acted like a blushing virgin he had not taken her maidenhead. He had believed it all an act, but now her confession made everything clear.

No, he had never meant to marry her, and now she had given him the means to keep her for as long as he wanted without going through with his promise.

"My darling," he said, gathering her in his arms, "we'll solve this mystery together, and then we can be married."

"But if we can't . . . oh, Michael, I'm so frightened!" she cried clinging to him.

"Don't be, darling, I'm here now. You're not alone anymore."

Walter Loomis waited in the sumptuously appointed study for the return of Michael Lawrence. The man certainly knew how to enjoy his wealth, Loomis thought. Nothing but the best. Loomis had returned from his mission in St. Louis without even stopping to change. He knew Michael Lawrence did not like to be kept waiting, and the news he brought was of utmost importance. He had no regrets: Lawrence paid him well for his efforts, and his ferret face twisted into an ugly grin at the thought of his reward for all the records on the woman's case he had stolen. What was she to Michael Lawrence? His new mistress, no doubt. But she must be pretty special to inspire such interest in a man like Lawrence, a ruthless rogue beneath that charming, urbane exterior. And to this facet of the man's nature there was no better witness than Walter Loomis.

His musings were interrupted by Michael's arrival, who went straight to the point without a preamble. "You got it?"

"Yes, sir," Loomis replied and handed him the report.

Michael's face did not betray his emotions as he read the doctor's notes. When he finished, he regarded Loomis, who waited expectantly.

"Are these all the records?"

"Yes, sir."

"What else did you learn?"

Loomis shook his head. "Nothing. No one knew anything about her."

"The doctor?"

"Nothing there."

"Go back and find out who she is, where she came from."

"Yes, sir."

"Don't spare any expense, and keep me posted."

"Yes, sir."

"And, Loomis, this is important," Michael said, putting an end to their meeting.

"Good night, Mr. Lawrence."

Michael waited until the man went out before he unlocked the safe he had hidden behind a large painting, put the report inside, and relocked it. Then he returned to the bed-chamber where Chantele was sleeping, her hair spread over the pillow like a mantle. He stood by the bed, regarding her face and stroked her silken cheek.

"Whoever did that to you," he said quietly, "I'll find him."

Fourteen

Willy Braun, a frequent visitor to their suite in the Burnet House, was also a constant companion on their excursions to the Rhineland's restaurants, beer gardens, and other places of entertainment, and in the small hours of the morning when they were coming home, he suggested a visit to Bucktown.

"Bucktown?" Chantele inquired.

"Slums," Willy replied with a grin.

"A sewer," corrected Michael.

"You can't say you've seen all of Cincinnati until you've gone slumming in Bucktown," Willy said.

"Forget it," Michael said, "I'm not taking her in there."

Willy sulked.

"There's nothing to see but a collection of sleezy saloons, brothels and filth," Michael said, "and we could get a knife in our backs at any time. Do you still want to go?" he asked Chantele.

She shook her head. She had seen enough poverty and misery during the last two years, and she did not derive any pleasure from other people's misfortunes.

"You're getting worse than a schoolmarm," Willy complained. "Do you think she hasn't seen any of that before?"

Chantele stiffened.

"Shut up, Willy," Michael said harshly.

"Shut up, Willy," Willy mimicked. "She's your mistress, not your wife, and she's been around, haven't you, sweets?" He tried to tickle her chin, but Michael grabbed his wrist before he could touch her.

Michael signaled to the driver to stop. "Get out, Willy."

After Willy stumbled out of the coach, Michael turned to Chantele. "I'm sorry darling," he apologized for his friend, "he was drunk."

"It doesn't matter, Michael," she said in a quiet voice.

"Victoria, you are my wife," he said putting his arms around her, "even though we have to wait to be married."

"I know, Michael," she said with a sigh, resting her head on the hollow of his shoulder.

Chantele did not see Willy Braun until a week later, when they met by chance at the James Book Store. She had just purchased the latest copies of the *Atlantic Monthly* and *Godey's Ladies Book* when she ran into him. He removed his hat in greeting.

"Hello, Willy."

"Uh, hello, Victoria," he said uneasily, and then, "I'm sorry about the other night. I guess I had too much to drink."

"It's all right, Willy," she said, and noticing the bruises he bore, she inquired, "what happened to your face?"

He touched a bruised cheek, watching her curiously. "I had an accident," he replied. "May I escort you?"

"Of course."

They began to walk away from the shop and Willy seemed to be somewhat edgy. "May I buy you a cup of tea?" he offered.

"That would be lovely, Willy."

"There is a cafe not far from here," he suggested, "We could walk."

"If you wish," she agreed. "I could use the exercise."

Involved in their conversation, she was unaware of where they were going until she realized that the buildings were becoming shabbier and shabbier. "Is it much farther, Willy?" she inquired beginning to worry.

"No, it's just around the corner."

The street on which they turned was a ramshackle collection of dilapidated framehouses, and the stench emanating from the open sewer was suffocating. Garbage and human waste floated on water as black as ink.

"Where are we?" she inquired, alarmed.

"Why are you afraid, Victoria? You've seen this and worse, haven't you?" he said taking her arm. "You can fool Michael with your airs and fancy accent, but you're not fooling me."

"I don't know what you're talking about, Willy. Please let me go!" she cried, trying to pull away.

"You're no better than those," he said pointing at a couple of prostitutes leaning against the wall of a half-rotted dwelling. "Only your price is higher." And pulling her to him he added, "I'm just as rich as Michael, Victoria, I can pay your price and he doesn't have to know."

"You are crazy!" she cried, trying to pull

away from his grasp, but he had a strong hold on her. He pushed her against the wall and began tearing at her dress. There were a few people around but no one paid much attention to her struggles.

"Willy, please, let me go!" She could smell the whiskey on his breath when he put his face close to hers. He tore her blouse open and pinched a nipple, making her cry out in pain. "Either you do it here with me, or I throw you down in the gutter and take you there," he hissed viciously.

"Michael will kill you!"

"Michael won't know."

She took a moment to collect her wits. No help was coming. "Very well, Willy," she said ceasing her struggles.

He released his grasp only for a moment, but that was enough; her knee came up against his groin, and Willy bent over and fell to the ground clutching his crotch.

Chantele ran as fast as her legs could carry her. She couldn't believe this had happened. Someone stepped in her way and she just pushed him aside and continued her frantic run. The stench of Bucktown still clung to her nostrils even after she had left that human sewer behind and made her way back to the bookshop. Her carriage was still stationed where she had left it, and she climbed onto it and began to cry hysterically, not even noticing when it went into motion. Then, she tried to collect her thoughts. Her dress was torn, how could she hide her condition from Michael? He would kill Willy if he learned what had happened. She couldn't tell Michael, and she prayed that he would not be at home when she got there.

He was not, and she scrubbed from her skin all traces of Bucktown, and she was still in her dressing gown when Michael arrived and came into her room.

"Leave us, Louise," he dismissed the maid. He sat by her side and kissed the curve of her shoulder. "You smell good enough to eat," he said opening her robe, and as he did, Chantele remembered the bruise Willy had left on her breast. "I must be more careful with you," Michael said putting his finger to the bruise.

"It's nothing, darling," she said nervously.

"Anything that mars your beauty is important to me," he replied. She thought he was going to make love to her, but he did not. "Let's have dinner at home tonight, do you mind?"

"Of course not, darling."

"Don't bother to dress," he said meaningfully before he left the room.

She let out a sigh of relief; he didn't know or suspect anything. The whole episode was like a nightmare, and she buried her face in her hands. "Oh, Michael, my love," she said to herself, "I can't let anything happen to you!"

Michael excused himself when a visitor was announced during dinner and Chantele was on pins and needles, but he seemed to be in good spirits when he returned to the table.

"Anything important?" she inquired.

"Just a trifle," he said. "More wine, darling?"

"Please."

Her hand was shaking and he inquired, "Are you all right? You seem a little edgy tonight."

"I'm all right," she lied, "just a slight headache."

"Oh? How was your day? Did you go out?"

She put the glass down, afraid to spill the wine. "Just for a little while."

"Shopping?"

"Window shopping."

"Bored?"

"No, I'm not bored."

"I have to take the overnight packet to Aurora," he said, and after a pause added, "I'd like you to come with me."

"Oh, yes, Michael," she replied eagerly. It was just what she needed, to get away from Cincinnati with Michael before he learned what Willy had done.

They stayed in Aurora for two days, and upon their return to Cincinnati she was shocked to learn that Willy had been murdered during one of his excursions into Bucktown.

"He was fool going there," Michael said.

"The place is a trap, and anyone venturing in there is risking his life."

Michael watched her, apparently unconcerned. No, she had no suspicions. He had kept her in ignorance of his activities. But little happened in Cincinnati that Michael didn't know about; he had a good number of paid informers everywhere and had known of Willy taking her to Bucktown and of her subsequent flight moments after. She had tried to hide the episode from him and only confirmed it by her nervousness. At first, Michael had been puzzled. Why was she protecting Willy? Then, he realized it was not Willy she was trying to protect, but himself.

Too bad Willy had not learned his lesson, after the first warning—that no one touches what belongs to Michael Lawrence.

The murder of young Willy Braun caused a tremendous stir in Cincinnati. His assassins had vanished into the human sewer of Bucktown, and angry voices were raised demanding that something be done to rid the community of the scourge of humanity that infested that section of the city. Michael had an air-tight alibi and was not overly concerned. He had been miles away when the murder had been committed. His influence and his wealth protected him from any open accusations, but still his name was whispered with undesirable frequency. It was almost like New York all over again, he reflected, but with an important difference; now he had more experience and knew which string to pull at the right time. Nevertheless, it was getting time to go home, to pay back all those who had made him leave town under a cloud of suspicion. His father was dead now; there was no one to stop him.

And Victoria. She could be an instrument in his plans. He would make her the most desired woman in New York, the most famous, and then he would claim her. He missed the excitement of parading a famous beauty as his latest conquest, the envy it created.

"I want you to go back to the theater, Victoria," he said one day.

"Are you sure?"

"Positive," he replied, "But not here in Cincinnati. I'm taking you to New York."

"New York!" she exclaimed, aghast. "But, Michael, all your interests here . . ."

"I have interests in New York, too."

"You're doing this for me, Michael," she said covering his hand with hers. "You don't have to, you know."

He raised her hand to his lips. "I'm doing it for both of us, my darling."

Rodney Hackett was a very shrewd young man. Even though the name Victoria Page was meaningless in New York, it was changed to

Ariane Bentley. A clever publicity campaign was launched to excite the public's imagination. Chantele's British accent inspired Rodney, and he took advantage of the American public's fascination with European aristocracy to add an adequate amount of spice to the legend he was creating at a time when companies based at each theater imported famous foreign stars to add lustre to their marquees. Rodney began by circulating the rumor that Ariane Bentley was the stage name selected by a daughter of the English nobility whose vocation for the stage had led her to defy her family, that she had selected New York to make her debut in America because her appearance on the London stage would not be tolerated. Even before her arrival in New York, her name had become a household word.

Chantele was frightened by the charade, but Michael was delighted.

"Everyone is dying to see you," Rodney announced, brushing aside her objections. "The theater is sold out through the entire engagement. People can't resist a daughter of the English nobility defying her family and her class. Half of New York is trying to guess which family you really belong to while the other half thinks they already know."

Chantele was far from being convinced, but Michael wanted her to be the most famous actress in New York, and by this time she had learned that what Michael set out to do, was done.

"We're just laying the groundwork," Rodney said, showing her the newspaper articles praising her beauty and talent a few days before her scheduled arrival. "And that's only the beginning. My office has been flooded with invitations from all the important people trying to beat each other to the punch."

"Oh, Rodney, I'm frightened," Chantele confessed. "What if someone recognizes me as Victoria Page? I'll be exposed as a fraud."

"Don't worry, my love, we've covered all the bases," Rodney assured her. "A story has already been prepared in the event that happens, which is unlikely." Then, he added, "Tomorrow the newspapers will carry the story that you arrived secretly in New York, and that a press conference has been scheduled for next Friday. The timing is important, since your debut is the following week."

"I wish Michael were here," Chantele said dolefully. She had seen him only on occasion since their arrival in New York, and she missed him.

Rodney was cognizant of Michael's plans, and aware of his reputation, was very pleased with the arrangement. Any premature connection between Michael Lawrence and the rising actress would only damage the image he was trying so hard to create for her. He felt sorry for the girl; she was obviously in love with the man and didn't know the darker side of Lawrence. But then, it was not his place to tell her.

In her elegant hotel suite, Ariane Bentley received the reporters and granted her first interview in New York.

"Miss Bentley," one of the reporters said, "there are persistent rumors that you belong to one of England's most aristocratic families and that they disapprove of your acting career. Is that true?"

Rodney had drilled her well. "My family disapproves, it's true, but I love the theater and always wanted to be an actress."

"Have you ever played drama, Miss Bentley?" another reporter inquired.

"Yes, I have, but I prefer comedy. I like to make people happy, make them laugh."

"Is that what you plan for your engagement here, Miss Bentley?"

"We have planned different shows, some comedy, and something new we like to call 'extravaganzas,' with beautiful costumes and music."

When she began to tire under the strain, Rodney came to her rescue. "That will be all for today, gentlemen. The lady starts rehearsals tomorrow and needs her rest."

There were exclamations of disappointment,

and Chantele addressed the reporters, "Thank you, gentlemen, for your most kind and warm welcome," she said graciously. "I've been looking forward to this visit to your lovely city and trust that we shall meet again soon. A repast has been prepared as a token of my gratitude for all your kindness."

Applause followed her statement as she left the parlor and returned to the bedchamber, where she sat on the bed and clasped her hands on her lap to stop them from shaking. Oh, how she longed for Michael! She felt so lonely without him, despite the retinue of servants and secretaries who followed her around.

"I'm just being silly," she told herself. "He loves me, he'll be back." She dismissed any doubts that Michael had tired of her. Why else would he stage this charade if he didn't love her and want her happiness?

Rodney breezed in bubbling with excitement. "You were magnificent, my dear," he said giving her a hearty hug. "They were absolutely taken with you. All you hear out there is how beautiful and charming you are."

"A charming fraud, that's what I am."

"A creation, not a fraud," he corrected. "That's just a part of the game, darling, don't feel so guilty. From now on you are Ariane Bentley, a noble and daring beauty whose love for the theater has cost her the support of her aristocratic family," he declaimed. "They'll eat it all up, believe me."

When she didn't appear convinced, he said, "Forget it. Get some rest now, because tonight you're making your first public appearance."

Every move she made was reported by the bevy of reporters who followed her each time she stepped outside her hotel suite. After her photograph was published, women began to copy her hairstyle, and her clothes and jewelry became the favorite drawing-room topic. Bets were placed and guesses made as to her real identity; copies of her photograph were sold as soon as they appeared in the market, and when rehearsals began, Chantele was glad to get away from all the personal appearances that demanded so much pretense on her part.

"But you are a star, darling," Rodney reminded her, "not just an actress."

She was showered with gifts and invitations, wined and dined by the elite, and constantly surrounded by servants and bodyguards who protected her from curious mobs wherever she went. Rodney remained her faithful companion; but she longed for Michael.

The night before the opening, Chantele dined with Rodney in her suite and retired early. Her future as an actress would be decided soon. Had it all been in vain? Could she carry the weight of the principal character? These and other worries plagued her and she tossed and turned in her bed, unable to sleep. She heard the door of her room open, and she sat up with a start when a shadowy figure stepped inside.

"Victoria?" said a familiar voice.

"Michael!" she cried out, "Oh, Michael!"

He was crushing her in his arms and kissing her hungrily.

"Oh, Michael, I've missed you so!" she said between the kisses.

He released her only long enough to shed his clothes. He spoke little, but his lovemaking was as deliberate as always, achieving her total surrender.

"It's been too long, Michael," she said, her amber eyes delving into his before she covered his lips with hers in a long and searing kiss. "Oh, darling, don't leave me again!"

"It won't be for long," he said holding her tightly against him. "I'm making a great deal of progress, and after tomorrow you'll be the toast of New York."

"I wish I could be so sure."

He brushed her hair from her face and touched her cheek. "Nerves?"

She nodded.

"You'll be fine, my sweet," he said and kissed her softly. "Sleep now."

Chantele sighed with contentment and snuggling close to him slipped into the land of golden dreams. And she woke up alone.

There was not enough space in her dressing

room for the flowers that continued to arrive. The theater was packed. And Ariane Bentley was terrified. She couldn't even remember what the play was about.

"You'll be fine once you're on," Rodney kept repeating. "I'd be worried if you were not nervous."

Chantele's hand was shaking so much that her maid had to apply her makeup. The memory of her first performances was haunting her tonight, more strongly than ever.

By tomorrow I'll be the laughing-stock of New York, she thought, and Michael will never want to see me again.

"Five minutes, Miss Bentley," a voice said with a tap on her door.

Chantele broke into a cold sweat. "Why did I ever agree to this?" she lamented.

"Because you love the theater," Rodney replied soberly, "and because you love Michael and want him to be proud of you."

"I'll disgrace him," she said biting her lip and fighting back tears.

Rodney put his arm around her shoulders and walked her out of the dressing room. By the time they had reached the sidelines she appeared calm and detached. They waited for her cue. It came, and she walked on stage. Rodney watched her without surprise. He had known all along that she'd be all right.

Actors, he mused, what a strange breed.

The new comedy was light and well paced, and well performed, and even the skeptics agreed that a new star was shining brightly in New York. The cast answered seven curtain calls.

"I knew you would do it!" Rodney said warmly when she left the stage. "Listen to that applause, Ariane. Michael's money didn't buy that." And then Rodney revealed that he had arranged for appearances in Brooklyn, Albany, Boston, and Philadelphia, which provided an agreeable surprise.

"Marietta!" she cried at the sight of her friend. The two girls embraced and Marietta regarded Chantele with admiration.

"You look fabulous," she said admiring her clothes and jewelry, "and happy."

"I am happy," Chantele admitted. "But tell me about yourself. Are you appearing in Philadelphia?"

"No," Marietta said shaking her head, "I'm . . . between engagements at the moment."

They were now in Chantele's suite, cup of tea in hand, and Marietta glanced at her surroundings with admiration. "This is where you truly belong," she said. "I've thought about you often. The way you fled from Michael Lawrence . . . I've never been so frightened in my life as I was when I returned your ring to him." She had expected him to roar with anger, but she had been even more frightened by his coldness. "Still, things turned out well for you," she added.

"Not until Michael found me," Chantele said. "I was in Pittsburgh, down to my last penny and no prospects when he appeared."

"And now you are a star," Marietta interposed. "I told you he would do anything for you."

Chantele smiled, shaking her head. "Something like that," she admitted, "but it was really his idea." She paused before she added, "I love him, Marietta, and I believe he loves me. We are to marry."

"Marry!" Marietta exclaimed, visibly astonished.

"Yes," Chantele replied. "He asked me to marry him in Pittsburgh and I had to tell him the truth about me. He has hired someone to investigate my past, and we'll be married as soon as we can. But enough of me," she said after a small pause, "tell me about yourself. Did you leave the Raines company?"

"In Chicago," Marietta replied after a small hesitation.

"What happened?"

"You'll find this hard to believe," Marietta said, blushing, "I fell in love."

Chantele waited for Marietta to continue. It was obvious from her friend's expression that the experience did not have a happy ending.

"I met a man who made me forget all the

rules I had lived by and tried to hammer into you. Jimmy was like no other man I had ever met before, and when the company left Chicago, I stayed with him. I didn't know then that he was a gambler. He took all my money, sold all my jewelry, and after all that was gone, tried to talk me into selling myself for his benefit. Thank God I had enough sense to run away as fast as I could."

"I'm sorry," Chantele said taking her hand.

"I'm all right," Marietta said shaking her head and becoming her cheerful self again. "You told me once you were a survivor, and now it's my turn to say that I am, too."

Chantele brightened. "How would you like to work with me?"

"With you?"

"Yes. Michael is building a new theater in New York, and we are forming our own company. We expect to open next year, and we can take turns as the leads."

"That's wonderful!"

"Oh, Marietta, I'm so glad I've found you again!" Chantele said squeezing Marietta's hand. "I've missed you so!"

After a long, often disheartening search, Walter Loomis had succeeded, but Michael Lawrence was not going to be pleased with the news regarding his lady's past.

Loomis handed the report to his employer,

who shuffled quickly through it and said, "In a nutshell?"

"The lady's name is Chantele Marquandt," Loomis began. "Originally from Paris, France. Good family, old nobility from what I was able to learn. She was married to Colin Marquandt, the only heir to a large fortune and a plantation north of New Orleans."

"How long were they married?"

"A little under a year. She was very ill and lost a child, and her husband sent her to New Orleans to recuperate. There was a scandal involving the lady and another man. Her husband tried to strangle her in front of many witnesses. There was a duel in which both participants survived, and when the lady disappeared, her husband was charged with her murder and arrested, but he escaped before the trial. No one has heard from him since."

"Any family left?"

"Annette Marquandt, the husband's stepmother, and her son by a previous marriage who was adopted by Leon Marquandt, the father, shortly before his death."

Thoughtfully, Michael ambled across the room and poured whiskey into a glass without offering a drink to his employee, who waited expectantly.

"I want you to find him, Loomis." Michael said after a pause. "And when you do . . kill him."

It was to be expected. Michael Lawrence was not a man who would run a risk of an estranged husband popping up unexpectedly like a jack-in-the box and coming between himself and his lady.

After Loomis was gone, Michael settled himself behind his desk and went over the report carefully. Who had tried to kill Chantele Marquandt? The husband? No, he immediately discarded the notion. The man would have killed his wife in anger. There was a considerable fortune involved. Someone had carried out a very clever plot to dispose of all the Marquandts. The step-son Robert? No, too young. The step-mother? Of course, it had to be. Michael smiled to himself and then remembered that other report locked in his safe describing the condition in which Chantele had been found in St. Louis. At this moment, he wasn't sure whether he wanted to kill Annette Marquandt or thank her for what she had done.

But the entire affair boiled down to Chantele Marquandt being dead, murdered by her husband. And Ariane Bentley belonged to him.

She came out to meet him when he returned to the party. "You were gone a long time, darling," she said locking arms with him.

"Just a little business I had to take care of, my love."

"You work too hard," she chided him

gently.

"I know, darling," he replied raising her finger to his lips. "But no more business tonight, I promise."

She regarded him lovingly and smiled.

Michael never asked himself if he loved this woman. It was enough that she belonged to him. Seeing the light in her eyes when she looked at him, as she did now, was as thrilling to him as the moment of possession, something he had never experienced with any of the other women he occasionally enjoyed. He had taken his time, planning and scheming his return to New York, until he had control of the people who counted. When he had appeared on the scene, Ariane Bentley was the most admired and desired woman in New York, just as he had planned. And she had come to him when he claimed her, to the envy and dismay of those who had shunned him and could not do anything about it now that he knew how to use the power that was his.

"The major was looking for you a few minutes ago," she said scanning the room. "Ah, there he is, standing by the fireplace."

"I'd rather stay here with you," he whispered, his eyes delving into hers. "Or better yet, I have a mind to take you upstairs."

"Oh, Michael," she laughed, "what will our guests think?"

"That I'm the most fortunate man," he

laughed, "But you're right. Let's get rid of these people early, my love. You and I have a date that won't keep.

Ariane Bentley's extravaganzas were a tremendous success that filled the theater night after night, and after several weeks of continuous performances, she would retire to the estate Michael had purchased for her on the South Fork of Long Island, a welcome respite from her hectic life in the city. Michael's visits were usually brief, but Chantele treasured the quiet solitude of the country setting and took long walks along the deserted beach, enjoyed swimming in the ocean and horseback riding, and sketching the lovely surroundings. Before returning to New York, Michael had mentioned that the investigator he had hired to uncover her past had found a new lead which seemed promising. But he had said that before, and after more than a year she was wondering if Michael was only trying to raise her waning spirits.

But it was too lovely a day to brood, and this morning she gathered her sketching pad and charcoals and set out on her horse to capture a certain cove she had spotted during a ride with Michael, where trees and fallen logs provided a marvelous background to the pounding surf.

Since the time she had played Julia in *Two Gentlemen from Verona,* Chantele had discovered the freedom afforded by male attire, and here in the country, where no one could see her, she wore boy's clothes during her rides. Now, donning her favorite brown wool breeches and a vest over a plaid red-and-brown shirt, she tucked her hair under a brown cap and rode out on the handsome chestnut mare she had named Drusilla. She galloped away from the house and then set the mare down to a walk. The air was crystal clear and the trees were sharply delineated against the azure, cloudless sky. She breezed in the tangy, salty air and could almost hear the sound of the surf on the beach. Suddenly, two men on foot came out from behind a clump of trees and intercepted her path. Startled by their sudden appearance Drusilla reared, and Chantele had her hands full just trying to stay in the saddle.

"Are you crazy?" she cried angrily when one of the men yanked the reins from her hands. Without a word, the man yanked her from the saddle and Chantele fought him, ineffectively pounding his broad chest with her fists. Her captor's arm went around her waist like a band of steel, and, panting with exhaustion, Chantele looked up into eyes of a color she had never seen before and that were blazing with anger. The man's face was set in hard, grim lines that made her tremble.

"Who are you?" she demanded trying to hide her fear and something, perhaps surprise, flashed through the strange eyes of her captor.

Fifteen

The room was moving when she woke, and Chantele realized that she had been taken aboard some sort of vessel. She shuddered at the hatred she had seen reflected in the blazing eyes of her captor. Her husband? Was it possible? Someone had tried to kill her before. Had he? If only she could remember . . . All the years she had been searching for her past, and now that it had caught up with her, she was frightened.

She tried the door and found it locked. Where were they taking her?

An eternity passed before the door was unlocked and Colin came in.

"You never expected to see me again, did you?" he said in French. "That was a very clever scheme you devised. Was it your idea, *madame,* or your lover's?"

She stared at him, unable to answer. What was he saying, what had she done? Whatever it was, she had to find out before admitting to anything.

"I don't know what you're talking about," she said in English. "I've never seen you before in my life. Who are you? What do you want? If it's money you're after . . ."

"Stop it!" he cut her off. "I've had enough of your pretense, Chantele."

"Chantele?" she repeated. "My name is Ariana Bentley. What do you intend to do with me?"

"What I'd like to do is kill you," he said taking one step toward her, making her quail. He stopped, clenching his fists and ran a hand over his face. "Don't try my patience, Chantele." Then, he turned his back on her and walked out.

It had taken him a long time to find her. And he, who had vowed to drag her back to

New Orleans to clear his name, was not sure, seeing her again, if he would be able to keep himself from strangling her. She had fooled him once with that false innocent quality that was still a part of her. Did she really think he would fall for her act, denying she was his wife? Was her heart so shallow that she believed a man would not recognize the woman who had been the center of his life, the woman he had held and loved? She was embedded in his mind and in his heart. She had been only a girl then, and now she was a woman in the full bloom of her beauty; coming face to face with her again had shaken him to the very core of his being. How could he look upon her without remembering . . . amber eyes shining with passion . . . sultry lips whispering soft words of love . . . No! He could not allow himself those memories. She had betrayed him, she had cost him his honor and almost his life.

Even knowing her for what she was, after all she had done, it was hard to imagine that beneath that angelic appearance beat a ruthless, cheating heart. In Michael Lawrence she had found a kindred spirit, if what Jim McDaniels had said about Chantele's new lover was true, that he was a man who did not stop even at blackmail to gain his goals.

Jim had warned him that taking Chantele from him would be like taking a morsel away from a hungry tiger. The man regarded Ariana

Bentley as his most precious possession. Her
New York townhouse was well guarded, and
only the South Fork estate, her retreat, afforded the opportunity to approach her. Colin
had been reluctant to accept Jim's help, but
without it, abducting Chantele would have
been impossible. Michael Lawrence's paid informers were everywhere, in every stratum of
society, and little went on without his
knowledge. Only Jim could be trusted, and
Colin trusted him like a brother.

Chantele tried to collect her wits about her.
Her husband's accusations had left her
bewildered, but one thing was clear: the man
meant to kill her, and she was not about to sit
still and wait for him to do it. He had forgotten
this time to lock the door, and she could see
the shoreline through the porthole. She was a
good swimmer, and she feared the man more
than she feared the sea.

Chantele removed her boots and stealthily
tiptoed out of the cabin. She could not see
anyone on deck except the man at the helm,
whose face was turned away. It was now or
never: the longer she waited, the farther from
the shore they would get and, quickly, before
she lost her courage, she made a dash overboard. Before diving into the icy waters, the
wind carried the cry of alarm, and emerging on
the surface she saw the the yacht was changing

course. They had seen her. She tried not to panic, to keep her strokes even, but the shore was much farther than she had believed and the yacht was now coming toward her. Her woolen clothes weighed her down and her limbs began to tire, but she kept on and on until a hand reached out of nowhere and grabbed a handful of her hair. Where she got the strength to fight him she didn't know, but she struggled to free herself.

"Stop it, you little fool, or we'll both drown!"

"Let me go!" she cried continuing her struggles. She didn't see his fist, only felt it before everything went black.

She had been stripped of her clothes and lay naked under a blanket when she woke, and shivering with cold she heard footsteps approaching. Colin came in with a steaming cup of coffee in his hand, which she accepted without a word.

"For your information, *madame,*" he said while she sipped her coffee, "there are sharks in these waters."

She tried to cover her fear with bravado. "I'd rather feed the fish than stay here waiting for you to kill me."

She thought he was going to strike her, but he did not.

"There's nothing I'd like better," he said,

"but I need you alive."

She held back a sigh of relief. "What are you going to do with me?"

"I'm taking you back to New Orleans."

"New Orleans? In this boat? It will take for ever!"

"I've waited four long years, *madame*. A few more weeks will be of no consequence. Are you in such a hurry to get back to your lover?

"Michael will kill you!"

"I've no doubt he will try, but I don't kill easily, as you well know."

"You are talking in riddles. Why New Orleans?"

"I'm getting tired of your pretense, Chantele."

"I'm not pretending!" she all but screamed. "I'm not your wife, how many times do I have to tell you?"

He seized her by the shoulders and shook her, spilling the coffee and the blanket dropped to the floor. She stood, frozen in terror, as his eyes wandered over her naked body.

"Damn you!" he said jerking away, as if touching her had burned him. He turned his back on her and went to the dresser, where he pulled a bundle of clothes and flung it at her. "Cover yourself," he said tersely and walked out. She heard the door being locked.

She could not stop trembling. Even after she had put on the heavy clothes, she was shivering with cold and fear. A musky male scent clung to the sweater she wore. His scent. Her husband. He was taking her back to New Orleans, she thought and laughed bitterly. In all her travels, that was one place she had missed. He would not kill her, at least for now, she reflected, as she tried to untangle her hair. He needed her alive. Why? Her mind was full of questions, and she had to find the answers before she told her husband the truth. Her husband, she repeated to herself. The word had a foreign sound. Until now, she had no other husband than . . . Michael! She had not thought of him since her abduction, she realized. He would be sick with worry, searching for her. But Michael was her lover; her husband was this mysterious stranger who hated her and wished her dead.

Later in the evening she heard someone unlock the door and give a light tap.

"Enter," she bid, and waited expectantly. Her husband would not have knocked before entering.

"Mr. McDaniels!" she exclaimed recognizing the tall and gangly man who came in bearing a tray with her dinner.

"Hello, Miss Bentley," he said sheepishly.

"What are you doing here?"

Jim deposited the tray on a small table and shuffled his feet, like a little boy caught with his hand in the cookie jar.

"Why are you doing this to me?" she said when he didn't answer.

"Colin is my friend," he said finally.

"The man is insane, Mr. McDaniels. He claims I'm his wife and I've never seen him before in my life. I don't even know his name."

"Colin Marquandt," Jim said regarding her curiously.

She was pensive. She and Michael had met the McDaniels socially. Perhaps with a little patience she could sway him in her favor.

"Miss Bentley . . ."

"Ariane, please," she interposed. "Such formality seems a bit out of place in this situation, don't you think?"

He nodded, smiling sheepishly.

"Why is he dong this, Jim? What did his wife do that he hates her so?"

"Don't you know?"

"Jim, please! I've been abducted by a complete stranger who claims he's my husband, who has made accusations I know nothing about. How can I convince you that I am not Chantele Marquandt?"

Jim swallowed hard, unable to look away from her imploring eyes that were filling up with tears.

"He's going to kill me, Jim."

"No, he won't hurt you, I promise."

"Will you help me?"

Jim was no fool; he knew what she was trying to do. "I'm sorry, Ariane," he said shaking his head, "I can't."

With her head bowed and a tear running slowly down her cheek, she presented the most desolate picture he had ever seen. It was easy to understand how Colin had lost his heart to her, Jim mused. In spite of his cynical views on love, Jim knew his friend to be a romantic at heart, a man who saw things in black and white. He could not really blame him; women had always found his looks, his charm, and his fortune too attractive, and numerous affairs had left him wary. Chantele was a puzzle, a set of contradictions. It was more than her rare, delicate beauty that inclined Jim in her favor; there was a softness about her, a disarming vulnerability that he could not associate with Colin's version of his wife's betrayal. But there was her involvement with Michael Lawrence, a relationship he had never been able to understand even when he knew her as Ariane Bentley.

Behind that innocuous exterior, Jim was a perceptive man who had witnessed his friend's conflicts, knowing that one day Colin would realize that no man can live another's dream, that he had to follow his own star to fulfill his own destiny. That was now behind him, but he had paid a high price for the lesson. What the future held in store, no one knew. Only one thing was sure: the next few weeks would decide their fate.

Jim was glad to see that Chantele had eaten her dinner when he let her out of her cabin an hour later. She didn't seem to be in the mood for conversation, and they strolled the deck in silence. At the helm, Colin watched them.

"Tell me about him," Chantele said finally, looking past Jim at the silent silhouette. "What kind of a man is he?"

"A good one," Jim replied without hesitation, "unbendable, perhaps, but strong, and he demands more of himself than of others."

"And who goes around abducting strange women claiming they are his long-lost wives?" she said wryly.

"He's not like that at all."

"Tell me more about that paragon," she said flippantly.

"Don't, Ariane."

She seemed repentant. "I'm sorry, Jim." She paused before adding, "I really want to know about him. Did he love his wife or is he seeking revenge just to satisfy his injured pride?"

"He loved her."

Had he loved her with the same intensity he hated her now, she mused. "What happened, Jim?"

When he seemed to hesitate, she said, "If I'm to be blamed for whatever happened between them, I might as well know what that was. Please, Jim, tell me all you know."

"He found her with another man . . ." he began reluctantly. "He almost killed her in front of witnesses. Then, he challenged the other man to a duel. The man survived his wounds, but Colin was arrested for the murder of his wife."

"But how . . ."

"She had disappeared during the night and the gown she had worn that evening was found in his room, torn and bloodstained. It was a setup. She framed him for her own murder before running away with her lover. She must have figured that if he survived the duel he would not survive the hangman."

My God, she said inwardly, had she really done all those things? No wonder her husband hated her. "Did he . . . love her very much?"

"I believe he did," Jim answered. "It's funny," he added after a brief pause. "Colin was always very cynical about love, but I always suspected that once he fell in love, he would do it completely. He's a man of strong passions, Ariana, with him there are no half-way measures."

"So he hates her now as much as he loved her once," she concluded.

Jim regarded her in silence.

"Who was the other man?"

"A gambler, from what I understand."

Chantele fell silent, running through her mind all she had learned of what had happened in New Orleans. "Jim, will you be my friend?" she said suddenly.

"Ariane, I . . ."

"I'm not asking you to help me escape, Jim," she interposed. "I understand your loyalty to your friend. But I do need your protection. He hates his wife and you said yourself he's a man of strong passions. He almost strangled me this afternoon," she added, and Jim gasped. "I'm afraid he'll kill me before we reach New Orleans. Please, Jim, will you protect me? For his sake as well as mine. You're the only one I can trust!"

He could not deny her request; after all, he was partly responsible for her being there.

"I promise, Ariane."

"Thank you, Jim," she said gratefully and kissed his cheek. "I can't ask for more."

From his post at the helm, Colin saw it all. Damn her, she was already working her wiles on Jim. He had to get her to New Orleans quickly.

Chantele saw little of Colin as they continued to sail near the coast. She had discarded any thoughts of escape; after all, she had spent the last four years searching for her past, and distressing as it may be, she had found it.

She had tossed and turned for hours after

Valerie Giscard

they had dropped anchor for the night when she heard footsteps overhead. Was it Colin, she asked herself. She had tried to approach him on several occasions meeting only his hostility. Quickly, before she lost her courage, she pushed the covers aside and left her bed. She found a robe in the dark and on bare feet left the cabin and went out on deck. The night was clear, and the moon cast its light upon the waters sketching a silver path. She looked about and saw the tall, lonely silhouette leaning against the railing of the afterdeck.

"Colin," she called softly and immediately saw him stiffen.

"What are you doing here, *madame?*" His icy tone almost made her quail.

"I couldn't sleep either," she said tentatively, and then added quickly, "I just wanted to talk."

"We have nothing to talk about," he said gruffly, turning his back on her.

She felt her resolution weaken but tried to summon her courage. "On the contrary, Colin," she said, "we have a great deal to discuss."

He turned to face her and crossed his arms over his chest.

"I've been thinking about your accusations," she began warily, watching his reactions. "I'll do whatever you wish me to do. I'll go to New Orleans and convince everyone that

I am really your wife."

When he didn't answer, she continued. "I might as well tell you the truth," she said, encouraged by his silence, "I didn't before because I was frightened. It is possible I may be your wife, I just don't know."

"What story are you concocting now, madam?"

"Not a story, Colin, the truth. Will you listen to me?"

He made no reply.

"I don't know who I am," she confessed. "Four years ago I was found in St. Louis not knowing my name or where I came from."

"Really, Chantele," he said impatiently, "considering your talent for the dramatic, I expected better from you."

He turned and began to move away, but she ran after him and placed a restraining hand on his arm. "It's the truth, Colin," she cried, "Why won't you believe me?"

He paused, and regarding her upturned countenance, for an instant was caught in the spell of her amber eyes shining in the moonlight. She smelled of woman and sea. How could she still have such hold on his emotions? All these years he had tried to cast aside the memories of her that would not go away. Leon had accused him of weakness, voicing the secret fears he had always carried in his heart; the belief that it was his own weakness that had prevented him from breaking away and led him to accept a life he had so despised. Even after finding Chantele with Lucas, he had been unable to kill her. After the duel he had found himself willing to believe in her again, and her deceit had almost destroyed him.

In the years of struggle after his escape from prison, Colin had discovered his own strength, and aside from Chantele's betrayal those could have been the happiest years of his life, free from the bonds of duty and tradition he had carried. He had panned gold in icy mountain streams, fought cold, hunger, and disease and had not only survived, but made a successful new life in California. He had proven to himself that he had no need of L'Esperance or the Marquandt fortune, a realization that had restored his confidence and self-esteem. But the call of the land had been strong, and he had invested the profits from his thriving business in a large ranch he had baptized as Nueva Esperanza. A fateful name, Nueva Esperanza, new hopes for a new life that he had no right to begin until he had found his wife and regained his honor. He had set out to find her, and the photograph of Ariana Bentley he had seen in Chicago had led him to New York and Jim McDaniels, his old friend from university days in England. It had been Jim who had warned him of Michael Lawrence's power and ruthlessness. Colin had nothing against the man; he only wished to settle his score with his wife. And here she was again, with quivering lips that spoke only lies.

"I believed in you once, *madame,*" he said icily, "and was almost hanged for it." With this, he turned and walked away.

Chantele stared at his retreating back, unable to move. She refused to believe she could have been such a monster. If only she could remember what their life together had been . . . Even now that she feared him she was aware of the strong attraction she felt for him. Questions and more questions ran through her mind, but only he had the answers. Somehow, she had to make him tell her.

He avoided her during the days, and at night she listened for his footsteps hoping for another chance to speak to him alone as they had before, and determined that this time she would get her answers.

Immersed in his thoughts, he did not hear her approach and was startled when he looked up and found her standing there. "Get back to your cabin," he said tersely.

But she made no move to obey and he also remained where he was. Only the sounds of the water lapping against the hull broke the pervasive stillness until she said, "Were we happy, Colin?"

"What kind of a question is that?" he bristled.

"Please, bear with me," she said. "Pretend

for a moment that I can't remember anything about our lives together." And encouraged by his silence she asked, "Was our marriage arranged, Colin?"

"No," he admitted gruffly.

"How did we meet?"

Why did she insist on twisting the knife, he said inwardly. But two could play the game, and wrestling with his emotions he answered her questions. But in the telling the memories became real, and the night and her nearness were working their magic.

"Did you love me, Colin?" she asked softly.

He didn't know how she came to be in his arms, and his lips were on hers in a searing kiss that went beyond passion, that was more a revelation of his longings, and she gave herself to that kiss that erased all notions of time and place. Only this moment existed, nothing else.

Suddenly, he pushed her away. "Witch!" she said in a strangled voice. His face was grim when he said, "It won't work this time, Chantele."

"Colin, I . . ."

"Get out of my sight," he said through clenched teeth. "You make me sick!" He turned his back on her and heard the paddle of her bare feet on the boards, running away. His knuckles turned white as he held on to the railing with all his might. Damn her, he cursed under his breath, she could still work her magic. In spite of everything she had done . . . he still loved her.

Blinded by tears, Chantele ran into the cabin a flung herself on the bed. Colin's kiss and subsequent rejection had thrown her into such a state that she couldn't stop crying.

For an instant she had had a glimpse of what their love had been. How could she had lived with him, lain in his arms, and carried his child without loving him? No, she must have loved him then as she did now, because she did love him. What else could this overwhelming feeling be other than a love so strong that she wanted to save him even if it meant her life? Her feelings for Michael paled by comparison.

"Oh, my God," she exclaimed sitting up with a start, "Michael." Colin's presence had erased Michael from her thoughts. Perhaps it was true that she was fickle and shallow. She had loved Michael, even considered herself his wife for almost two years and she had cast him out of her mind without a second thought when Colin had kissed her. Had she done the same before? Was she still the same heartless creature who had destroyed his love and turned it into hatred? But he still loved her; in that kiss Colin had told her what he denied even to himself. A warm flush invaded her, imagining the love that had been theirs. She had to make Colin love her again as he had loved her once, because only then would she be whole again.

It was difficult for Chantele to reach a man

who treated her with icy contempt, and yet, every day spent near him made her love grow stronger. She was grateful for Jim's company during that time, and unable to reach her husband, it was to him that she appealed. Jim listened to her recount of the last years and remained silent when she finished her story.

"I tried to tell him, Jim, but he did not believe me," she said dejectedly.

"You can't really blame him," Jim said gently. "He's been to hell and back since then. Colin is a man who feels deeply, Chantele. There has been a great deal of grief in his life, and your love was the best thing he ever had. Losing it, the way it happened, would have destroyed a lesser man."

"But he didn't lose it, Jim. I love him."

Jim regarded her warily when he asked, "And Michael Lawrence?"

"I thought I loved him," Chantele admitted. "I don't expect you to understand, Jim, but I was desperately lonely when Michael came into my life. After two years of searching, I still didn't know who I was. Michael was very good to me. He gave me love, security, and a new purpose to my life." She paused before she added, "He asked me to marry him, but I could not. Not until I knew about my past."

"And now?"

"It's Colin I love," she answered quietly. "Even if he lets me go after we reach New

Orleans, I could never go back to Michael. If
only I could prove that I'm telling the truth
. . . Oh, Jim, I don't want to lose him, not
again!'' she wept.

If Chantele was telling the truth, it was obvious she knew nothing of Michael Lawrence's
true nature. It was possible; the man had
enough cunning to keep her ignorant of his
darker side. Her grief seemed genuine; she was
either a consummate actress or telling the truth.
Jim decided to give her the benefit of the
doubt.

"There might be a way to prove your story,"
he said tentatively.

"How?"

"The doctor who found you in St. Louis."

"Of course," she bright, "Dr. Spinner! But
do you think Colin will listen?"

Jim had tried to help his friend without in-
terfering between him and his wife. But if
Chantele had also been a victim and she could
prove it, they were dealing with a completely
new problem. In the heat of passion Colin had
been unable to see beyond Chantele's betrayal
to the possibility of a more sinister plot. They
had to go to St. Louis. Dr. Spinner, if there
was one, held the key to unlock the mystery
once and for all.

"He'll have to," Jim said.

Meanwhile, in L'Esperance, Annette was
busy altering the plantation books to conceal
her manipulations. Everything had gone wrong

from beginning to end. First, Colin had escaped from prison, cheating the hangman; as long as he was alive, the estate was held in trust by the bank. She had expected that with all the Marquandts gone she would be the logical heir, but even from his grave Leon had thwarted her dreams of grandeur. Robert was to be the heir after Colin was pronounced legally dead, while a small trust fund had been set aside for her. Annette had been outraged at the terms. All her careful schemes had failed to bring her the riches she believed were her due, but upon reflecting on her situation she had seen the way to salvage at least something for herself.

She had sent Robert packing to school in France while, as his legal guardian, she managed the plantation. It had taken four years of forfeiting the books, of squeezing every cent out of the backs of the slaves to accumulate a sum that did not begin to satisfy her greed. And now she was running out of time; Robert was making noise in France demanding to celebrate his twenty-first birthday in L'Esperance, and to top it all the threat of civil war was becoming more real every day. Didn't the fools know that war meant the destruction of profitable plantations and valuable property?

She heard a commotion outside the study and before she was able to put the books aside the door opened and a stranger walked in, catching her by surprise.

"Sit down!" Michael said curtly when Annette began to rise.

Annette froze. "Who are you?" she said.

"That, madam, is irrelevant," Michael replied. "I'm here to tell you that Colin Marquandt is probably on his way here with his wife."

Annette blanched, and Michael continued, "Yes, Mme. Marquandt, I'm sorry to disappoint you, but Chantele is very much alive. I must say, your plan was very clever. It might have worked had you chosen your hired help more carefully."

"You have no proof that I . . ."

"I don't need any," Michael said with a wave of his hand. "There is no need to pretend. I have neither the time nor the inclination to argue with you. At any rate, that is not why I am here."

"If it's money you want . . ."

"Lady, I can buy you ten times over. No, I'm not here to blackmail you. What I want is your cooperation. I want Colin Marquandt dead, as much, or more, than you do."

"Why?"

"Because I want to take Chantele back with me. She's been my mistress for the last two years, and if you are wondering why she never returned, I'll tell you. When she was found in St. Louis, her memory was gone."

"Then, how . . ."

"Do I know about you? I had her past uncovered, but she doesn't know it. I had no desire to inform her that somewhere she had a husband who had been accused of her murder."

"I see . . . but Colin has managed to find her."

"It's an educated guess. She disappeared recently, and I have reason to believe her husband is responsible."

Annette's confidence was beginning to return. This man was an unexpected ally. "And you think they are coming here? Of course," she added thoughtfully, "Colin would want to clear his name with the authorities."

"That's what we are going to prevent, madam. I have my men with me. Marquandt will never leave L'Esperance alive."

Sixteen

No one at the Lord Baltimore Hotel recognized the young woman dressed in boy's clothes as the same Ariana Bentley who had charmed audiences only months before. Colin had agreed to their trip to St. Louis, but he still could not bring himself to trust his wife. He would not let her out of his sight during their brief stay in Baltimore, but sharing a room with her and seeing her in different stages of undress proved to be an ordeal.

Pretending not to see his discomfiture and perfectly aware of her effect on her husband, Chantele played the part of the eternal female to the hilt. She longed for his arms, to dispell his doubts, to make him love her. She found herself fantasying that if Colin made love to her she would remember, and that feeling persisted even after she had called herself a fool for believing it. But by the time she had been outfitted for the trip and they were on the train to Cincinnati, Colin was still keeping his distance.

The journey was long, the train uncomfortable, and when they boarded the steamboat for St. Louis, Chantele was grateful for the softness of a real bed. Colin had no such luxury, stretched out on a chair and shifting uncomfortably to accommodate his large frame. Resentfully he glanced at his wife, sprawled on the wide bed with room to spare. He could not remember when was the last time he had had a decent night's sleep; the train journey had left him weary, and he eyed the empty bed space wistfully. Finally he got up from the chair, stretched out on the bed with a contented sigh, and immediately fell asleep. Through the stupor of sleep his senses became aware of the warmth of another body pressed against his. He woke to find Chantele snuggled up against him, and cursing under his breath he pushed her gently toward the other end of the bed. Again he settled down to sleep; but sleep was elusive this time, and he was about to return to the chair when Chantele turned in her sleep and threw an arm across his chest. Colin remained immobile, but uncomfortably conscious of the caress of her breath on his skin, the fragrance of her hair, fearful that any movement on his part would wake her. The softness of her face in response brought back memories of other times when they had been side by side, filled with the exquisite languor of their lovemaking.

If he had any sense, he would return to the chair, he told himself, and yet he remained, unwilling to move away. There had been no one like her for him, before or after. The women he had bedded in the last four years had meant nothing.

Chantele snuggled up even closer. When he saw her eyes fluttering, he feigned sleep.

For an instant, Chantele was disoriented and regarded her husband with surprise. His eyes were closed, but the tatoo of his heart under her hand betrayed his wakefulness, and she smiled inwardly. She touched his cheek gently and traced the contour of his lips with the tip of her finger. When he opened his eyes and she saw no trace of anger or hate in them, she was afraid to speak, that words would only break the spell of this moment. She traced his face with gentle kisses before her lips covered his in a long and soulful kiss that made the years disappear into this magic moment of passion and love, tenderness and desire, that blended their bodies and their hearts into one dream of paradise.

Later, holding her still and feeling the beats of her heart against his, Colin found himself praying that tomorrow would bring the proof of her innocence. If only he could believe in her once more, but even after all those years the memory of Chantele in Lucas's arms continued to torment him. Of Michael Lawrence . . . he could not bear to think.

The St. Louis levee was as crowded as she remembered, but the city had grown considerably since the last time she had been there.

"Everything looks so different," she said.

"When was the last time you were here?" Jim inquired trying to make conversation in an effort to break the tension. Colin had maintained an irritable silence all day, and Chantele could not conceal the fact that she was on edge.

"Three years ago," she replied. "It's over there, the house on the corner."

A feeling of foreboding invaded her when she saw that the shingle by the door did not bear Dr. Spinner's name.

"Are you sure this is the house?" Jim inquired, seeing her dismay.

"I'm positive," Chantele said, eyeing her husband warily. His face showed no trace of emotion.

"Perhaps they will be able to tell us where we can find Dr. Spinner," Jim said ringing the doorbell.

The few seconds felt like hours, and finally a black servant opened the door.

"Good evening," Colin said "We would like to see Dr. Lukas."

"The doctor is having his supper, sir."

"May we wait? It's important."

"Yes, sir," replied the Negress standing aside to let them in. She showed them to a parlor where Chantele recognized some of Dr. Spinner's furniture.

A grandfather clock standing in a corner ticked away the minutes. No one spoke, and the room was fraught with tension when a stocky, middle-aged man walked into the parlor and the visitors sprang to their feet in unison.

"Good evening, gentlemen, madam," the man said affably, "I am Dr. Lukas. What can I do for you?"

"We apologize for the intrusion, Doctor,"

Colin said, after acknowledging the greeting and introducing himself and his companions. "We are looking for Dr. Spinner and hoped you could tell us where we can find him."

"I'm sorry, Mr. Marquandt, but Dr. Spinner sold his practice to me last year, before he went West."

"I see," Colin said thoughtfully. Out of the corner of his eye he saw Chantele waver on her feet. "Did Dr. Spinner leave any of his medical records with you?"

"As a matter of fact, he did," Dr. Lukas replied, "but I'm afraid those records are confidential, sir."

"Please, Dr. Lukas," Chantele pleaded reaching for the doctor's hand, "I was under Dr. Spinner's care four years ago. For the love of God, please, help me. Let my husband see those records!"

Dr. Lukas was taken aback by her vehemence and his face reflected his puzzlement as he looked from one visitor to another. "It's highly unusual . . ."

"It's a matter of life and death!" Chantele cried.

Dr. Lukes looked from her pale countenance to her husband's impassive face before he said, "Very well, Mrs. Marquandt."

She released his hand with a sigh of relief. "Thank you, doctor."

"Please, my dear, sit down," Dr. Lukas said gently. "Was the name Marquandt?"

"No, it was Victoria Page."

Dr. Lukas nodded. "Please wait here while I check."

Three pairs of eyes followed Dr. Lukas as he ambled out of the room and disappeared. Chantele was too edgy to sit still, and she paced the room while Jim fidgeted in his chair. Colin went to stand before the window, where he stood as still as a statue. His demeanor had been so cold and aloof after the night they had spent together, that Chantele was terrified of what would happen if she could not present proof of her story. He might as well kill her, because without him she didn't want to go on living.

Jim sprang to his feet when Dr. Lukas returned, and Chantele clutched at her heart when she saw that his hands were empty.

"I'm sorry, Mrs. Marquandt," Dr. Lukas said shaking his head. "There are no records under your name."

"Are you sure, doctor?" Colin said.

"Positive."

"But there must be!" Chantele cried.

"Thank you, Dr. Lukas," Colin said taking her by the arm, "and please accept our apologies for the intrusion."

"Wait!" Chantele cried pulling away from

her husband's grasp.

"Please, Dr. Lukas, can you tell me where we could find Dr. Spinner's housekeeper, Miss Pruitt?"

Dr. Lukas took a moment to think, scratching his gray hair as he did. "I believe Mrs. Spinner had been the doctor's housekeeper before their marriage, Mrs. Marquandt," he said finally, and added, "I'm sorry."

It was the final blow to all her hopes, and she let Colin take her by the arm and lead her out of the house. She did not even hear the words exchanged at the door, and the return to the steamboat was all a blur. When she came out of her limbo they were back in their stateroom, and she turned to face Colin, who was regarding her with disgust.

"Please, Colin, you must believe me," she implored. "I told you all I know. Dr. Spinner told me I was more dead than alive when he found me. My memory was gone, Oh, God, how can I convince you?" she sobbed. Her legs refused to support her and she fell to her knees before him, crying bitter tears.

"Spare me your dramatics," he said caustically.

She covered her face with her hands and he regarded her prostrate form at his feet before he turned away and walked out of the stateroom. After he closed the door behind him he could still hear her ragged sobs.

On the surface, business went on as usual at L'Esperance. Since Annette's takeover, fear had been an important part of everyone's life, as was hunger, and cold. Clothes had not been distributed among the slaves for years, and they went about in their rags and with empty bellies because food was also scarce. The vegetable gardens the slaves had tended in their spare time had disappeared because there was no time to be called their own; they worked from sunup 'till sundown, seven days a week, under the relentless whip of a cruel overseer. Even the laughter of children had disappeared; a shadow hung over L'Esperance. The presence of Michael and his thugs did not alter the situation much, except to increase Annette's irritability. She tried to remind herself that the man was an ally, that he would dispose of Colin. His handsome, urbane appearance did not fool her for one minute, and she feared Michael Lawrence as she had never feared anyone in her life. The man had traveled a considerable distance to take Chantele back with him and dispose of Colin, and yet there had been no anger in his voice or in his manner as he had given her a recount of Chantele's misfortunes at the hands of the ruffian she had hired to kill her, and this filled Annette with dread. Was he planning to dispose of her, too, after killing Colin? What was there to stop him?

Annette wished she had someone she could count on, but there was no one. Harris, the overseer, might be feared by the blacks, but Annette was realistic enough to know that he was no match for Lawrence's men even if he were not a coward, which he was. Even if Robert were here, he would be of no help. He was sure to side with Colin. What a disappointment her son was, she lamented. All she had was the small gun she had taken to carrying in the pocket of her skirts since Lawrence's arrival. It wasn't much, but it gave her a small measure of comfort.

Another day had gone by and still no trace of Colin or Chantele. Where were they? Why was it taking so long? The waiting was killing her, and she readied herself for another sleepless night.

"Annette?"

She whirled around toward the voice and her face turned pale at the sight of Colin. Chantele was with him.

"Colin!"

"Hello, Annette," Colin said evenly.

"How did you get here?" Annette said trying to recover her composure. Where was

Michael Lawrence, she said inwardly. Aloud, "I didn't hear a carriage."

"I'm still a wanted man," Colin reminded her. "I thought it was better this way. Where is Robert?"

"In school, in France," she said, and to gain time, "My dear, how good it is to see you again! And Chantele!"

Chantele had not spoken a word. This was the home she had shared with her husband, and the place was as unfamiliar to her as this woman who seemed so happy to see them again. Colin's step-mother, Annette.

Annette pretended ignorance of Chantele's condition. "What is it, my dear? Are you ill?"

Chantele bit her lip, and turning moist eyes to her husband shook her head.

"What is wrong?" Annette said feigning surprise, "Where did you find her, what happened, Colin?"

"That's what I want you to tell me, Annette."

Annette paled. Still, she forced herself to keep up her pretense, playing for time. Where was Michael Lawrence? "I don't know what you mean, Colin," she said evenly. "I haven't seen her since the night she disappeared."

"What a nice family reunion," came the voice from the doorway, and everyone turned in unison.

"Michael!" Chantele exclaimed.

He had a gun in his hand, and it was pointed at Colin's heart.

"Hello, darling," Michael said without taking his eyes off Colin. "Are you all right?"

"Yes," she replied, "But what are you doing here?"

"Waiting for you."

"How . . . how did you know where to find me?"

"It's not important, darling. All that matters is that I'm here to protect you."

"But it is important, Michael. You knew about my past, didn't you? Why didn't you tell me?"

"Because your husband tried to kill you, my love. I wanted to find him before he tried again."

"No, Michael, he didn't, he told me he didn't."

"And you believed him?"

"Yes!"

"But you still don't remember."

Chantele shook her head. "No."

"He tricked you, darling, but you don't have to fear him any more. I'm here now." He turned to the two men who had appeared behind him and said, "Take him outside."

"What are you going to do to him?" Chantele cried when the two men took Colin at gunpoint.

"Don't worry, darling," Michael said taking his eyes off Colin, and cold anger rose within him at the sight of her anguish.

"Colin!" Chantele cried and when she made to go after him, Michael grabbed her by the arm.

"Let me go!" she screamed trying to pull away, but Michael held fast. "Michael, please, don't hurt him!" she pleaded in earnest. "I'll do anything you want, but please, let him go!"

"You are coming with me, Ariane," Michael said tersely, and she let him take her by the arm and out of the house, followed by Annette. In the dark, they were only shadows. Shots rang out.

"Colin!" Chantele cried, struggling against Michael.

"Take her away!" Annette cried while Michael struggled to subdue the girl. "Take her away now!"

Somehow, the scene was suddenly familiar to Chantele. She was again at the New Orleans levee and Annette was telling the man to take her away and dump her into the river. Chantele stopped struggling and turned to Annette, crying, "It was you! It wasn't Colin who tried to kill me, it was you!"

Suddenly, there was a gun in Annette's hand. A shot rang out and everything came to a standstill. Annette's eyes widened, and she raised her hand to her breast, where blood was seeping through the bullet hole. She opened her mouth, but no sound came out and she sank slowly to the ground, where she remained still.

"Oh, Michael, it was her! She tried to kill me. Shc . . ." The flood of memories came rushing back, and she was again in the hands of the man who had raped her so brutally. "No! No!" she screamed before she slumped into Michael's arms.

Michael lifted her with ease, and bearing his precious cargo covered the distance to the carriage he had hidden in the shadows. After depositing Chantele on the seat, he climbed in after her and popped the reins. Everything had gone according to plan, he congratulated himself as the carriage covered the gravel driveway in the direction of the levee, where a paddle steamer waited. Colin Marquandt had played right into his hands, returning to L'Esperance.

He carried Chantele aboard the vessel, where he deposited her on the bed. Would she remember when she awoke? No matter; she would continue to be his mistress until he tired of her. His patience with her had been rewarded by her willingness to please him, but if she resisted, he had other means to make her submit. Still, it would be a shame to use force with her. She had been delightful when she had come to him voluntarily.

He gave orders to cast off and the paddle
wheels got into motion, churning water and
picking up speed. It was all over, Michael told
himself. Ariane Bentley was his, and no longer
was there a husband to dispute his possession
of her.

Suddenly a figure lunged out of the shadows
knocking Michael down. "You!" he exclaimed.
He fumbled for his gun, but Colin kicked it out
of his hand, looming over the fallen figure of
his adversary with clenched fists.

"Get up, Lawrence!"

Michael got up warily and looked about him.
Where were his men? Fist fights were not his
style, but he had some knowledge of boxing.
He blocked Colin's first thrust and retreated
out of his reach. He continued to move back,
and when Colin went after him and stepped into a circle of light, Michael saw that his shirt
was stained with blood. His incipient smile was
wiped out by a blow that seemed to have come
out of nowhere.

As the fight progressed, Michael realized that
it was not going to be as easy as he had expected. They were well matched in physical
strength even though Colin was bleeding from
a wound in his shoulder, and Michael sought
that spot to land his blows. The fight had
moved to the afterdeck when Chantele came
out and saw them. She followed, and her hand

flew to her mouth when she realized that Colin was losing blood and growing visibly tired. Michael reached for a club and raised it over his opponent's head.

"No!" she cried, "No! Stop it!"

For the flick of an instant, Michael lowered his defense as Colin's fist came up in an upper swing. Michael stumbled against the rail and toppled over the side. Chantele opened her mouth, but before she could cry out an agonizing scream stabbed the night.

"Michael!" Chantele cried, rushing to the side, but Colin caught her and held her to him.

"Don't look, kitten."

"Oh, Colin!" she sobbed, burying her face in his chest.

"It's over, kitten," he said gently, "It's all over now."

The paddle wheels continued churning, churning water that had turned crimson with blood.

Epilogue

"But how did you know it was Annette who tried to kill me?" Chantele inquired.

They were back in L'Esperance, and Michael's thugs had been safely locked away.

"After St. Louis, I began thinking . . ." Colin began.

"And I thought you didn't believe me!" Chantele interposed.

"I wanted to," he said regarding her fondly, "very much." He cleared his throat when he remembered Jim's presence and continued. "I realized that in my anger, I was blaming you for everything. But then I began to consider your story as the truth and things began to fall into place. The Marquandt fortune had never meant a great deal to me, but it was considerable enough to bring out the greed in others. With both of us out of the way, Annette and Robert had it all."

"Robert! And you suspected him, too?"

"At first," Colin admitted, "the thought crossed my mind, but I could not convince myself. It wasn't easy with Annette, either. I always thought a great deal of her, but then I began to remember Leon's illness, your own; Annette's hand was everywhere. She had to be responsible."

"I guess we never really knew her," Chantele said, shaking her head, "I thought she was so kind . . ."

"Well, she's gone now," Colin said. "Robert will have his hands full when he returns from France."

"What do you mean?" Jim inquired with interest.

"I intend to give L'Esperance to Robert."

"All of it?"

"All of it."

"You're going back to California?"

"Yes, Jim. My life is there now," Colin admitted. "But there is much to be done here. There is going to be a war, and there is no way the South is going to win it. We have to prepare our people for freedom, we can't just turn them loose. I think we owe it to them."

Chantele listened to the exchange and wondered. Would Colin want her with him in his new life? Now that the past was no longer a mystery, she remembered how he had sought another woman's embraces while rejecting her own. Was there someone waiting for him in California?

"I don't know about you two," Jim was saying, "but I'm calling it a night." He rose from his chair, stretched out his long frame, and stifled a yawn. "Good night, folks," he said, walking out of the room.

"Good night, Jim," Colin replied and turned his attention to Chantele. "You have been very quiet, kitten. Are you all right?"

She bobbed her head and then inquired, "When will you be leaving for California?"

"I don't know yet," he shrugged. "I suppose I'll have to stay here for at least a few months after Robert gets back from France." He regarded her soberly before he said. "Will you come to California with me, kitten?"

She could hardly believe her ears.

379

"I love you, Chantele," he said, going to her and kneeling by her chair. He took her hand and raised it to his lips. "I should have had faith in you, kitten. Can you forgive me, give me another chance?"

"Oh, Colin!" she cried throwing her arms around his neck. "I love you so!"

Their lips met in a kiss that absolved him of all his sins.

"I've been such a fool," he said stroking her cheek fondly. "I don't know what we'll find in California, my love. I've been gone a very long time, but I want to start fresh, just the two of us with no ties to the past, where we can establish our own traditions. Nueva Esperanza is not anywhere near this plantation when it comes to luxury, but if you . . ."

She touched the tips of her fingers to his lips. "I don't care if we have to live in a shack as long as we're together," she laughed happily. "All I ever wanted was to share your life, Colin, and all I ask is that you never shut me out again."

"Never!"

READ THESE PAGE-TURNING ROMANCES!

FASCINATING, PAGE-TURNING BLOCKBUSTERS!

BYGONES (1030, $3.75)
by Frank Wilkinson

Once the extraordinary Gwyneth set eyes on the handsome aristocrat Benjamin Whisten, she was determined to foster the illicit love affair that would shape three generations—and win a remarkable woman an unforgettable dynasty!

A TIME FOR ROSES (946, $3.50)
by Agatha Della Anastasi

A family saga of riveting power and passion! Fiery Magdalena places her marriage vows above all else—until her husband wants her to make an impossible choice. She has always loved and honored—but now she can't obey!

THE VAN ALENS (1000, $3.50)
by Samuel A. Schreiner, Jr.

The lovely, determined Van Alen women were as exciting and passionate as the century in which they lived. And through these years of America's most exciting times, they created a dynasty of love and lust!

THE CANNAWAYS (1019, $3.50)
by Graham Shelby

Vowing to rise above the poverty and squalor of her birth, Elizabeth Darle becomes a woman who would pay any price for love—and to make Brydd Cannaway's dynasty her own!

THE LION'S WAY (900, $3.75)
by Lewis Orde

An all-consuming saga that spans four generations in the life of troubled and talented David, who struggles to rise above his immigrant heritage and rise to a world of glamour, fame and success!

A WOMAN OF DESTINY (734, $3.25)
by Grandin Hammill

Rose O'Neal is passionate and determined, a woman whose spark ignites the affairs of state—as well as the affairs of men!

Available wherever paperbacks are sold, or order direct from the Publisher. Send cover price plus 50¢ per copy for mailing and handling to Zebra Books, 475 Park Avenue South, New York, N.Y. 10016. DO NOT SEND CASH.

WHITEWATER DYNASTY BY HELEN LEE POOLE

WHITEWATER DYNASTY: HUDSON! (607, $2.50)
Amidst America's vast wilderness of forests and waterways,
Indians and trappers, a beautiful New England girl and a handsome
French adventurer meet. And the romance that follows is just the
beginning, the foundation . . . of the great WHITEWATER
DYNASTY.

WHITEWATER DYNASTY: OHIO! (733, $2.75)
As Edward and Abby watched the beautiful Ohio River flow into
the Spanish lands hundreds of miles away they felt their destiny
flow with it. For Edward would be the first merchant of the river—
and Abby, part of the legendary empire yet to be created!

WHITEWATER DYNASTY #3: (979, $2.95)
THE CUMBERLAND!
From the horrors of Indian attacks to the passion of new-found
love—the second generation of the Forny family journey beyond
the Cumberland Gap to continue the creation of an empire and live
up to the American dream.

ENTRANCING ROMANCES BY SYLVIE F. SOMMERFIELD